1777

Another Chance

An American History Time Travel

Book 2

By

Michael Roberts

ISBN: 9798783100406

Imprint: Independently published

Proofreading by Phoenix Book Promo

Want updates and more from Michael Roberts?

Sign up for his newsletter here!

Prologue

November 2nd, 1777
Windsor Castle

Lord Frederick North, the second Earl of Guilford, the Prime Minister of England, and the servant, advisor, confidant of King George the Third of England, stood in front of the full-length mirror, evaluating his appearance. He wasn't alone in this self-serving exercise. Two servants stood behind him, dressing Lord North in his formal robes. One was his valet, the other a woman.

Lord North's wig wasn't on straight, and he uttered a *tsk* sound, sucking air through his teeth and into his mouth. The female servant noted what he was in distress about and moved to straighten his wig, without a single word spoken between them. She added a touch of white powder to cover the bare skin of North's head that had become exposed when the wig had been adjusted.

This servant seemed adequately efficient at reading his needs, all of them. A skill that seemed ironically uncommon among the common people. His stomach jiggled as he chuckled at his own joke, even if it was only spoken in his own thoughts. He made a mental note to repeat the joke to the king.

Although he'd called this particular servant to his silk sheet-covered bed last night, he still didn't know the woman's name, nor did he care to learn it. He would, however, make a note to have her see to his requirements every time he stayed at the king's palace. She was a little bulky, with thick shoulders, muscular arms, and a big ass, but he liked his women durable. The thinner servants bruised too easily, and he couldn't afford to have rumors of him being an abuser jumping from ear to ear in the palace. His eyes dropped to her ample cleavage. Unlike his wife, this woman had huge, soft breasts. His wife, Anne, hadn't been blessed in that area. He wished his wife had a chest like this woman.

Today, courtesy of a tight corset, her boobs pushed up and out of her yellow dress. It wasn't an expensive dress by any means, but like most of the serving ladies' dresses, it was designed to draw the eye to certain areas of the female body. She must have realized last night he liked the size of her breasts, as she was showing a little more today than she had yesterday. His valet sagely kept his own gaze averted.

Also, and most importantly, unlike his wife, this woman knew not to engage him in conversation whilst they were otherwise occupied. Oh, if only his wife were more like her. He thought back to the previous night and could remember her speaking to him twice. When she did speak, it was to inquire if she could do anything else for him.

His own wife seemed to be acquiring her own opinions of late. She seemed to have an opinion about everything these days. He'd noticed the older she became, the freer her tongue wagged in sharing those opinions.

He thought about pilfering this servant from the king's service and bringing her into his own household. She hadn't put up a fight last night, and he found her to be quite accommodating. She was eager to please him. Lord North had no illusions about himself. He wasn't a young man, nor did he have a body that women found desirable. If she was eager to please him, it was because she had hoped for some coin afterwards, and she wanted to finish the act as quickly as possible.

In truth, he cared not for her motivation, but for her service. He appreciated a servant who knew their place in the world, and maybe some secrets about the palace. Most fools thought servants weren't real people and said things in front of them that they'd not say in front of their own family members or confidants. As if the servants didn't speak the same language. Lord North knew servants were people, he just didn't respect them as such. Their eyes and ears worked as well as everyone else's, though they weren't smart enough to know they had such important information in their underdeveloped brains.

He'd learned long ago most servants possessed a treasure of information. Like a buried pirate's chest, that information had to be dug up. His valet was a superb example. He hadn't protested at the irregular servant helping Lord North dress this morning. He kept his head down, ears open, and was fiercely loyal to his lord.

Lord North had found himself staying at the Windsor Castle quite often of late. When he first became Prime Minister of England, he'd visited the castle once a month to discuss the royal financial books with the king. The royal debt was ten million pounds when he first started, before Lord North had devised a brilliant plan of how to discharge the king of that large debt four years ago. Up until then, the treacherous colonists in America had not paid their share of taxes, and Lord North had swayed the king to implement the Tea Act.

This additional tax should have been enough to pay off the Empire's debts and more. The plan was flawless, if in theory, but not in execution. He didn't live in the colonies and was forced to rely on others to implement his lucrative schemes. If only the colonists had complied and paid their lawfully ordered taxes. Who were they to question his wisdom or the king's commands?

Since the blasted Tea Party incident in Boston, the colonists had forgotten who their king was and had revolted.

The king sought to bring the traitors back into the fold, but it was Lord North who had convinced the king to force them to kneel to their betters. Not out of spite, but to ensure they never again tried to shake off the yoke of the British Empire's rightful rule. It was the best course of action for the Empire and, in the long run, for the colonists. The colonists were no better than willful children who had to be told how to live.

The Empire's debt was now over forty million pounds and rising by the day. Instead of the Tax Act solving the king's problems, it had made them four times worse. This was of no fault of Lord North's, of course, and surely the king knew that. The king, however, demanded answers for some hard questions, and it was Lord North's duty to provide those answers. Lord North would never allow someone else in the palace to provide information to the king that might falsely blame his actions and ideas for the revolt.

For a very specific reason.

Unlike the rest of the world, Lord North had seen signs the king was sick.

Not sick in any manner the royal doctor might help, rather that the king's mind had been slipping. Lord North had seen this before in others, although most were a great deal older than the king himself. Lord North had observed the king forgetting simple things, such as dates or names. The king's illness wasn't yet noticeable to most of the world. Those in the castle wouldn't dare attempt to speak to the king without an invitation from the king himself. Lord North knew, as the seasons turned, the illness would become more visible to others, and rumors of the king's declining health would spread like a plague.

Lord North's lips turned up at the corners as he smiled at himself. He'd learned how to twist the king into action by using words that caused the king to question the loyalty of others.

He shook his head a few inches as the buxom woman retrieved the red perfume bottle that smelled like roses. Although it was popular with many of the upper class, Lord North found it made him sneeze, and it was made in Paris. She set the bottle back down and touched a finger to the blue one next to it. That one smelled of lavender and was produced in London. Lord North gave a slight nod of approval. It wouldn't do to have the king recognize the smell of a popular perfume made by, if not quite public enemies, his very real foes.

Some people believed the king of France was the second most powerful man in the world. Wiser men of importance knew Lord North as the Prime Minister held that position.

The smile on his face faded as he considered the news he'd have to report to the king this morning. Word had returned to England about the British defeat at some God forsaken place called Saratoga. Lord North heard this Saratoga was nothing more than a field in New York. If it held any real importance at all, Lord North would have already known its location before this incident.

The king knew of this disaster, but what he didn't know yet was Lord North's spies had reported the French were talking with colonial diplomats named Franklin and Adams. North pursed his lips at this development. These conversations centered on the troublesome French joining this revolt and helping the colonists.

Troublesome, irritating French.

The French cared nothing for the colonists, but by helping the rebels, the French hurt England. Both King George and Lord North knew the French had secretly provided weapons and supplies to the colonists for over a year. The French people still desired revenge against the British after losing the Seven Year War. This Saratoga skirmish was incidental but might be enough to persuade the French to openly commit themselves.

The valet was tying off his cravat, but that didn't stop him from huffing out a sour breath laden with old herring and thick pudding directly in the valet's face. If the valet grimaced, North didn't notice. This Saratoga incident had him far too deep in his thoughts. Because, if the French helped the colonists, the war might last for years and cost the Empire tens of millions of pounds more. The royal debt would easily reach eighty or ninety million pounds before the rebellion ended. The king's only chance was for Lord North to convince him to double their efforts.

The king had already decided to send thirty-two thousand troops to bring the colonists back in line. Lord North had a plan to get the king to double that number. If they sent every ship they had to the colonies, then they could commit over seventy-five thousand troops. It would take four to six months to organize such a feat, but it needed to be done. The valet fluffed the cravat at North's neck, and he swatted the valet away like an irritating fly.

If he accomplished this feat with the king, the rebellion would end before the French committed themselves, allowing them to pull away from the conflict without losing honor and quashing this irksome and expensive insurgence. Then and only then could taxes be collected again. The colonists would first be made to pay for the cost of their rebellion, but after that, the taxes would continue and fill the royal coffers. Then the king could turn his sights back on the French and their lands.

The buxom woman stood behind North, tugging at his coats, both to adjust his appearance before he presented himself to the king, and to remind him to pay her coin. North shoved past the valet and reached for his velvet pouch on the dressing table and handed over a few shillings. She frowned at him.

"Come back this eve, and you'll see more," North intoned.

She gave an awkward curtsey, one that showed off her ample bosom, before departing his quarters.

As his valet finished with the rest of North's ministrations, he considered the biggest problem – the king's military advisors were tiring of the rebellion and the expense to continue it. They wanted the king to give up the Americas entirely, or at best, negotiate a new peace with fewer taxes. The cowards wanted to bring the English troops home and to cut the royal losses.

When the valet stepped back and bowed, indicating North's dress was complete, Lord North spun on one heavy buckled shoe and marched from his chamber, his mind a blur. Why did these advisers think England had soldiers if not to fight and die for their country? It was their duty and their honor to fight for the king, not the king's duty to keep them safe. Those thoughts urged him to walk with speed toward his meeting with the king. The king had been refusing their attempts to influence him, but how long would the king last if Lord North wasn't whispering in his ear?

November 3rd, 1777

Paris, France

At seventy-one-years old, Benjamin Franklin more swaggered than walked into his favorite restaurant, his cane in his right hand and the stunning Isabella on his left arm. He'd met the young lady at a party the night before, and she didn't want to leave his side. Her adoration seemed to represent the collective mind of France, and Franklin basked in it.

The Continental Congress had chosen Benjamin to go to France to represent them because of his ability to move the hearts and minds of his fellow men against the English. He found himself to be rather popular among the French and especially among the ladies. Being a landowner in the new country and a foreign diplomat here, and an enemy of the British Empire, only increased his popularity with the full hearted but beautiful women of Paris.

The French had long memories and had a deep love for hating the British and its royal family. It seemed like almost every woman in Paris had lost a son, brother, husband, or father in war with the British, in the land far from home and over the sea. What was called the French and Indian War back home, the French called the Seven Year War. The French had lost that war but had never forgotten it, and the women he encountered welcomed him as the Empire's newest enemy. To many of these ladies, Benjamin became a symbol for the new country. They wanted to show their support, and they did, quite often. Benjamin had no misgivings about himself. Yes, Isabella was young and beautiful, but how long until his eyes wandered to another beautiful young lady? With so many to choose from . . .

His gaze fell on the man he was here to have dinner with sitting at a table on the far side of the room. John Adams raised a hand to catch Benjamin's attention. Adams wore a disapproving look on his face, no doubt because of Isabella. Whether it was her age or because Benjamin had brought her to the dinner, it was too soon for Franklin to say. He'd no doubt have the answer to that question in short order.

"Benjamin," John Adams said, pulling out a chair for Isabella. At least he kept his manners. "Is this your daughter you saw fit to bring to our private meeting?"

Oh, not so many manners, Franklin griped inwardly. Apparently, Adams was upset about both her age and her presence. Many believed Benjamin was a grandfatherly figure until they met him in person. Benjamin was really a man who liked to be in charge and didn't mind letting others know. He only brought the young lady because Adams's letter instructed him to arrive alone. *Instructed.* As if Benjamin was Adams's apprentice or junior delegate.

Benjamin intended to make it clear to the young man that Adams didn't give instructions to him. The American delegates could not be seen fighting with themselves in public, and Benjamin was rather good at making his point with suggestive mockery.

"John," Benjamin said, leading Adams a few feet away from the table and Isabelle, his pleasant grandfatherly smile fixed securely in place. "If only I could resign myself to one woman like you have somehow managed your whole life. I'm afraid I've been cursed with the passions of a younger man. I so wish I could be tamed the way you have been, but I cannot. Additionally, I already had plans for this evening when I received your generous request for dinner."

"We need to talk about the two treaties," Adams said in an urgent whisper, ignoring Franklin's overt insults. "After the victory at Saratoga, the French are ready to sign both treaties. Or, I should say, they *were* ready to sign."

"Oh?" Benjamin asked, a moue concern crossing his wrinkled face. "Has there been a development I don't know about?"

"A very unfortunate one for us," Adams answered, keeping a fake smile on his face and flashing his eyes to Isabella.

Benjamin stepped close to the table and grabbed Isabella's hand. He lifted it to his lips and kissed her fingers.

"My dear," Benjamin coaxed in a soft tone, "my poor colleague here is frantic and in need of my guidance and assistance. Will you forgive me and allow us to have some time alone?"

"You promised me dinner, Benjamin," Isabella said as her dainty lips curled into a pout. Oh, she had mastered the look of spoiled indignation.

"Yes, yes my dear," Benjamin said. "I know I did, but my poor friend here is inconsolable."

"Very well," she said. "But I'll want a gift tomorrow."

Benjamin smiled easily as he helped her to her feet and watched her leave. Benjamin then sat in the chair Isabella had been warming a moment ago. Benjamin motioned for Adams to retake his seat and then leaned forward in a conspirator manner.

"King Louis was ready to sign the treaties yesterday, but today we received troubling word," Adams whispered, flicking his eyes around the room as he spoke. "One of the king's spies reported Lord North is campaigning King George to double the troops he commits against our new country. Seventy-five thousand soldiers."

"After the victory at Saratoga, it's not totally unexpected," Benjamin whispered back, his own gaze fiercely fixed on Adams. "And though it sounds unsurmountable, Lord North will not want to let go of the colonies and the future tax revenues they give that easily. Not without a fight. He's likely whispering in the king's ear at this moment as we speak."

"Agreed," Adams said. "The problem is Louis will not commit to send military force to the states to fight our war. He fears if the British send seventy thousand troops, he'd be sending his men to an unwinnable conflict. They've lost too many young men to the British already. I fear he's ready to abandon us."

"We'll need to act fast," Benjamin said.

"Yes, yes," Adams quickly said. "I have already located a ship that sails for New York in the morning. I've instructed one of our aides, the young boy, Matthew I think his name is, to pack and buy passage. I've prepared a letter for him to take with him, informing congress of this information and asking for direction on how they want us to proceed. The problem is you know some of the brainless cowards back home, with less backbone than men like us, will see this as another reason to change course and return to British rule and tyranny. Some would be happy to place British shackles back on themselves and our children."

Benjamin knew the younger man was right. This wasn't the time to assert himself as the senior delegate. However, the younger Mr. Adams could be a little too honest and forthcoming at times.

"Listen to me, John," Benjamin said, locking eyes with the younger man across the table. "You're right about two things, but you're also wrong about two others."

"I wasn't aware I'd discussed four different topics," Adams said.

"Oh, but you have, sir," Benjamin said. "You're right. We need to send a message. You're also right. This could make some cowards want to change course. I'm afraid you were wrong about sending this message to the Continental Congress. No, I fear this message must be placed in the hands of General Washington himself and no other."

"And the second issue I was wrong about?" Adams asked.

"We'll not be asking for advice on how to proceed," Benjamin said. "We, that is you and I, will think up a plan tonight and inform the General how we are going to proceed."

"Plan?" Adams asked. "What plan would that be?"

"Let's go and find out," Benjamin said as he stood up, putting his weight on his cane. "We must wake Charles and seek his advice."

Adams didn't need to ask who Charles was. Charles Gravier, the foreign minister and Count of Vergennes, had been a great ally, and earlier today had told them he was going to officially acknowledge the United States as an independent nation.

"I have an idea," Benjamin said. "But not the understanding of how we might accomplish it. We must seek his advice now, tonight, and ensure our message and plan are on that ship in the morning."

Chapter One: Basements Suck

Philadelphia, Pennsylvania

December 2nd, 1777

Lafayette, or Marie as he insisted I call him, lingered next to me at the window, facing Jonas's parents in the family's candle shop. As Lafayette faced the family, I stared out the window, watching the sun set in the horizon. Jonas's two younger brothers sat quietly on their chairs, listening intensely about their big brother, the second brother they'd lost at the hands of the British.

I relished the brief, beautiful moment of reprieve in watching the sun sink behind the snow-covered hills. A glorious inferno blazed with eye-popping reds, yellows, and oranges. It was fitting to watch the giver of life end its day, knowing it would rise again in the morning in a cycle of death and rebirth.

Jonas was a young man who had served his country well and helped me become a better person. He'd been under my command when he'd made the ultimate sacrifice and gave his life for a recently birthed country. His was a life that had ended abruptly and too soon. He wasn't more than a boy in my eyes, though he acted and fought like a fully grown man.

Lafayette had told Jonas's mother and father about the time the three of us had spent together and how their son had died. It should have been me who told his story, but Lafayette was much better with words. He had a distinct and loquacious ability to remember and recount Jonas's words, about how, as we had sat around the fire, Jonas told us about his family and the love he had for them. The memories and pride they held for their son were the only things they had left of him. Jonas was gone, and I could find no glory or beauty in his death. My loss, though, was but a sliver of the loss his parents were feeling. Lafayette had a way of bringing emotion to his voice and making those memories come to life for his parents in a way I never could have.

General Washington hadn't been able to leave his men at Valley Forge but had written Jonas's parents a letter for us to give them. Jonas's father had tried to read the letter, but his eyes kept filling with tears. Lafayette gently reached out and took the letter from his hand. Clearing his throat, and in his French accent, Lafayette read the letter to the parents, word for word in the first person, as if he were General Washington himself.

The General didn't write as a General and didn't talk about the loss of a soldier. Instead, he spoke as a father who, although didn't have any biological children of his own, he'd adopted his wife's two children and knew the love of a parent. The letter was from one parent to another. Washington didn't mention some greater good or discuss how men needed to sacrifice to ensure our victory in this war. No, Washington focused on their loss, and how he knew that, although his words could bring no solace to their sorrow, he wanted them to know he'd cried and prayed for them. The General wrote he'd written to his wife, and if Jonas's family ever needed anything, they were to write to her, and she'd forward any correspondence to him, no matter where he was.

Hot tears coursed down my cheeks as Lafayette read the letter, and my mind went back to the day Jonas was taken from us. I'd lost family and friends back in my own timeline before I got into that alien ship and was sent back into the past. I was not unfamiliar with the depth of that sorrow.

Growing up as a boy, I realized early on in life that, compared to most people, I had a noticeable lack of emotion. I was never one to fully understand words like empathy or sympathy. Not counting the day my wife was murdered by a British Officer, an act that set me on my road for revenge and retribution, I couldn't remember a single day I had allowed myself to cry.

Since the day I'd entered that half destroyed blue alien ship in the year 2021 and rode the time machine back to the year 1777 in hopes of changing our timeline and preventing the British Empire from ruling the world, I had changed as a person for the better. I was still a killer, trained in the twenty-first century, but that didn't change the fact I was somehow becoming a different person, a better person.

Meeting Annie was my first step back to humanity. Annie had been the first woman in my life since my wife had been violently taken from me by a British officer. Until I had met her, I believed I was destined to die alone. Then again, until I met her, I was okay with that destiny. Her two daughters, Molly and Regan, had filled a void I'd not known was there until they somehow imbedded themselves in my heart. Then I met Lafayette and Jonas, two young men filled with a zest for life. They were like two little brothers to me. Grown men, but still with much to learn. My horse Little Joe had also broken through some of my emotional walls. He'd become more than a pet or a horse. We had a bond I didn't fully understand or know was possible with an animal. He was more like support dog, a friend, rather than a horse, a mount to be ridden.

Lafayette, whose full name was Marie-Joseph Paul Yves Roch Gilbert du Motier de Lafayette, a rich aristocrat from France, had sailed to America searching for experience and adventure. And he'd found it. When I first met him, he gushed with arrogance, but the young man had grown so much since that day when Jonas and I rescued him from the British.

At some point, while I was deep in my thoughts, Lafayette had finished reading General Washington's words and handed the letter back to Jonas's father. It was dark outside now and past time for us to go. Informing Jonas's parents of the loss of their son was only the first of two missions. We'd also agreed to steal food from the British and bring it back to the men of Valley Forge.

Jonas's parents were helpful in our second mission. They told us where the British stored their supplies. The British had several warehouses on the outskirts of the city and they were filled with much needed food.

I moved deeper into the shop, where the back door was. I wanted to do another check of my weapons to ensure I was ready. Lafayette noticed what I was doing and started another check of his own weapons.

I wore my twenty-first century, green waterproof coat. It fell to my waist, designed to keep me warm while giving me full movement, yet it was cut and tailored to blend into the eighteenth century, as all the modern technology I'd brought with me was. I reached up and unbuttoned it. Underneath the coat, I wore my black leather vest lined with a bullet proof material. The vest had four brass buttons in the front and one larger brass button where chest pockets would be. The larger button was really a hardened C4 explosive shape charge.

My hand shifted down to my Tec-9 pistol, which sat in a late nineteenth century cowboy-style holster. The pistol was custom made by a gunsmith from the twenty-first century. He'd taken an eighteenth-century German flintlock pistol and stripped it down to the wooden frame. He'd hollowed out the wooden pistol as best he could, then he took a 9mm Tec-9 pistol machine gun and tore it apart. The smith fabricated new parts matching the Tec-9 but resized to fit in the flintlock and rebuilt the Tec-9 inside of the hollowed-out flintlock frame where it held a thin, six-round magazine. He also reattached the original hammer on the outside for looks. He attached a larger, copper, fake barrel over the real Tec-9 barrel, so it would fool anyone who looked at it if they didn't look too closely.

My hand moved up to the shoulder holster under my left arm. My Thompson Center Contender was tucked next to me. It was a single shot pistol used for hunting and competition shooting that shot a 30-30 Winchester rifle round. The weapon broke open and reloaded like a single shot shotgun.

I also had two twelve-inch-long matching knives. The blades were crafted of titanium, and the handles had deer antler grips on them. One was attached to the front of my gun belt while the second one sat at the small of my back.

My newest weapon was a three-foot-long double-edge British cavalry sword. The blade was straight and thin, maybe two inches at its widest point. It was razor sharp, but designed for stabbing, made to be held and used with only one hand. Lafayette was an expert swordsman and teacher. My last weapon was my throwing boot knife, but I didn't bother checking it.

I also had three high explosive grenades and my night vision goggles in my satchel, but that hung on the pommel of Little Joe's saddle, and he was near town with the three soldiers General Washington sent with us. My greatest weapon was also in my satchel, sitting in its waterproof case – my smart phone. It was useless as a phone with no one to call, but its computer chip contained a library of books I could call upon for knowledge.

We left the soldiers waiting for us about a mile out of town. Lafayette and I agreed we'd a better chance, the two of us. We wanted to go unnoticed. If we were spotted, it wouldn't matter if we had ten or a hundred soldiers.

Lafayette, for his part, carried his slightly single edge curved French sword, a large knife I had taught him how to throw, and like me, he started to carry two pistols. He'd become very skilled with his weapons.

We stepped out into the cold night, cold enough to see our breath, and made our way down the streets. Though it was dark out, the streets were busy with foot traffic. Merchants were still trying to sell their goods. One out of every three people was British soldiers. The nice thing was, we couldn't miss them with their red coats on, noticeable even in the dim light.

As we walked through the city, we saw at least one wanted poster for me on every corner. That was the second reason I wanted Washington's soldiers to wait out of town. The price on my head had gone up from two thousand to twenty-five thousand pounds. I had to do the math in my head. Most day-to-day products were paid for in pennies or shillings. Twenty pennies equaled one shilling and five shillings made a pound. You could buy a horse for twenty pounds, and the Empire was offering twenty-five thousand pounds for my head, a veritable king's ransom. Even the most loyal of soldiers might feel the temptation of turning me in for that much money.

The posters, tattered pieces of paper, indicated the king's offering of a reward for the criminal known as the Pale Rider. It explained that I favored a black vest and two pistols. The amount offered had increased, but there was one recently added item that was new. This poster now added I had a scar on my head going from front to back. My left hand reached up on its own accord towards my scar, but I caught myself, and brought it back down to my side. Besides being so damn cold, the ransom posters were why I wore my coat over my vest and guns tonight. I had also taken to wearing a black three-point hat to cover the scar.

I hadn't shaved since the day I'd stepped off that damn alien ship and was now sporting a beard and mustache. The look was new for me, and I didn't like it. It itched. I preferred to be clean shaven, but since the posters didn't mention facial hair, I figured I would let it grow. If the posters ever changed and included the beard, that's when I would shave.

Lafayette thought I should be proud to be recognized as the Pale Rider. I considered it a huge target on my back. No, I wouldn't be shaving anytime soon.

We made it to the outskirts of the city without being stopped or questioned by any soldiers. I figured they assumed I wasn't stupid or brazen enough to ever travel back to Philadelphia after the damage I'd done last time. That showed how little they understood me.

We located four warehouses on the south outskirts of the city, a few hundred yards from the water. Four soldiers guarded the front of the warehouse's large double doors. Several fires blazed, and the soldiers appeared more interested in staying warm than staying alert. We crept around the back side and looked through the gaps between the wet boards. The first warehouse seemed to be filled with muskets, gunpowder, and cannons. The next one overflowed with bags of grain, from floor to ceiling and wall to wall. The last two were empty. The soldiers opened the double doors to the last two as if they were getting them ready to load them up.

Two merchant ships had been moored to the pilings, and it looked like they had finished off loading the last of their cargo. Sailors and dock workers worked by torch and lamp light, loading up the six wagons in a line. The dock workers had to be cold and yelled at their fellow workers to finish the job. They wanted to go home to their families or to their favorite taverns.

Two horses pulled each wagon. A teamster and a soldier sat on every wagon. The teamsters seemed to be only armed with large knifes and pistols. The soldiers carried muskets with bayonets fixed on the ends of their barrels.

At first glance, I was a little surprised more soldiers hadn't formed up, walking with the wagons to protect the food. Then it seemed obvious they weren't worried. Thousands of soldiers were in the city close by, and they were only moving the wagons a few hundred yards to the warehouses where sixteen additional soldiers waited. If it was still daylight, they would have a line of sight from the docks to the warehouses. Whoever had planned the offloading had ordered it done while the sun was still up, and didn't bother to plan for the darkness to come.

Lafayette and I skulked down to the docks as the wagons rolled forward when we came to a fork in the road. One road went from the docks to the warehouse while the other fork broke off and went down river and away from the city. That road then went around and hooked up with the road where we'd left Washington's soldiers. I had Lafayette break off and start walking down the road while I continued towards the docks. I told him it would be less threatening if they saw one of us, but in truth, I didn't want him to see how I was going to kill them. I didn't really have what you might call a plan, but I figured I'd take the last wagon in line and ride off in the dark.

I had my suppressor attached to my Tec-9, so I could kill them with little noise. I walked down the road and let the first five wagons go by without so much as looking at them. My hat was pulled down low and the collar of my coat was turned up.

The sixth and last wagon overflowed with a mountain of potatoes, barrels of salt, and bags of flour. I didn't see any salted beef, but this would do for now. It was a far sight better than shoe leather. Two old brown horses pulled the wagon, but they didn't seem well taken care of. Pulling these wagons from the docks to the warehouse was the sum of their lives now. The soldier on the wagon looked bored and half asleep. The wagon driver was in his late forties and eyeing me. I doubt he saw me as a threat. It was more likely he was making sure I didn't grab any food off the wagon as they rode by.

With a shocked look on the wagon driver's face, I smoothly pulled out my Tec-9 and fired two quick shots. The *THUNK THUNK* of my pistol, followed by the sound of two men falling off the wagon and onto the snow-covered ground, was the only noise I had made. I climbed onto the wagon and grabbed the fallen reins. The driver and soldier in the wagon in front of me never turned around. The little sound I had made was covered by the men at the docks yelling about going into town and the cold wind that howled in the night. I kept the wagon moving slow and steady until I reached the fork. My deer skin pants prevented the dampness of the wagon's wooden bench from soaking through, but not the coldness of it. My legs were freezing.

I turned the horses to take the fork and kept going. The wagons ahead of me didn't notice anything, and it seemed like a clean get away. Life wasn't complicated if you strived to keep things simple.

I picked up the horses' speed to a canter and continued down the road until I caught up to Lafayette walking along the side of the dirt road. I pulled the wagon to a stop alongside him, and he jumped up, settling onto the bench next to me with a smile on his face.

"That was easier than I thought it was going to be," Lafayette stated in his accented English.

"We're not out of the woods yet," I told him. "And that trick won't work again. They'll have more soldiers from now on."

We needed to regroup with Washington's soldiers and then hightail it back to the fort. The British would have noticed the missing wagon by now and would be sending soldiers after us. The British army, for the most part, consisted of foot soldiers, so they had little chance of catching up with us. As we got near the spot where I'd left Little Joe and Washington's men, I realized something wasn't right. I slowed the wagon to a stop and listened. Lafayette opened his mouth to say something, but I held up a hand, stopping him. Something was missing. No birds, but more than that, I had given orders for the men to keep a look out. Someone should have made themselves known to us by now.

Lafayette and I stepped down from the wagon and moved closer to where I had left our group. Lafayette pulled his two pistols, thumbed the hammers back, and peered into the trees, ready for someone to jump out at us. I found a circle of rocks with the burned down fire in it that the men had used for warmth. I didn't see any other sign of the men or horses. Lafayette located tracks of men heading into camp and then tracks that led down to the road and towards the city. Blood drops splattered the ground on top of the white snow. Not a pool of blood as if someone had been shot or stabbed, but more of a thin spray, like someone who'd been punched in the face or maybe butt-stroked by a musket.

Someone had captured them and taken them away.

"Well, shit," I said under my breath, following the tracks with my eyes.

"There's nothing for us to do, Thomas," Lafayette said.

He had assessed the situation well. He was still looking at the tracks in the snow with his eyes, then looking over at the valuable cargo in our wagon.

"They might be already dead by now," he continued. "This food is too important. I don't want to leave them anymore than you do, but we've no choice."

Little Joe was gone, so the British had him as well. If that wasn't enough reason for me to go back into the city, then the fact the British now had my grenades and night vision was. I couldn't let those weapons fall into British hands.

"I have to go back, Marie," I said to the younger French soldier.

"If you feel strongly about it, I'll go with you."

"No, my friend," I said. "You're right about the food. It's too important. You head back to the fort and don't stop until you get there. I'll catch up to you if I can."

He stood open-mouthed, not knowing what to say and wanting to convince me otherwise as I walked back down the road that led to the east side of the city. I was glad we'd stopped a mile outside of the city and not farther.

"Don't worry about me, Marie," I yelled back to him. "They'll be following you and those wagon tracks, not me."

Lafayette realized I was right, and any soldiers coming after us would follow the wagon. His job, driving the wagon, was no safer than mine. He ran for the wagon, and I had a feeling those poor horses were going to be pushed harder than they had been in a long time.

It took me almost an hour to walk the one mile in the snow. The wind kicked up again, and I thanked God for my twenty-first century gloves. This was the main road into the city, so the snow was firmly packed down, making the cross-country trek easier.

My gloves were thermal, but they were thin, so I still had full use of my fingers. Ice clung to my beard and mustache, adding to my reasons why I wanted to shave.

The city was quieter now than it had been a few hours ago. The snow had started falling, and the wind raced through the streets and whipped between houses. I had no idea where they had taken Washington's men. If I couldn't find them, I'd search the stables for Little Joe.

I had walked up and down half the city with no sign of Washington's men, and then I turned another corner. Little Joe and four more horses were tied to a hitching post in front of a tavern appropriated by a platoon of British soldiers. My satchel no longer dangled from Little Joe's saddle horn. If the satchel had been with Little Joe, I might have cut my losses and rode out of town, but I couldn't leave without it.

The tavern was a standard, three-story red brick building, longer than most of the taverns in town, so I was guessing the hotel and eating area were larger than normal. The British allowed the tavern owner to still serve alcohol and meals to customers, but the platoon of soldiers had taken up residency in his rooms. Their command staff had ordered them to pay for their drinks, but the tavern owner was forced to feed the men for free.

Only two men walked out of the tavern, but no new customers entered the establishment. Anyone with the good sense God gave a goose would be home right now, either in front of the fire or in bed under the blankets. What that said about me, I didn't want to think about.

I opened the door and walked in as quickly as possible, shutting the door behind me. With the wind ripping through the open door and blasting the room, everyone in the place paused what they were doing and stared at me. Acting casually, I shook out my coat and stomped my boots, which gave me the time to make a quick scan of the room and my surroundings.

It was a normal if large tavern, with a red oak bar in front of me and a tall, skinny bartender behind the bar. The bar itself consisted of long, thick red wooden planks, held up and laying across large wooden barrels. Four colonists stood on my side of the bar, drinking from large wooden cups. A large fireplace overwhelmed the opposite wall and two older men sat in front of it, warming themselves in rocking chairs. Six round tables took up the rest of the room, with chairs sat evenly spaced around the tables.

Between the six tables were at least twelve soldiers. They ate out of bowls with wooden spoons. Muddy footprints and small puddles of water covered the floor. A thin cloud of smoke hung in the air from the coal oil lanterns. Off to my right was another room with two long, picnic-style tables. That had to be the main dining room, but I only had a view of half the room, so I couldn't see how many people were in it. Off to my left, two sets of stairs ascended into the depths of the tavern, one going up and one going down. It was common for a place like this to have a basement for storage.

The lanterns and fireplace put out a lot of light but not for that part of the room. Dark shadows filled the barroom against the walls where the flickering yellow light from the fireplace didn't reach. Heady scents of beer and cooking meat hung in the room, with an underlying fishy odor coming from the kitchen behind the bar.

After a few seconds, the room lost interest to me, and heads turned away as men fell back into their private conversations. The room grew loud again as the buzz of conversations picked back up. I walked up to the bar and asked the barkeep for an ale. He slid a large wooden mug over to me, and I dropped two pennies on the bar. I needed to figure out if the soldiers took Washington's men upstairs to the rooms or downstairs to the basement. I made my way over to the wall next to the stairs and sat in a lone chair submerged in the darkness of shadow. I had not seen the chair when I first walked into the tavern. It was a good place to go unnoticed.

With my back to the wall, I had a good view of the entire place. The colonists at the bar were engrossed in whatever they were whispering about while the soldiers at the tables focused on the food in front of them. None of the soldiers carried their muskets with them, so they had to be staying at the tavern. With no reason to bring their muskets downstairs to eat some mutton stew, they'd left their muskets in their rooms.

One of the old guys in front of the fireplace appeared asleep while his friend pretended to read a book. He held the book up as if he were reading it, but he'd not turned the page since I'd walked in. I couldn't see his eyes from where I was, but his nose pointed at me and not the book in his hands. If his nose was pointed at me, then his eyes were as well. He wasn't a farmer or merchant – he was too clean, and his clothes were too upper class for that. His thin, wire-rimmed spectacles looked expensive. He had a blanket over his lap and legs, but he didn't appear to be cold. Was he partial to having a blanket on himself, or was he hiding something under the blanket? I figured he must be the owner of the tavern and was looking over the man he'd never seen before who had entered his place.

A muffled noise from downstairs came up behind me. I listened closer, trying to drown out the noise of the main room. Someone was yelling. They were downstairs, but if I moved from this chair, I would draw the attention of the whole room. I drank my ale, acting as if I was doing anything other than looking for a way to go downstairs. The older guy in front of the fireplace kept watching me, but now he also turned his attention to the rest of the room. One of the colonists from the bar set his cup down on the bar and put his coat back on. I leaned over the side of my chair and surreptitiously set my cup onto the floor.

The colonist walked to the door, and as soon as he opened it to leave, cold air blasted the room again. The light in the room dimmed as the wind thrust the open flames in the fireplace to one side. As when I walked in, heads turned to the front door to include the man next to the fireplace. I stood up and sauntered to the stairs that led down to the basement.

The stairway was too dark, and the lower stairs disappeared into blackness, but the sounds of snoring reached up to me from the bottom. My first five steps downward went better than I could have hoped for. My sixth step, on the other hand, ended with a creak of boards. I froze in place as my eyes adjusted to the darkness. A soldier stood at the bottom, next to a closed door. He leaned against the wall and his eyes blinked, like someone who abruptly awakened.

I pulled my knife from the front of my belt and made it to the bottom of the steps in three quick leaps. Grabbing his coat with my left hand, I brought the butt of my knife down onto his head like a hammer, knocking the red coat out before he'd a chance to give warning. He had my satchel over his head. Sliding my knife back into its sheath, I lifted the satchel from him. My grenades, night vision, and phone were still in the leather bag. The guy most likely saw them but had no idea what they were.

I slid the soldier quietly down to the floor and away from the door. Muffled voices from deeper inside the basement got louder. I slid my coat off and dropped it to the floor. I pulled out my Tec-9, holding it ready in my right hand, and turned the doorknob, pushing the door an inch with my left. Light from the basement shone through the crack and I peered inside. Several men stood around the perimeter. The General's men crouched on the floor with their backs against the wall and their hands tied in front of them. I counted seven red coats in total facing away from me. The particular red coat doing the talking was an officer. Whenever he turned his body, lamplight reflected off his silver buttons in a perfect line down his chest. A large lantern hung on the wall from a peg two feet from the door, providing enough light for the whole room.

The officer yelled at the General's men. He kicked one of his helplessly tied up prisoners in his side. This officer behaved like the same British officer who had murdered my wife – using violence on the helpless to make himself feel like a big man. I'd assumed he wanted to know where General Washington was, but I was wrong. He was asking the men about me. He wasn't doing this for the war or in the name of his king. He wanted the reward for my head, nothing more.

That desire was going to cost him his life. I removed my hat and dropped it on the unconscious soldier at my feet. Reaching into my satchel with my left hand, I pulled out my night vision goggles and slipped them on my head. I stepped into the room and around the door. No one had turned my way yet, so I slowly pushed the door closed. Taking one step to the side, I blew out the lantern and pulled my night vision down over my eyes, turning them on.

Darkness engulfed the room. Curses erupted from the void, and rustling told me the British men spun around to face the door. Most of them looked straight at me, but it was too dark for them to see me.

"One of you, go open the door for light," the officer yelled.

In the green haze of the night vision, one of the men stepped forward, and I shot him. He fell back into the men behind him, and in that one second of light, in the flash my shot provided, they saw me standing between them and the door.

"Get him!" one of the red coats yelled.

Switching my pistol to my left hand, I drew my sword. The red coats had their knives out and searched the dark for me. Another soldier ran for the door, and I thrusted my sword into his chest. He screamed and fell onto his back. The officer drew a flintlock pistol and cocked back the hammer. If he fired the pistol, the whole tavern would come down here. I shot him, and he collapsed against the wall, then slid to the floor.

The soldiers saw me again with the flash of light and rushed towards me. I ran the first man through with the sword and shoved him into his two friends. The officer on his back was still alive and raised his flintlock. I fired my last two rounds into his chest, and his head slumped over as he died. One of the soldiers saw me as my pistol flashed twice more and he bore into me, pinning me against the wall. He punched at me until I thrust the blade of my sword through his chest and out his back.

One of the last two soldiers found the door and opened it, flooding the room with what little light there was on the stairs. I holstered my pistol and drew my knife as he spotted me. He turned to run, but the General's three men had not been sitting idle this whole time. Two of them, with their hands still tied, had brought down the last soldier and had killed him with his own knife. The other man ran at the soldier who had opened the door and pulled him backwards into the room. A knife slid across the soldier's throat, and he was dead. I yanked my night vision off my head and stuck it back in my satchel.

The General's men had kept their heads. None of them yelled or panicked. They managed to pull in the man on the stairs and closed the door, leaving it open only a few inches to give us some light to see by.

"I told them you'd come," the youngest of them whispered in awe as the soldiers cut themselves free.

"Great," I said. "Now we need to figure a way out of here. Any ideas?"

One of them took the officer's flintlock pistol from his lifeless hand as the others gathered knives. They looked at me to answer my own question.

"Ok," I said. "None of the men in the tavern have muskets, so we can run for the door. Our horses are hitched right outside. If we can get to them, we should make it out of the city."

Turning my back on the men, I reloaded my pistol and picked up my jacket. One of the men had retrieved my sword and handed it to me.

"You'll need a weapon," I said to him. "Hang onto it until we're safe. Line up at the door. I'll go first. Everyone stays quiet and walks up the steps as carefully as you can. I want to be at the top of the steps and running for the door before they know what's going on."

I handed my jacket to the youngest man and then pulled my Thompson Contender from my shoulder holster.

I opened the door, stepping onto the stairwell and froze in place after my first step. At the top of the stairs stood the old man who had been watching me from the fireplace. The old man held a flintlock pistol in his right hand and a lantern in the other. His eyes went wide as he saw my black vest and two pistols. Recognition covered his face. The flintlock pistol in his hand dropped to the floor. His shaking hand raised in the air as one boney finger pointing at me. I ran up the steps, and on my third step, the old man found his voice and managed to start yelling.

"Pale Rider!" he hollered. "It's the Pale Rider!"

I didn't want to waste a bullet on him, so I shoved him out of the way as I ran by him. It was too late. The rest of the room was on their feet and moving towards us. I raised my two pistols, trying to look menacing. I pointed my Tec-9 at the closest man, and he froze in place. I pointed my Thompson at the man behind the bar, who was reaching for something large under a towel. When he saw my Thompson was pointed at him, he straightened, his hands resting on top of the bar.

"Anyone moves, and I'll kill every one of you!" I shouted. "I am the Pale Rider, the bringer of death."

No one in the room moved any closer. They were busy looking around, waiting to see if anyone had a musket or flintlock. None of them had their muskets, and common soldiers weren't issued flintlock pistols. As I yelled at the room, Washington's three men ran behind me and out the front door. As the last one ran out, I raced for the outside myself.

"First man to step through the door dies," I called out to the room.

Footsteps could be heard upstairs, and the thumps of boots running down the steps came my way. Holstering my Tec-9, I snatched a lantern and threw it against the stairs. The lantern broke, and liquid fire sprayed out, covering half the steps. One of the closer soldiers took that as his chance to be a hero and ran at me. I shot him in the face, and he collapsed onto his back. Two more soldiers stepped forward, and I had my Tec-9 back out before they took their second step. They wisely decided not to take a third but searched the other men, hoping someone else was dumb enough to move forward. I could see they were hoping I'd waste my shot on someone else. Neither moved any closer, and neither would ever know I'd have shot them both if either had tried.

One of Washington's men was on his horse and holding the reins of Little Joe for me. Another yanked on the reins of Lafayette's horse. I jumped on Little Joe's back, and we rode out of the city like the devil himself was after us. It only took three or four seconds for musket fire to break the darkness. As we raced through the winter night, I wondered how this story was going to be exaggerated with every telling of it. How much did the reward for my life just go up? On the brighter side of things, I now had a reason to shave. Those wanted posters would include my facial hair from now on.

We rode in a full run for about a half mile, then slowed the horses to a steady gallop. I stopped the men and held out my hand to the soldier who carried my sword. He handed it back to me, then looked back the way we'd come.

"Don't worry," I announced. "It's too soon. They don't have a lot of horses; most are foot soldiers. They'll have to find some horses if they want to come after us."

The men took solace in the fact that they didn't see anyone pursuing us. They'd be coming soon, and I didn't want to wait for them to find us. I wanted to bring the fight to them.

"Keep going hard for another half a mile," I told the group. "Then slow the horses so you don't tire them out. I'll catch up to you."

"What will you be doing?" one of the men asked.

"Waiting here for them," I said. "If no one comes down the road in the next hour, I'll ride hard until I catch up to you."

Several of the men argued until I held up a hand, stopping them.

"Go now," I said sternly, pointing down the road.

As the men rode off, grumbling loudly, I turned Little Joe into the trees and found some thick bushes covered with snow to hide behind. After checking my guns, I climbed off Little Joe and brushed him off with the horse brush from my saddle bags. It took them longer than I'd thought it would, but the soldiers were racing my way. I had been waiting for about twenty minutes before the sounds of horses galloping at full speed came from the direction of Philadelphia. I patted Little Joe's neck and whispered in his ear as they rode by to keep him calm. I didn't want him panicking and giving away our hiding spot. I counted ten men as they passed me. Then, climbing onto Little Joe's back, I kicked him into a run.

We broke through the bushes. Snow flew in the air like a cloud, and I went after the posse. Little Joe had rested and caught his breath while we waited for the soldiers to ride by, so he was faster than the British horses. It didn't take long for us to catch up to them. They were riding in pairs, and as I closed in on the last two, I pulled my Tec-9 out of its holster.

Shooting at a target on horseback at a full run is harder than you might think. John Wayne might not have ever missed when he did it, but I wasn't shooting blanks, and these weren't actors I was up against. My first round I shot too soon, and though I was twenty feet back, I had missed completely. Thankfully, with the suppressor on my pistol, the soldiers never heard the embarrassing bad shot.

I kicked Little Joe harder and in a burst of speed, we closed within ten feet of the last two horses in the column. I fired again, and this time the rider on my right arched his back and lurched off his horse. The man riding next to the fallen soldier saw his compatriot fall and twisted around to look back. I fired once more and struck the second man in the chest. The man plummeted off his horse backwards, landing hard on his head and rolling. The two horses, now having no riders to press them to keep going, slowed and fell behind as I rode in between them.

I only had one bullet left in my Tec-9, and reloading my pistol on horseback wasn't an option, so I holstered my gun and drew my sword. Little Joe was still going strong, so I pushed him, and we rode up between the next two riders. They caught me as I swung my sword in a back hand swing at the rider to my right. I struck his upper chest, and although my sword may not have cut deeply into his skin, I did knock him backwards off his horse. He tumbled head over feet in the sloshy snow as I twisted my body and drove the point of my sword into the side of the rider on my left. This time my sword sunk deep, and he screamed. I pulled my sword out, and while he didn't fall off his horse, he did yank back on the reins, causing his mount to slide to a stop. He was out of the fight, but his scream caused his fellow riders to look back and discover me.

The remaining six horsemen reined in their horses, and as they were stopping, I kept going. I rode between them and swung my sword for the lead on the right. I figured the leader had to be in the front. I didn't know if he was the one on the right or left. Coming at them from behind didn't give me a view of their rank, and I was going too fast to see, anyway. My sword was in my right hand, so I swung for the one on the right.

My blade bit deep into his neck and opened a sickly gash, causing blood to pour out, like a sink overflowing with crimson water. I halted Little Joe and swung around to face them.

They wore looks of shock and horror on their faces. They were supposed to be chasing me, not be chased by me. The man I had sliced held his throat with his right hand as thick blood gushed through his fingers. His eyes rolled back, and he collapsed off his horse, undoubtedly from blood loss. He, I now saw, wasn't the leader. I had chosen the wrong man. The horseman next to him was the officer.

As they stared at me in shock, I reacted more quickly, sheathed my sword, and drew my Tec-9, firing my last round and killing the officer. As the officer fell from his horse, I scrambled to holster my Tec-9 and draw my Thompson. I fired and killed the man who was behind the fallen officer. That left only three soldiers still on their horses. Shoving my Thompson back into the holster under my left arm, I again drew my sword. I thought about drawing my knife with my left hand, but like I said, I'm not John Wayne. Unlike the Duke, I wasn't able to put the reins between my teeth and ride. I needed to control Little Joe with my left hand.

To my surprise, the three remaining soldiers turned as one, as if they had practiced it like a choreography, jerked hard on the reins and spun their horses around in a one hundred-and eighty-degree spin. I screamed my war cry, and they laid their boots on the sides of their horses, riding off in a flurry of mud and snow. I gave chase, screaming for about thirty seconds. Then I reined Little Joe in, satisfied the soldiers had lost their taste for blood.

They'd go back to Philadelphia and report how the Pale Rider had killed seven of them, and not wanting to admit they ran like cowards, they'll say I somehow disappeared like the mist, or whatever rumors were going around about me these days. My personal favorite was that the natives had taught me their magic, and I could shape shift into animals.

After reloading my pistols, I turned Little Joe around and headed back down the road at an easy trot. It'd take me hours to catch up to the men, then tonight and into the morning to find Lafayette.

The snow came down harder with large, thick flakes, and though we were miserable, I was happy to see it. The British wouldn't be in a rush to send more men out after us, and if they did, the newly fallen snow would cover our tracks.

Halfway back to Valley Forge, we caught up to Lafayette and the wagon. He was still running the horses hard, but I had him slow down to a walk. If we stopped in this storm, we might freeze to death. We pushed hard through the night and next morning, making a slow go of it. In the deep snow and mud, the wagon slowed us to a snail pace, but there was nothing to be done about it, since we were in this trouble in the first place because of the wagon. Well, because of the food on the wagon, but at this point, I wasn't going to argue any difference.

I ordered Washington's three men to ride ahead and let the men at Valley Forge know we were coming. I didn't want them to see the wagon and think we were the British. News of the wagon would spread, and that would also help with the men's morale. Washington had started running short on food, and men were going to starve to death if something wasn't done. I was already planning our next raid.

When we finally rode into the camp, General Washington was sitting on his horse, Nelson, waiting for us. He resembled a marble statue, sitting straight and proud, not moving. Fresh snow covered his hat and shoulders, but he pretended not to notice. He'd never voiced it in words, but it was important to him to always appear strong in front of his men. If they lost faith in him, the war was over. That I understood very well. In a very real way, he was the embodiment of the war. He held these men together like a weld, in a way the hope of freedom from the British could not.

Those who had screamed for freedom from oppression and declared war and independence presently lay in warm dry beds surrounded by their families, while these men who had no voice slept in the cold, far away from their homes. In my timeline, General Washington had been captured in Philadelphia and hung in the streets. The war was as good as over on that day. The rest of the colonies had fallen like dominoes. When I saved his life, and changed history, I truly had no way of knowing how much I had changed it. Dr. Rock, a historian in my time, had explained that Washington's death was the beginning of the end for the colonists. At the time, I didn't really believe that one man's life could be such a driving force for a whole nation to rally behind.

Now I knew differently.

I rode up to the General who nodded briefly in greeting.

"I'll need a word with you and Marie," he said.

Lafayette jumped off the wagon, letting the soldiers take it to the supply area as he grabbed the reins of his horse tied to the back of the wagon. We followed the General to one of the few wooden buildings in the camp. Lafayette and I shared a tent, but the General had a room in this log cabin-like structure. When we arrived, the General yelled for a soldier standing by the front door and ordered him to take our three horses to the barn.

As we stepped up to the front door, the General thanked us for the much-needed food.

"I'm sorry, General," I interrupted him. "We should have tried for more. At the time I thought it was more important to get one wagon with less chance of being caught, but now, after seeing the men's faces, I regret that decision. We should have tried for two wagons."

"Perhaps," Washington said. "Then again, perhaps not. Either way, you mistook their smiles. My three soldiers have been regaling them with stories about you since their arrival."

"Oh?"

"They tell a story about being captured and taken down into a basement," he continued. "A basement in a tavern filled with British soldiers. They also talked about a knife fight in the dark between you and seven men. Then they say you attacked a dozen soldiers, single handedly, on horseback."

"In all fairness, sir," I countered, "your men killed two of those first seven soldiers. And it was only ten soldiers on horseback, not a full dozen."

"Fairness you say," he repeated my words in a sardonic tone. "In all fairness, you never should have tried to rescue those men, and every one of them know it. You should have cut your losses and headed back for the camp with the food. But no, not the famous Pale Rider. You send Lafayette away with the wagon, and go back into the city on foot, to get those men, alone. They are starting to believe the fantastic tales about you."

"As am I, General," Lafayette said. "Although, my time with Thomas has me believing *Bringer of Death* is a more accurate name."

I didn't know what to say and pursed my lips. It wasn't like I could tell them the truth. That I would have left his men and came back to camp, except the British had my horse and satchel. Those they could *not* have.

"I have good news and bad news for you," Washington said. "The bad news can wait a few hours. The good news is in there, behind this door."

He opened the door and motioned for me to enter first. I stepped in and right in front of me was Annie. Her wild red hair was impossible to miss; in fact, it drew the eye to her. My heart leaped, trying to escape my chest. I couldn't believe my eyes. Old Ben, Molly, and Regan stood behind her. They were smiling, and Annie rushed to me.

"Thomas," Annie yelled with excitement in her strong Irish accent.

We met somewhere in the distance between us. I hadn't known I'd moved forward until she landed in my arms. Public affection wasn't socially acceptable, but I didn't care who saw us. We were locked in a deep kiss that I didn't want to end. Old Ben stood back, politely giving us our moment, but Molly and Regan were under the belief it was their moment as well and joined in the hug, locking themselves to my legs.

"What's this?" Annie asked as she pulled back, rubbing her palm over my face, feeling the beard.

"It's temporary," I answered. "It will be gone soon, so don't get used to it."

"Too bad. I like it."

"What are you doing here?" I asked. "How did you get here? Why…? Is everything ok?"

"Shush," she said, putting a finger to my lips. "One question at a time. We are fine. The British were looking for us, so we had to flee. I didn't know where to go and remembered you said you were going to Valley Forge to meet with General Washington, so we came here."

"Mother and Grandpa stripped our farm and the Johnson farm of its blankets, food and animals," Molly added, trying to help her mother explain.

"We filled two wagons," Regan added. "Grandpa and I drove one wagon, and mother and Molly drove the other wagon."

I glanced over to the General who grinned slightly and nodded.

"They brought us much needed supplies," Washington added to the story. "I had some of my staff officers double up and made a room for them. They'll have to share a room, but it's better than a tent."

The smile on my face sunk and then disappeared as I stared into the General's eyes. He was a good man, and a fine leader, but he could also be shrewd. He should have sent them away right when they got here, or at best told me they'd have to leave in a day or so. Instead of sending them away, he'd ordered a room emptied for them at the expense of his officers. Annie and her family were in danger here and would be taking up beds and eating the food meant for fighting soldiers. He wanted something big from me and having me in his debt made it a lot easier for him to ask. My stomach dropped as all this sank in.

"What is it, Thomas?" Annie asked, seeing my face change with emotion. "Is something wrong? I shouldn't have followed you. I'm sorry, Thomas. I didn't know what else to do."

"No, no, no," I said, trying to ease her mind. "You did the right thing. I'm happy you're here. But I need a word with General Washington before we speak. Go to the room the good General has set up for you, and I'll be there shortly."

Ben stepped up and with a nod, offered his hand to me. We shook hands and without a word, he began peeling the girls off my legs. Annie kissed me again and then turned away, taking her family to their room.

"Ok, General, do you want to do this now or in private?" I asked with a hard edge to my tone.

I may have liked and respected the man, but I knew when I was being played, and he was playing me hard right now.

"Do what, sir?" he asked in an oddly light tone.

"Oh, I think you know what I'm talking about," I responded. "I want to know now, before I talk to Annie and her daughters. Before I go in there and make promises I can't keep."

The General nodded. "Very well, Thomas. I had thought to ask you for another favor. You are the only person I believe qualified, but I wasn't sure if even you could accomplish it. Not until my men told me about the tavern."

"And the whole getting Annie a room and not sending her away?" I pressed.

"I'll admit, I thought you'd have a greater chance for success if you weren't distracted with that concern. This way, you'll know the whole family is safe. I give you my word to look after them."

"Greater chance for success at what?"

He motioned for me to follow him as he turned and walked farther into the building. I followed the General to what was once a library but now served as his war room. I waved Lafayette to follow us. I didn't know what was going on in the General's head, but I trusted Lafayette and wanted him there in case I needed advice.

Washington took a seat at the long table and motioned for us to take seats on the opposite side. Maps, orders, and lists covered the table like a parchment tablecloth. Some of the lists bore names of those who had died this week of starvation or sickness. Washington reached into his coat and withdrew an envelope. He reopened the envelope and pulled out three pieces of paper folded in half.

"Mr. Franklin, Benjamin Franklin, was sent to Paris to represent the United States as our first ambassador of sorts," Washington told me, handing me the letter.

The way he said the man's name made me think Franklin must be important. It reminded me of the James Bond movies. Should I know this Franklin? Not in my timeline.

"*Monsieur* Franklin?" Lafayette asked, his words tinged with disbelief. "I have met him. I found him to be a brilliant and true gentleman."

I'd never heard of this Benjamin Franklin guy. Lafayette and General Washington were apparently familiar with the man. As I opened the letter, I wondered if he was giving me the letter so I'd know he wasn't hiding anything from me, or was he hiding something and gave me the letter so I wouldn't consider that very question. I was becoming a suspicious person. People in my time seemed to assume gentlemen from this time in history were forthright and honest. The longer I was here, the more I realized powerful men in any timeline will use people to get what they wanted. In the General's case, winning the war was what he cared about.

"Mr. Franklin has been trying to get the French to align themselves with us and join in our fight," Washington explained. "After the battle at Saratoga, the world saw it was possible to defeat the British. Upon reading about Saratoga, King Louis was ready to commit his country and resources."

"I knew it was only a matter of time before my countrymen joined us in this fight!" Lafayette declared triumphantly, as he slammed his fist against the table, a smile plastered on his face.

Dr. Rock had been right. She said if I'd help the colonists win the battle of Saratoga, the French would join the war. I had accomplished the first two of my three missions. Save General Washington, help win the battle of Saratoga, and make sure the colonists won the battle at Yorktown. Washington was safe, so he would lead the Americans. Saratoga had been won, so now the French would join in the war.

The battle of Yorktown was my final objective.

"However, Mr. Franklin reports the Prime Minister of England, Lord North, is convincing King George to send seventy-five thousand troops against us," Washington said as I read the letter.

Seventy-five thousand troops were twice as many as Dr. Rock had said the British would send. It was going to be difficult and grueling to win the war up against thirty-two thousand troops, but if they sent seventy-five thousand, the colonists would have no chance.

"Mr. Franklin is certain the king's other advisors are against sending so many soldiers," Washington said. "Mr. Franklin is not one for secrets or hidden plans. He believes that secret government plans, like vines grown in the dark, wither and die. Only those vines in plain sight and bask in the sun shall grow strong. I say this so you can imagine my surprise when I read his correspondence."

I was reading the letter while I listened to Washington. So far, the letter made sense, but then, I had no idea what Washington was talking about.

"It reads King Louis of France will not commit his navy to our cause, if King George sends so many soldiers," I said.

"You see our problem," Washington said as if that explained everything.

"Yes," I answered, "only, I don't understand what you want from me. I'm not a diplomat."

Lafayette laughed at me. "You're a diplomat with those guns. I've seen you end many battles with them."

"Yes, very funny Marie," I said. "But that's not what Mr. Franklin needs right now, is it?"

"Keep reading," Washington instructed. "Turns out, you're exactly the kind of diplomat whom Mr. Franklin thinks he needs."

I handed the first page to Lafayette as I read the second page of the letter. Franklin stressed the importance of this missive being burned and never spoken of again. He had a plan that wasn't worthy of being written down in the new country's history. Then I read his plan.

"He wants you to assassinate the Prime Minister of England?" I asked with no small measure of incredulity.

"Yes," Washington said flatly.

"King Louis would never agree to such an act," Lafayette said. "I know the king, and he would never resort to this course of warfare. There are rules to warfare, after all."

"King Louis didn't agree to it," Washington told him. "He has, however, implied he will still commit his forces to the war if Lord North was no longer the king's adviser and Prime Minister."

I kept reading the letter while trying to listen to the General. Franklin wrote the assassin had to be from America. King Louis didn't want to know the details, claiming it was below the crown to be a part of it. The king made it clear he also wouldn't risk having a French citizen captured or killed in such an attempt. If the attempt failed, then the French would look incompetent. If Lord North was killed, and it was later learned that the assassin was a French subject, King Louis would be blamed, and the French would be dragged into another war on their own lands again. The king may also be concerned the British might retaliate and send an assassin of their own, targeting him. King Louis preferred the idea of fighting the British in foreign lands. The British would be away from their supply routes, and French lands would go unmolested.

"I noticed Mr. Franklin didn't spell out this plan of his," I commented.

Washington shook his head. "No. The man I send will have to get that information from Mr. Franklin himself."

"And he mentions a favor. But doesn't say what kind of favor or for whom the favor is for." Favors could mean big trouble. I had learned that lesson long ago.

"On the last page," Washington pointed out. "It doesn't answer your question but says he has a contact who can get whoever I send into Windsor Castle and close to Lord North. For a price."

"That's good news," I said. "If the doing the favor itself doesn't get the man you send killed before he has a chance to get near the castle."

Washington gave me a tight grin. "You should be flattered. Franklin requested you by name. Your reputation has made it all the way to France."

I handed the second page to Lafayette as I read over the last page. I could read it again for details later, but right now I was searching for my name. Was the General messing with me, or did this Franklin guy in Paris really mention me by name? Halfway down the page, two words jumped out at me like an angry snake. *Washington's Assassin.*

"I'll go with you," Lafayette proclaimed before I even agreed. "I know every inch of France. I know Monsieur Franklin, and I'm a close friend of King Louis."

I shook my head. "No. Plus, I never said I would go."

"The Pale Rider has improved morale in the camp and struck a chord of fear in the heart of every British soldier," Washington said. "If he were to go to England and kill Lord North, think of the fear you would spread here and in England. King Louis would be inspired. The king might join the fight based on your actions alone. If the Pale Rider were seen and blamed, then the French wouldn't be implicated in the assassination."

My eyes went wide with disbelief, and I lifted them from the parchment. "You want the British to know it was the Pale Rider who did this act? You talk about the Pale Rider as if he's a friend of mine I can ask to do this for you. General, *I'm* the Pale Rider. You want me to go to a strange country, take the blame, and have the reward for my life doubled? Tripled maybe?" I didn't call him crazy outright, but I'm sure he could tell I thought as much from the tone of my voice.

The General didn't even flinch at my outcry. "Yes, you're the one they call the Pale Rider, Thomas. But the Pale Rider is now more than a man. He has become a symbol, an idea even. He's bigger than just you."

"Maybe," I said, resigned. "But I'm the one they're trying to kill."

"It would help relations with the French," he answered in a flat tone, as if he wasn't asking me to commit suicide. "Neither the British nor the French know your real name. Throw away your guns and black vest after the deed is done, and they'll never know who you are, or I should say who the Pale Rider was."

Like I would throw away the guns or vest.

But Washington was onto something. It was my fault King George was now planning to send twice as many soldiers. I was supposed to kill a bunch of soldiers, and save Washington, not travel across the ocean to sneak into a real castle and assassinate a Prime Minister. My life was too complicated.

Once I'd heard a saying I could never remember correctly. Something like a butterfly flaps its wings in Brazil and causes a hurricane in Texas. I had become that butterfly.

I had played with history and changed the timeline, and maybe now I'd prevented my wife Jenny from being killed. No, not killed, murdered. And not for certain. Until I had that certainty, I had to go to Paris and meet this Franklin guy. If I didn't go, then everything I had done might be for nothing, and Jenny might still be doomed.

But I didn't necessarily *like* to willingly play the part of Washington's Assassin.

If I was being honest with myself, I didn't mind killing soldiers who were helping England to rule the world one day. While I never enjoyed taking a life, I didn't have nightmares after, like others I'd known. What really concerned me was the fact I *wasn't* disturbed by it. Jenny and my best friend Aden always thought I was a good man, but I never saw that in myself. I was more bothered that I didn't have nightmares or remorse than I was about any deaths at my hand. I always thought if I *were* disturbed by it, by the killing, it might indicate I really was a good person who only did what he had to. Since I wasn't bothered by anything I'd ever done, I wondered, was I a bad person?

The line between justice and revenge was so thin I couldn't see it anymore. Luckily for me, I didn't care. My plan was to get justice and stop Jenny from being murdered. If I couldn't save Jenny, then I'd seek revenge. Either way, I was going to Paris and killing Lord North. His future was a big part of my past. I was going, and I knew it. General Washington seemed to know it as well.

"You don't speak French and will need an interpreter," Lafayette said, breaking my train of thought. "I've also been to Windsor Castle twice. You need me, Thomas."

I didn't want to be the cause of Lafayette's death. My mind scrambled to think of a good reason why he shouldn't accompany me, but I couldn't think of anything.

"No, Marie," I tried to protest. "This is going to be too dangerous."

"Thomas, men must make their own decisions," Lafayette said. "The British killed my father in the seven-year war. I came here seeking revenge against the British for my father. This is the best way I can hurt the British. Do not deny me this."

He was right; I did need him, and I couldn't do it without him. I nodded in acknowledgement.

"How do you suggest we get to Paris and this Franklin gentleman?" I asked Washington.

"You will need to capture a ship," Washington said as if that was the most common thing to do. "Any of our American ships would be sunk before they got close to Europe. You'll need a British owned ship. I've already ordered my officers to go through the camp and find at least two hundred soldiers with sailing experience. I've the perfect man to captain the ship and get you to Paris. He promised he can have you there in less than six weeks. You leave in two days."

I stood up to face General Washington.

"Ok." I accepted the task begrudgingly. "I'll do what needs to be done. But I have some terms."

"Name them, sir," Washington said from his seat.

"First, I'll have your word of honor that you'll see to Annie and her family's safety until I return. Longer if I don't return."

"You have it, sir," Washington said formally. "That is the whole reason they're staying here now."

"Second, I'm in charge. This captain you have may command the ship, but I command the mission. This is to be made clear to him. On the water, I decide what we do and as captain, he'll decide how we do it."

"The Scotsman will not like that," Washington said in a clipped, knowing tone. "They can be temperamental. But I'll set pen to paper and have those words written down as an official command. Any more conditions?"

"Just one more. I don't think the British are going to willingly give up one of their ships. I rather think they'll give chase. I have a few ideas about it and will require certain supplies."

The General leaned to the side and yelled for one of his aides, Alexander. A tall, young Lieutenant Colonel entered the room with a rolled-up piece of paper and a small ring-sized box in his hands.

"Thomas, I believe you've already met Lieutenant Colonel Hamilton?" Washington asked with a wave of his hand.

"Yes, sir," I answered. "We met shortly after the Battle of Saratoga."

Hamilton offered a wide, friendly smile and nodded in greeting.

"Alexander, Thomas will provide you with a list of items he requires for his mission. Please see they are filled."

"Yes, sir," Hamilton replied.

"Other than Mr. Adams and Mr. Franklin, no one outside of this room can know about this mission," General Washington said, fixing us with his gaze, one by one. "Not even the captain or the crew of the ship."

Hamilton held up the items in his hands to the General as a reminder of something. The General stared at them and suddenly smiled.

"Yes," Washington said. "I almost forgot. I've one condition of my own, Thomas."

The General took the paper from Hamilton. "Franklin will try bulling you if I send you to Paris as a civilian. I also can't require a captain in my new Navy to subject himself to the orders of a private citizen."

Washington handed the paper to me to read and took the small ring box from Hamilton's hand, opening it up. Two small, gold maple leaves the size of quarters sat in the box.

"I also don't like you running around as a civilian picking your battles and choosing your fights," Washington continued as I read the paper.

"You're making me a Major?" I asked, a little too loud.

I was getting a commission in Washington's army? What the –?

"Yes," Washington answered. "Congratulations Major Nelson. You'll also be promoted to Lieutenant Colonel upon your return."

Chapter Two: Long Goodbyes

I woke up with my arms wrapped around Annie. We were in my tent, still nestled under several wool blankets. The sounds of male voices talking, footsteps crunching through the several inches of snow, and a hammer pounding on a piece of metal permeated the thick cotton walls of the tent. Hamilton had been kind enough to allow Lafayette to sleep in his room, giving Annie and me privacy and time to discuss our future together. That was if I remained alive to *have* a future with her. I didn't tell her the details of my mission, but I had informed her about my being drafted in the Army and that I was going away for several months.

Through the crack in the tent flap, daylight broke the horizon, and I squinted against the light

Lafayette told me yesterday Hamilton had asked him to recount our battles together. Hamilton had also wanted to know about any of the battles I might have talked about being in. The Lieutenant Colonel was most interested in where I was from.

Lafayette had been more than happy to recount everything to Hamilton. I didn't mind until Lafayette told me Hamilton had written down every word of every story. I would need to talk to Hamilton and ask him to remove my name from those stories and give the credit to better known men. Men who *should* appear in history books.

Annie was already awake. She laid there with her eyes open, gazing at me with her soft eyes.

"Good morning," I croaked.

"You snore," Annie replied, smiling.

"How long have you been awake?"

"A while," she answered. "I didn't want to wake you."

Her finger gently traced the scar on my head. The injury I'd suffered no longer physically hurt me, but pain filled her eyes every time she saw it.

She stood up, still naked, and gathered her clothes. The soft skin of her back, legs, and breasts were covered with goose bumps from the frigid air. I laid back and enjoyed watching her dress. I wanted to grab her by her thin waist and pull her down to me, to make love to her again, but duty called. I needed to find Lafayette and General Washington. She wanted to get back to her daughters before they woke up. I waited until she finished dressing, not wanting to take my eyes off her before I dressed myself.

"Do you have a uniform, Major Nelson?" Annie asked me in a coy tone.

"No," I answered. "I made the General agree to two conditions to my enlistment. The first condition was I'd *not* have to wear a uniform."

She rubbed the back of her hand against my chin, feeling how smooth it was.

"I miss the beard," she said with a sad look on her face. "It really did look good on you."

Old Ben had lent me his straight razor yesterday, and Annie had patiently shaved my face. I had never used a straight razor before and feared cutting my own throat.

"It will grow back," I said, laughing. "If you liked it so much, maybe I'll keep it next time."

Seeing the smile grow on her face with those words, I was doomed to not shave again after this war was over.

As I dressed, I checked my weapons and equipment, and took stock of my ammo and medical supplies. I still had plenty but had been burning through both faster than I had expected to. I planned on taking my satchel with everything I could carry in it. Everything else that I didn't think I needed or didn't have room in my satchel for, I placed in my backpack and asked Annie to keep it for me. I made her promise to burn the backpack and everything in it if I didn't return to her. I didn't want to wake the girls, so I also asked Annie to say goodbye for me. We stepped out of the tent, our boots crunching in the snow. I buttoned up my jacket as we walked. Annie pulled one of our blankets tighter around herself.

Men lined up into two columns, ready to start on the march that would last today and tomorrow. The men had been told to take off their uniforms and wear whatever clothes they had with them. Most dressed like sailors. Several wagons were at the tail end of the column with food, barrels of water, and other items I'd asked for. Among many problems we might face, we weren't going to be able to resupply before we sailed, so I wanted six weeks of food and water.

I noticed most of the men ready to march were the older men. Not old men, but older. Many of the soldiers in camp were sixteen to twenty-five years old. These men appeared to be hardened men in their thirties. I wasn't sure if that was intentional or not. These men had scarred faces and calloused hands, and more than one man was missing some teeth.

General Washington, Lafayette, and Hamilton stood at the head of the column, next to a man I'd never seen before. He dressed in civilian clothes like everyone else but stood like an officer. His clothes were more expensive than the rest of the men's clothes were. Washington and Hamilton wore their full uniforms. Lafayette held the reins to Little Joe and two more horses, and it was only the second time I'd ever seen Lafayette not in his blue French uniform. His left hand kept scratching and pulling at his new pants. I had a feeling Lafayette tucked his uniform into his saddle bags.

I kissed Annie one last time and watched her walk into the cabin. I didn't take my eyes off her until the door shut behind her. I could feel more than one set of eyes on me, but I didn't care who saw. Once she was inside with the door shut, my chest heaved as I inhaled deeply through my nose and blew out of my mouth as I thought about how much I was going to miss her. Breaking my gaze from the log cabin, I turned and walked up to the group of men waiting for me.

"Thomas," Washington said, with a smile on his face and pointed his right hand at me. "May I introduce Captain John Paul Jones? Captain Jones, this is Major Thomas Nelson."

John Paul Jones was a fit-looking, dark-haired man with capable hands and an intense gaze, which was presently fixated on me. Washington had put a little emphasis on the title *Major* in our introduction. I guess Captain Jones wasn't crazy about me being the boss, and Washington was throwing out a little reminder. For his part, Jones kept his composure and smiled as he offered his hand.

"Major," Jones said in acknowledgement, giving a small tip of his head.

"Call me Thomas."

"One hundred and seventy-five men," Washington said. "All these men have sailing experience. Four of them are carpenters, like you requested. Don't forget to leave a few men behind to report how things went."

"Yes, sir," I said.

"Are you sure about their attire, Thomas?" Washington asked with doubt in his voice. "If these men are captured in civilian clothing, they'll be shot or hung as spies."

"It's the only chance we have, sir," I told him. "Otherwise, there's no reason to go at all."

"Very well, Thomas," Washington said, resigned. "I'll trust your judgement. God be with you."

"Company!" Jones yelled out.

He got the men's attention and was about to order them to forward march. He stopped with a lung full of air and made a show of blowing it out before putting on an apologetic face.

"I'm sorry, Major," Jones said mockingly. "Would you prefer to give the command, or would you like me to?"

So that's how it's going to be.

He was mad I was in command and planned on being childish about it. What was with the eighteenth century and everyone wanting to take command away from me? Lafayette tried it when we first met, and now Jones. I didn't have the time or patience for this bullshit and was going to put an end to it right now. I took a step forward, and Washington patted me on the back, then gave my arm a little squeeze.

"Like I said," Washington said as he walked away. "I trust your judgement."

From the look in his eyes and his choice of words, he'd known what was going to happen and didn't wish to witness it.

"Lieutenant Colonel Hamilton, with me, if you please," General Washington yelled as he walked off a little faster than normal.

The General didn't want his aide Hamilton to witness this either. Hamilton's head swiveled back and forth from me to Jones as he walked away. He was a bright one and knew he had missed something important. To his regret, he knew he was going to miss more.

"Captain, we need to talk," I said.

"Yes, Major," Jones said, oblivious to my mood. "Or would you prefer Pale Rider?"

"Keep poking that hornet's nest," Lafayette muttered under his breath, obviously enjoying this repartee.

"You can call me Thomas or Major," I said coldly. "Follow me please."

"Now, Major?" Jones asked. "We should be going. Can it wait?"

"No, Captain," I answered. "Now."

Without looking back or checking if he was following me, I marched away, my boots crunching down in the snow as I headed for the backside of the closest cabin. After I walked around the cabin and made sure we were out of sight of most of the men in the column, I stopped and spun to face him.

"Is there a reason we needed to talk back here?" Jones asked.

"Yes," I bit out. "I don't want you to lose the respect of your men."

"And how would I lose their respect?" he asked me, his eyebrows lifting.

Before I was Washington's assassin, I was Aden's security specialist. Before that, I was a police officer. But before that, I earned money bare knuckle boxing, and I was incredibly good at it. I now drew on that point in my life and the experience I had gained to clear up any misunderstandings between Jones and me.

"John," I started off.

"Captain Jones, if you please, Major," he corrected me.

"Captain," I started off again, taking a deep, calming breath through my nose. "Captain, I know you're used to dealing with officers who are considered gentlemen," I told him, trying to sound patient and reasonable. "I know you gentlemen are good at being passive aggressive and acting snippy, like a bunch of wet nurses with dried up tits, but I don't have time for that. Nor do I have time to earn your respect in the days to come. We have a ship to capture and a fleet to avoid. Then, when we reach Paris, the hard part for me will begin."

"With all due respect, Major," Jones countered, as his hands curled into fists and his eyebrows dropped low between his eyes. "What makes you think you're qualified to give me any orders? Everyone knows you were granted the rank of Major only because you're Washington's personal assassin."

And with those words, I stepped forward, rotating my body to the left, and using my core and arm muscles together as I'd been taught many years ago, drove my right fist up hard into his solar plexus. It connected solidly. Jones doubled over as the air in his lungs exploded out of him in a whoosh. He dropped to his hands and knees, vomiting on the ground.

He began to panic at not being able to breathe. His head kept jerking back, like he was dry heaving in reverse. He tried over and over to suck in air but wasn't able to. I'd seen the same panicked look before. Never in the boxing ring against opponents who knew to tighten their stomachs, but a few times on criminals who'd resisted arrest and mistakenly chose to fight. I believed I'd made my point and went down on one knee next to him, placing my left hand on his back.

"It's ok, Captain," I said. "You'll be fine. Slow down and take small breaths. Don't panic, and you'll be fine in a second. Just focus on taking small breaths."

After a few more tries, he was able to suck in a small bit of air. Then another and bigger breath. He started breathing normally and stood up on shaky legs.

"I shall report this to General Washington," Jones said between gasping breaths.

I swung another right fist, this time aiming for his jaw. I didn't put much of my power behind it. I didn't want to break his jaw, after all. His head snapped to the side, followed by his body, as his already weak knees buckled, and he dropped to the ground, onto his face. The snow helped break his fall. I dropped to my knee again and turned him onto his side. I slapped his face, calling his name. His eyes blinked as he came to, looking confused.

"Stand up," I said, grabbing his left arm and pulling him to his feet. "Choose your next words carefully. It'll be hard for you to keep your dignity if you leave here with blood on your face."

I brushed snow off his shoulders and straightened his uniform. He was visibly upset, and his mouth worked – afraid to say anything. Snow clung to the right side of his face and head. Vomit stuck to his chin and lower lip. I wasn't about to wipe that off for him.

"Look, Jones," I said firmly. "I didn't want this. But how did you think this was going to go when you insult and purposely antagonize a man whose only actual skill is fighting? Think, man. You went out of your way to upset a man you refer to as an assassin. Now I'd like to be nice and try to be friends but as I said, I don't have time for that."

Jones laughed as if he knew something I didn't. The vomit on his lower lip quivered.

"You half-witted buffoon!" he yelled as spittle shot from his mouth. "I may walk out of here with blood on my face, but you'll hang for this. You're in the Colonial Army now and you have struck an officer twice. You, sir, now fall under military law. General Washington himself can't save you from this."

I grabbed him by the throat and pushed him forward, slamming him against the cabin. The back of his head bounced off the log wall with a resounding *thunk*. My right knee came up and collided with his balls. He doubled over again, and I let go of him as he plunged to the ground. Groaning, he laid on his side, unable to move, then suddenly and violently vomited again.

Lafayette chose that moment to walk around the corner of the cabin to check on us. He took one look at the captain on the ground and swiveled around without a word, retreating to the column faster than he came.

"I told him not to poke the hornets' nest," Lafayette muttered to himself, barely audible as he walked away.

Reaching into my coat, I pulled out the paper Washington had given me. It wasn't the appointment to Major I'd first read. It was the new one I had him write for me. My second of two conditions, which I thought of as my fail safe. Going down on one knee again in front of Jones, wet snow and mud seeping into my pants, I held the paper out in front of him, several inches from his face.

"This says I've been appointed to the rank of Major," I explained. "Read the date on the warrant."

Jones had to pull his head back a few inches to get a better look at the paper. His eyes squinted as he scanned the document, stopping at the bottom.

"It says December seventh," Jones coughed out. "I don't understand."

"Today is the sixth," I told him flatly. "I'm not in the Colonial Army until tomorrow. I don't fall under your code of conduct. I'm still a civilian, and therefore, I fall under civil law. There'll be no hanging today. At worse, you could have me arrested. But the General needs me so he'll let me go, and I'll still have my mission and a different captain to master the ship. After today, I'll be a Major. However, for you to bring charges against me, you'll have to admit under oath you were out of uniform, in a time of war. That would make you a spy, like Washington said. In short, Captain, if we ever need to have this conversation again, I'll kill you and dump your body without hesitation. Do you understand me?"

He still didn't know what my mission was but knew it was important. The question he'd have to ask himself was, what was more important to General Washington and the Continental Congress? His services or the unknown mission? Jones was still lying with his face in the snow, but after a few seconds of thinking, he made a nodding motion with his head.

"Good," I said. "I'll be with our men waiting for you. Take your time, compose yourself, and for God's sake, wipe the vomit off your lip. You're an officer."

I stood up and walked back to the column. Lafayette stared at me as I returned. I took the reins and climbed into the saddle, mounting Little Joe. Lafayette and I sat on our horses for another ten minutes waiting, neither of us saying a word.

Captain Jones finally walked from around the cabin toward us. He kept his eyes straight ahead, not looking around. He focused on his horse as if the rest of us didn't exist. I was glad he was going to be riding a horse, because he was walking slowly and a little funny. His balls were going to take some punishment bouncing in the saddle, but I didn't think he could keep up walking, and he'd be fine by the time we reached Philadelphia. Jones slowly climbed onto his horse and, for a minute, his face blanched whiter than the snow. I thought he might throw up again, but he managed to maintain his composure. His shirt and hair were wet from the melted snow, but all in all, he looked little worse for wear.

The British had docked an armada of ships in the harbor at Philadelphia, and we were somehow going to take one. Jones kept insisting it would be impossible to capture a ship still in the harbor, but that was why Washington ordered *me* to do it, and not him.

"When you're ready, Captain," I said, letting him know to take charge.

"Thank you ... sir ... um ... Major."

He now knew I wasn't a Major until tomorrow morning but couldn't bring himself to use my name yet. I hoped this was going to be the end of our problems. I didn't want Jones as an enemy, but I didn't have time to try to win him over, either.

Other than the wagons, Jones, Lafayette, and I were the only three who had horses. The rest of the men were on foot, so the going was slow through the snow and mud. Captain Jones rode in silence, and I didn't try to engage him in conversation. I wanted to give him time to cool off and lick his wounds, not look like I was rubbing his ass-kicking in his face.

I let him decide when and where we made camp. I didn't care for the first spot he picked out, but it was defendable, so I let it go. I ordered him to go around and check on the men who were marching on foot. They needed to trust and respect him if he were going to command them on the ship. He wasn't going to earn their respect by sulking like a child. I asked Lafayette to talk to him, so he wasn't an outcast. Lafayette knew how to talk to men like him – self-inflated men. They spoke the same language.

"We need to bring him back into the decision-making process," I told Lafayette.

I had broken Jones down. Now I needed to build him back up.

The next morning, Jones called me Major in greeting, and I took that as a good sign. Hell, I took the fact that he didn't try to kill me in my sleep as a positive indication.

We arrived at our destination midday on December eighth. We ordered the men and wagons to make camp and rest south of Philadelphia and a few hundred yards from the water's edge. Captain Jones, Lafayette, and I trekked on foot to scout the harbor. We walked in the snow-crusted sand, staying close to the water.

Jones and Lafayette weren't accustomed to pretending to be anything less than professional soldiers but followed my lead. We kept our distance from the city and got close enough to see the ships. Seagulls flew over our heads, crying. I threw a few rocks, and the birds flew down, hoping for food. The tangy scent of salt and fish was strong in the air. Half a dozen row boats sat in the ocean carrying men fishing with frosted nets or crab traps on deck. A shiver went down my back about how cold that water had to be.

At least a dozen ships were anchored in the harbor. Jones used his telescope as he looked the ships over. I had my range finder out as I wracked my brain, trying to think of a way to capture one of the ships.

One ship was anchored in the middle of the water, away from the rest. It appeared to be the easiest one to capture since it was segregated. It had three decks of guns, and her sails were down. I wasn't sure what it was doing there. The captain anchored her in a bad place. She was practically in the way of any ships coming or going into the port.

"How about that one?" I asked, pointing to the massive mountain of a ship.

"That would be the HMS Sandwich, Major," Jones replied. "That would also be a worse choice to make. She has three decks of guns. Ninety guns total. She's being used as a floating battery. No ships sail in or out of the harbor without her captain's permission. She's anchored east for a reason. She has forty-five guns facing any ship wanting to leave the harbor, and forty-five guns facing any ship wanting to enter it. Half her crew is awake during the day and half are awake at night. And she's your first problem to overcome, because she'll blow us out of the water when we try to leave the harbor."

"I'm impressed, Captain," I said. "How do you know all that?"

"Her name's written on the side," Jones said. "I know the Sandwich has ninety guns and the only reason to anchor her in the middle would be to block the harbor."

Jones pointed to the two closest ships to us tied up to the first dock.

"That's the Dublin and Lenox," Jones said. "They are carrying seventy-four guns. They'd be good choices, but they have a lot of men on board, and I don't think we could take either one before reinforcements came. If we did manage to capture one of them, the HMS Sandwich would end us as we pulled away from the docks."

Jones's telescope moved down the line of ships as he read off the names.

"HMS Cornwall and that is the HMS Ajax," he said. "They also carry seventy-four guns. I would love to have the Ajax. She's beautiful. But the same problem as the others. We need more men to sail them, and I don't see how we could capture them anyway."

I was now glad Washington had picked Jones to captain our ship. I thought he was going to be more trouble than he was worth, but I didn't know anything about these ships, while he knew a great deal.

"There's the Vengeance," Jones continued, pointing. "There's the Resolution. She's an Elizabeth class ship."

I had no idea what an Elizabeth class ship was or why I should care. She was big and had a lot of guns on her. That was about all I could see.

"Those ships there are your next problem, Major," Jones said, pointing to two more ships. "HMS Defiance and Vigilant. They are Intrepid class ships. Amazingly fast. Unless we take one of them, we'll most likely not be able to outrun those two on the open sea."

Jones named off a few more ships that he seemed to know by sight. But he'd skipped two of the ships that were smaller than the rest and had fewer guns but looked sound. They were tethered to the dock nearest the grain warehouse. They weren't there the last time I was here, but they were in the same spot as the ship that had dropped off the supplies I'd stolen. Men were offloading supplies by hand and stacking them onto wagons. Soldiers stood around watching the loading of supplies this time, more of them than last time.

"You were right, Thomas," Lafayette said, pointing to the soldiers. "They learned."

"What about those two?" I asked.

"HMS Jupiter and HMS Ariel," he said. "The Jupiter has fifty guns, I think, and the Ariel only has twenty-six guns."

"What's wrong with them?" I asked, pointing with my chin. "Can we make do with one of those?"

"I'd rather go for a bigger ship with more guns," Jones said. "We're going to have to fight our way out of the harbor."

I thought about it for a few minutes, looking over the ships. Those two were the only two I thought we'd a chance of taking and holding long enough to get our supplies onto.

"We need to think about this in a different way," I said. "It's going to have to be one of those two ships. Let's work backwards."

Lafayette and Jones locked eyes, then looked at me as if I were crazy. No one in this time period would ever work a problem out by starting at the end instead of the beginning.

"Let's say we can't fight our way out," I said. "Then the first problem would be to find a way to get out of the harbor without a fight."

"That would be nice, Major," Jones said. "I don't see how that is going to be possible. If you could convince the British to give us a ship and let us pull away, the HMS Sandwich would still sink us."

"So, the Sandwich is our problem?" I asked.

"Our first problem," Jones answered, then corrected himself. "Actually, it's our last problem, because we need to capture a ship and hope we've enough men still alive to sail it before we get near the Sandwich."

"No, Captain," I countered. "The Sandwich is not our last problem. It's our first problem."

"How is that, Thomas?" Lafayette asked.

I flicked my chin at the captain. "Ask Jones. He's the one who came up with our solution."

"Captain Jones," I said, getting his attention. "Under your assumption that we can get the British to give us a ship and let us pull away from the docks, which of those two ships should we go after?"

"It doesn't matter, sir," Jones answered, his face screwed up in confusion. "This is crazy."

I was losing him again. He was trapped in traditional thinking, and as soon as I started thinking outside the box, he took it as incompetence.

"An answer, if you please, Mr. Jones. That's an order."

"Well," Jones said, thinking about my question, "normally, I'd say the Jupiter. It's bigger and has more guns, and we've enough men to man her. However, since your question involves us not fighting our way out, then I assume we'll have to run. The Ariel is faster. In fact, of those ships in the harbor, I'd bet only the HMS Defiance and Vigilant are faster than her. We also have more than enough men to man her."

"Really? More than enough? How many men could you spare and still sail her?" I asked.

"She's a Sphinx-class vessel," Jones answered. "More of a frigate. Normal complement for a ship that size is one hundred and forty men. I'd expected to capture a bigger ship like the Ajax or maybe the Resolution. I brought one hundred and seventy-five men for that reason. I could lose thirty-five or forty-five men and still sail her."

"Good," I said, nodding. "Last question. What will happen after those men finish offloading those supplies?"

"They'll replenish her supplies with food and water and whatever else the captain feels he needs," Jones answered. "Then they'll get the ship ready to sail. I don't see any ships in the harbor waiting to offload. The Ariel most likely sailed into the harbor a few hours ago. Her captain might keep the ship tied up to the dock for the night. He may let his men go to town and drink for a few hours. It's what I would do. They'll make sail at first light and head out into open waters."

The screams of seagulls caught my ears, and I glanced up again at one of the small fishing boats out on the ocean. The men were throwing fish parts into the water, and the birds were in a frenzy. A plan was starting to form in my head.

"Marie, how many barrels of gunpowder did we bring?"

"Twenty full barrels, ten empty barrels, thirty feet of fuse, and twenty clay jugs of coal oil," Lafayette answered from memory. "We took almost all the coal oil from Valley Forge. Hamilton was visibly upset about it and didn't want to give that much up. I had to go straight to the General to get that much."

When we'd left Valley Forge, I had a few initial ideas of what we might need and how those items might be used, but now that I was face to face with the problem, I wished I'd asked for more.

"Let's get back to the camp," I said. "We need to come up with a plan and prepare. We attack at sundown."

Chapter Three: Pick A Ship

I strolled up to Lafayette, who was organizing his men and making sure everyone knew their part in the plan. Lafayette held a finely made, beautiful, deep red musket, longer than a standard musket. I had liberated that musket several weeks ago from a British sniper named John Brooks, who'd tried to kill me. He failed, but not for a lack of trying.

I took a second to wonder if the man was still alive. The last time I'd seen him, he'd been accidentally shot in the stomach by one of his own men. I gave him a horse and let him ride away toward the nearest British outpost. He was a determined man, so I figured he may have made it to a doctor in time.

Taking my eyes off the fine musket, I looked over to the sun that had dropped over the misty horizon, and then to the moon already climbing the night sky, giving us ample light to see. I could still make out Lafayette clearly. The moon was going to be a large full moon tonight and would provide a lot of light. This was good for us, but it was also good for the enemy.

"Are you ready and sure of your part?" I asked him.

"*Oui,* Thomas," he answered, exasperated, which made his accent heavier. "You have asked me three times now. I've my men divided up into two groups. The first group has left already. They'll have their part completed before you get on board. They know to make their way back to Valley Forge on their own. I have several men in a good place to watch so they can make a report to General Washington. Little Joe is with them. I made sure they knew you would have their heads if anything happened to him. My second group and I are heading out now. Give us a fifteen-minute head start, and we'll be ready. We'll watch for the signal. Don't leave without me."

We shook hands, and as I pulled away, Lafayette pulled me in for a hug.

"Be careful, *mon ami*," Lafayette said affectionately. "I still have a lot to learn from you."

"See you on board," I said, disentangling myself. "Watch for the signal and don't be late. I'll need you with me in Paris."

He straightened and walked away, stopping next to the wagon with his group of men. They were going to walk towards Philadelphia, taking ten barrels of gunpowder and clay jugs of coal oil with them. I was surprised at the swelling of pride in my chest as I looked at this young man who I'd come to think of as a little brother. He was a fine leader, and I had seen him grow with wisdom since we'd been together.

Captain Jones stood with our second wagon. He had the food and water supplies, plus the empty barrels and extra barrels of gunpowder. I walked up to him and peered down into the wagon. A hundred muskets rested at the bottom of the wagon. Two of our men were covering the contents of the wagon with a blanket.

"Most of the men are already in the city. They know to make their way to the harbor," Jones said without being asked. "They should be safe. Without muskets, they'll look like dock workers. I've given orders for them to stay close enough to be at the ship within minutes of seeing the signal."

I nodded at him. "Good. I'd like more, but that might make anyone who sees us suspicious. You handpicked your ten best men who can get the ship ready while we wait for the others?"

"I don't know all the men," Jones said. "But the ten I picked out seem to have the most experience, including Lieutenant James, my first mate."

"Get the men ready. We move out in fifteen minutes," I commanded.

***

Captain Jones and I marched down the dock like two men doing business. I didn't notice any men on the decks of the two ships tied to the pier for the warehouses, so Jones might have been right about most men being in town. The wagon rolled fifty feet behind us, with the men walking behind it. The soldiers on the docks appeared more concerned about protecting the larger warships than the smaller, already offloaded supply ships. A dozen or more soldiers stood in front of the HMS Ariel, talking lightly and trying to keep warm. I guess they weren't too worried since they didn't so much as glance our way.

We made it to the gangway leading up to the main deck of the Ariel, and Jones removed his hat. At that signal, our sailors at the wagon lit two torches. That was the main signal Lafayette would be waiting for. He and his men had buried or hidden the ten barrels of gun powder in the sand and at different places near the ships. Ten of his men were assigned to light the six- to twelve-inch-long fuses. An eleven-inch fuse took one minute to burn down to the end, so that timing gave us thirty seconds before the first barrel exploded and one minute until the last explosion. We'd left twenty men in the woods with muskets to open fire on the guards and fake an attack.

"Wait here until you see me signal you," I told Jones.

We didn't have time to mess around or allow anyone a chance to give warning. I walked up the ramp and was met by two sailors clutching cudgels and who demanded to know who I was and what business I had there. Without so much as blinking, I smoothly pulled out my Tec-9 with a noise suppressor attached. I fired one round into the first sailor's chest and then another into the chest of his very surprised partner. Their bodies hit the deck hard and might have given alarm to any sailors below.

I didn't have time to worry about that now.

I stepped to the side of the ship and waved at Jones to walk up the gangplank. Twenty men rose up in the grass and snow between the water and the city. Nineteen muskets fired at the same time, and five of the soldiers in front of the Ariel fell. Only nineteen muskets fired because the twentieth man held two flintlock pistols and wore a black vest. His vest didn't look anything like mine, nor did the man look anything like me, but he was a man holding two pistols and wearing a black vest. People would see what they wanted to see.

This was Lafayette's idea. He noted the man's vest once when he took off his coat. Lafayette gave the man one of Lieutenant James's pistols, as well as one of his own. Lafayette gave the man his own French flintlock and kept his finely made red oak, English-made flintlock. The flintlock had once belonged to a Major Campbell, who was now dead. Lafayette had taken the pistol and gave it to our now dearly departed friend, Jonas. The fine flintlock pistol was something for Lafayette to remember Jonas by. I doubted Lafayette would ever part with this pistol, even if it wasn't French made.

"The man said he'd be proud to pretend to be the Pale Rider. He couldn't wait to tell his family about it," Lafayette had told me.

I thought the man was a damn fool. That vest made him a target.

I'd initially said *no* to the idea, but Lafayette pointed out it would add to the confusion and scare the British. I agreed and wondered how much the price on my head would go up after this.

Men raced around in a panic and screamed as the British soldiers returned fire at our men. Soldiers yelled, "Pale Rider!" as they pointed to the man pretending to be me. Our men turned to run back into the woods, and the first barrel exploded. It was the farthest from the ships and the closest to the city.

Our men yelled that we were under attack and that Pale Rider was here. Jones's sailors from the below grabbed muskets from the wagon and ran for the Ariel, as our sailors from the city also rushed our way.

The next barrel exploded a little closer to the ships. The British soldiers were still firing into the woods and confusion took over as the city awoke to the chaos.

We had left a clearing from the city to the ship for the men to run and not worry about being killed by our own explosions. A hundred men sprinted from the city, shouting that the explosions were cannon fire and the Pale Rider was trying to sink the ships. Two more explosions blasted and killed a few soldiers who happened to be running by them. Smoke filled the air, darkening the moonlight as British soldiers ran for the tree line, chasing our men.

The sound of footsteps behind me caused me to spin around to see twenty barefooted men run up on deck from below. Some had swords, but most held knives or clubs. Jones, to his credit, didn't hesitate. He fired his flintlock at one and then drew his sword. Our sailors raced down the docks as if to help, demanding to launch the ships before the Pale Rider sunk them. One of the British soldiers below actually helped our sailors untie the front rope, then the soldier ran to regroup with his platoon.

Well, damn. I'd told Jones earlier we would get the British to help us launch the ship, but I meant it figuratively, not literally.

I fired my last four rounds, killing four of the ship's crew. Pulling my sword and knife, I rushed to fight next to Jones. He'd killed another with his sword but was overrun by more soldiers when I ran a crew member through with my sword. The real crew of the Ariel hollered to the soldiers on shore that they were under attack, but with the musket fire and explosions and general turmoil, their voices were drowned out. Two more explosions and twin fireballs lit up the smoky night.

Between the musket fire, exploding barrels of gunpowder, smoke and fire, men yelling, and most of the city being awakened from their sleep, confusion and panic seemed to rule the night. The ground between the ships and the city filled with dense smoke, covering our true intent. I'd ordered the men to set jugs of coal oil on top of the barrels, so as the barrels exploded, fire would also rain down and add more black smoke into the air.

Our sailors, led by Lieutenant James, filled the deck of the ship, and the fight with the original crew of the ship ended in a barrage of musket fire. Captain Jones didn't hesitate—he gave orders to the men to get underway. To the British, we looked like the Ariel's crew, trying to save our ship. The last four barrels exploded one by one, and sand was thrown into the air and fire covered the ground. The last four were the closest, designed to separate us from the soldiers. I wanted a wall of fire between us and the British force now running this way from farther down the beach.

As our sailors from the city reached the ship, they grabbed muskets and barrels of food, water, gunpowder, or the larger empty barrels out of the wagon and brought them on board. Lafayette stomped up and down the dock, giving orders and counting men as they ran by. Jones ordered two of his men to cut the second rope and cast off. Lafayette was the last man to board the ship, jumping on as it pulled away from the dock. Lafayette still had his saddle bags over one shoulder.

"How many?" I yelled to Lafayette.

"Not counting you, me, Jones, and your ten men," Lafayette answered, as he added the numbers in his head, "one hundred and twenty-five."

With my ten men, we had one hundred and thirty-five sailors. We'd started with a hundred and seventy-five. Twenty were the men who opened fired and ran. Five were the part of Lafayette's crew who weren't coming with us, and three had our horses and would report to Washington what they saw. We should have had one hundred and forty-seven men with us. That meant twelve men were either killed or didn't make it to the ship before we cast off. They knew if they couldn't make it to the ship for whatever reason, they were to go back to the city and blend in until they could return to Washington.

Bells rang in the night as the ships in the harbor called their men to battle stations. The crew of the Jupiter tried to launch their ship as well but they, like the Ariel, had given their men leave in the city and only had about ten men trying to do the job of fifty.

Jones yelled for the crew. "Make sail!"

I didn't need to be a sailor to know what he meant, since the crew busied themselves freeing the sails and wrangling them into place. Jones steered the ship but yelled for James to replace him. They brought the ship into the wind and headed straight for the HMS Sandwich.

Now came the hard part.

“I pray your plan works,” Jones yelled at me. “If not, we’ll be sunk as soon as the captain of the Sandwich realizes we’re trying to pass.”

The HMS Sandwich didn’t know what was happening on shore, but her captain was making ready for battle. The wooden shutters covering the cannon ports had lifted, and the cannons pushed forward into place. It was too dark to fire at us at this distance, but the moonlight would help them as we sailed closer.

Jones and I stood together at the prow of the ship, our eyes locked on our telescopes. The crew of the Sandwich rushed around on deck. I located the captain, who remained at the stern of his ship, studying us with his own telescope. Bringing my telescope view to the prow of his ship, I found what I was looking for.

“What’s our range?” I asked Jones, as I used my range finder on the ship myself.

“Five hundred yards,” Jones estimated.

My range finder said four hundred and seventy yards, but that was close enough for me to trust him. I pulled my Thompson and laid down on the bow of the ship.

“Call out the range, Captain, if you please,” I said to Jones.

The Ariel was catching full wind in its sails and picking up speed. The HMS Sandwich fired one cannon at us. The splash hit the water about a hundred yards in front of us and thirty yards to our port side.

"That was either a warning shot to turn around," Jones observed, "or they're finding our range to open up a full broad side and sink us."

"Range?" I asked as I aimed in on my target.

"Four hundred yards," Jones answered.

Then Jones yelled back to Lieutenant James, "Hard to starboard."

The ship pulled hard to the right, heading towards shore and the front of the HMS Sandwich. Forty cannons fired from the Sandwich as one. The ship was hidden in a cloud of smoke and darkness. Splashes struck the water around the Ariel as several rounds hit the main deck, destroying parts of the railing and killing men. Another hit the side of the ship, blasting a three-foot-diameter hole fortunately above the water line.

"Hard to port, Mr. James," Jones yelled back to his lieutenant.

I had to admit, Jones kept his composure under fire. He was zigzagging us to make it harder for the Sandwich to get off a good shot. The ship lurched to the left and away from shore.

"Three hundred yards," Jones told me in a low voice.

I fired my Thompson into the night but didn't get the desired effect.

"How long until they fire again?" I asked.

"About one minute," Jones said. "Minute and a half if we're lucky."

I reloaded and aimed it again. We were getting close but shooting a pistol and hitting a man size target at night, from three hundred yards out, while on a moving ship going forward while also going up and down into the waves, wasn't an easy task.

In my head, I counted down backwards from sixty. I needed to hit my target before the Sandwich opened with another broadside. They couldn't miss us again with how close we were, and we wouldn't survive another barrage.

As my countdown reached ten seconds, cannons on the Sandwich shifted, pushed forward again into their firing position.

"One hundred yards," Jones announced.

I took a deep breath, letting out half the air in my lungs, holding the rest. I pulled the tension out of the trigger and knew it was only going to take one more pound of pressure to fire. The Ariel went nose down into the water, then came back up. It held the high part of the arc for a second before dropping back down into the water again. In that one second, where the ship was at its high point, I pulled the trigger again. The recoil of the Thompson pushed back on my hand. The gun jerked upward as a small explosion caused the barrel to rise.

My bullet flew through the night, impacting with its target.

Before we'd walked down to the docks, Lafayette's first team had been tasked with stealing two of the fishing rowboats we'd seen in the daylight. They had placed the rest of the barrels of gunpowder and coal oil onto one boat and towed it out to the Sandwich with the second boat. They did this quietly, with no torches or lamps. They'd managed to tie the boat to the thick hemp rope attached to the Sandwich's anchor. That boat now rested against the Sandwich, held in place by the rope tied to the chain. Captain Jones had never heard of this being done in naval history, so it was something no one would expect.

None of the sailors aboard the Sandwich would be able to see the small boat unless they went to the chain and looked straight down. Anyone not on the Sandwich who might see the boat would assume the captain of the Sandwich knew about it and most likely ordered it tied there.

The darkness was vanquished for a bright two-count, forcing me to squeeze my eyes shut as the barrels on the boat exploded as one giant blast. The lamp oil added to the explosion and sent out a bubble of fire in all directions.

Cannons from the Sandwich fired at us, but it was too late. The explosion had not only lifted the front of the ship up but had pushed it to the side. Men on our ship yelled and cheered as they realized we now had a chance. We were no longer at the side of the ship but more to the front of it. The cannons sent their steel cannon balls harmlessly into the water.

A giant hole appeared in the front of the Sandwich's hull. It was hard to see with the black smoke, but the screams of the crew carried far across the water. Splashing also carried to our ship, but I didn't know if it came from debris hitting the water or men jumping overboard.

We were fifty yards from the prow of the ship, moving through the black acrid smoke. The front of the ship was taking on water while the upper deck was still on fire. Several feet of the thick steel anchor chain now hung limp and broken from the upper deck.

Captain Jones ran back to James and took over the steering. Like a real-life David and Goliath story, we glided by the ship three times bigger than us that now laid wounded and stranded in the water, limping towards shore as she took on water and hoped not to sink. The men on board may have seen us but no longer cared what we did as long as we didn't open fire on her.

I stood up high and took off my jacket, letting the men of the HMS Sandwich see me in my black vest. For no discernable reason, more for effect than anything else, I pulled out my Tec-9 and held my guns high in the air for them to see. Washington wanted me blamed for the upcoming assassination, so I needed them to know Pale Rider absconded with their ship. I spotted the captain of the Sandwich, who was staring straight at me. Most of the men on his ship were too busy putting out fires or trying to save the gigantic ship to notice me. Yet, a few of the sailors stopped what they were doing and pointed at me excitedly.

As we passed the massive vessel and raced for the open waters, our sails billowed. Captain Jones seemed to sense the best angles to fully capture the absolute maximum amount of wind we possibly could. As I laid out my plan to him, Captain Jones warned me that he wouldn't head straight to Paris. He was going to follow the tides and winds until the British were well out of sight. Then he'd set course for France.

Lieutenant James had half the crew climbing ropes and shifting the sails. I had no idea what they were doing or what difference their actions had on the ship. Instead, I made myself useful trying to help the crew in treating the wounded, throwing the dead overboard, and clearing the ship of debris.

When that was done, Lafayette and I searched the ship from top to bottom, looking for any of the original crew who may have been hiding. The only person we located was the cook, who was well past drunk and passed out in his hammock. After waking him up so he had a chance of survival, we threw him over the side and into the dark, freezing cold water. I figured one of three things was going to happen. He might live long enough to make it to shore, get eaten by sharks, or die of hyperthermia. My money was on hyperthermia or maybe hyperthermia followed by eaten by sharks.

Lafayette took a group of sailors to start on repairs to the several gaping holes in the side of the ship. I had only known about one of the holes. The two new holes weren't as bad but needed to be sealed up just the same. Really, there was no such thing as a *good* hole in a ship.

I found the captain's quarters and first mate's quarters next to one another on the main deck behind the wheel of the ship and searched them for any useful items. I noticed some brandy, gold coins, and the British Captain's uniform scattered around the room. Searching the desk, I found the captain's diary and some maps, but I left them for Captain Jones. I decided Captain Jones and I would share this room while Lafayette and Lieutenant James shared the first mate's quarters.

We sailed deep into the night, as Captain Jones refused to leave the wheel, not trusting anyone else to our escape. I appreciated that he did this. He was a pompous ass, true, but Washington was right – he was an exceptional sailor.

I walked to the stern or aft of the ship and gripped the railing. The wood beneath my palms was smooth and strong. I took a second to marvel at the craftsmanship of the ship builders in this century. These ships weren't only functional; they were like pieces of art. How did they get the wood this smooth? How much time was spent sanding and polishing these ships to get the wood to feel like glass? Then man, in his ultimate wisdom, took these ships and pitted them against each other in battles to the death. Not only killing the men who sailed them, but sinking or destroying these giant pieces of floating art.

Blowing out a deep breath, I brought myself back to the here and now. I gazed out into the great dark ocean behind us. The bright lamps flickered on what had to be ten different ships following us, and those lamps formed a loose, zig-zag pattern. The fastest and closest of them were still out of range to fire their cannons. It was too dark to tell if they were catching up to us or falling behind. Lafayette sauntered up next to me and patted me on the back.

"You did it, Thomas."

"No, Marie. We did it, together. But the job's not done yet. We still need to make our escape, and the British seem a little upset with us."

I pointed to the lamps in the distance that bounced up and down as the ships rose and fell with the waves. The lamps, or rather the ships, did manage to stay in their loose line. Two of the ships appeared to be closer than the rest.

"The main damage has been fixed good enough for now," he replied. "We are not taking on any water, and the sailors tell me they can do a better job sealing up the side of the ship once we do get away and drop sail for a few hours. The damage to the main deck looks bad, but it's not as bad as it looks. Some of the sailors will work on that tonight. They don't need us to drop sail for these repairs."

"Good," I said. "How many men did we lose?"

"Ten," Lafayette answered in a clipped voice. "That brings the crew down to a hundred and twenty-five men. The captain said he will make do. He wanted me to warn you it will be tough going if we lose too many more."

That was not in my plans. I flicked my gaze to Lafayette. He had two pistols on him again. He'd given one away, so he must have raided the ship's magazine and picked up another pistol. It wasn't near as fine as the one he'd given away, but it looked reliable.

"Three, maybe four hours until sun rise," I told him. "Let's go talk to the captain."

***

I didn't know what the morning would bring, so I told Jones I was going to get a few hours of sleep. I instructed Lafayette to wake me if anything else happened. Jones ordered Lieutenant James to sleep as well, so James could relieve him in the morning. I pulled Jones to the side for a private meeting and asked him to reconsider.

"It's not an order," I said to Jones. "You do what you feel is best as captain, but when the sun comes up, we'll need to outrun or fight those ships, and I'd like you rested and in command."

Jones nodded and changed his directive, ordering his first mate to take command and to wake him thirty minutes after sunrise. We went to the captain's quarters, and I showed Jones the maps and journals I'd found.

"They may prove useful," Jones said, flipping through them. "I'll read them later if we're still alive."

He grabbed the British uniform, presumably to throw it out, when I placed a hand on his arm.

"I may need that later."

"For your mission?" he asked.

"Yes."

He knew better than to ask more. The General had ordered him not to ask any questions about the mission itself. This was to be the mission that never happened. Well, the British would know, but it would go down in history as the assassination committed by the criminal known as Pale Rider, and nothing to do with the Continental Congress. Jones let it go at that.

Jones puffed up his chest. "I wanted to tell you, that had to be one of the best shots I had ever seen with a pistol. My biggest concern was if you missed again, we'd be sunk before making it to open water."

"I know," I said. "That was my biggest worry as well."

"Have you ever made a shot like that before?" he asked.

"From a moving ship? No, never. It was a first for me. That was why I missed the first shot. We are only alive because you kept us afloat long enough for me to get off a closer shot."

His eyebrows flew up on his forehead. "A closer shot? We were fifty to seventy-five yards away."

I realized too late a normal flintlock was only able or accurate for only half that distance. It was a close shot for me with my Thompson, but with a flintlock at night, it was truly an impossible feat of marksmanship. No wonder he was amazed. He peered down at my shoulder holster and the Thompson tucked in it.

"May I see it?" he asked, pointing to my pistol.

"It's custom made from Germany," I lied. "I promised the gunsmith who designed it not to show it to anyone. You know how those German gunsmiths are about their secrets. At least until he mass produces it."

He had no idea what I was talking about, but not wanting to admit his ignorance, he nodded his understanding.

"Very well then, Major," Jones said. "The sun will be up too soon. I suggest we get some sleep while we can."

Two hammocks hung from the ceiling in the captain's quarters. Jones asked if I had a preference to which one I wanted. I shook my head, not seeing a difference. He picked one, and I rolled myself into the other. Sleep overtook me in minutes.

Chapter Four: Saved by the Jolly

The hammock swayed back and forth with the motion of the ship. The ship would rear up as it climbed through and over the waves, only to crash back down into the dark, churning water on the downward side. The motion repeated itself over and over again in a never-ending dance. Every time the ship tilted up, it would right itself, then overcorrect and fall back downward, the hammock rocking one way, then the other. The sounds of waves hitting the hull of the ship made for a soothing, almost hypnotic, sleep.

Somewhere in the darkness, I dreamt I was with Jenny. No, it wasn't me with her, but a man who resembled me. The man she was with was a different version of me, and she was alive and happy. The alternate version of me looked happy as well. He was softer, the visage of a man who'd not grown up learning how to throw knives or was forced to earn money bare knuckle boxing for the entertainment of British officers. I couldn't help but be happy for her and for the alternate me. How weird is it to be happy for yourself who wasn't you?

Lafayette's voice permeated the darkness. He called out my name, but I didn't open my eyes. I didn't want to leave this dream, but in the back of my mind, I knew I needed to. I fought to focus on his voice and claw myself towards wakefulness, then slowly forced my eyes open. Normally, I woke quick and easy, always being on guard. Between the knowledge of us being on the open sea, safe from ambush, and the rocking of the hammock, I'd slept harder in the last few hours than I had since coming to this century. It had been days since I had last dreamed of Jenny. My dreams were filled more and more of Annie now. I wanted to hold on to not only the memory of Jenny, but of the memory of every dream I had of her since I'd never see her again.

Light came through the five huge, closed windows in the back of the cabin. The frames of the windows were bright with colorful stained glass. The sun's morning rays penetrated the glass and filled the room with yellow, red, and blue beams of light.

I turned my head, finally remembering where I was and what had happened a few hours ago. Lafayette knew better than to shake me awake and had called out my name from several feet away. Captain Jones was fully dressed and pulling on his boots. I had also slept fully dressed except for my boots. I sat up and rolled out of the hammock.

"Report," I rasped at Lafayette as I put on my boots.

"The ships are still following," Lafayette said. "Two of them are closing on us. They'll be in range to fire on us soon."

I walked over to the closed windows. Footsteps stomped on the wooden planks behind me, telling me Jones and Lafayette were following me. I opened the middle window as Lafayette, then Jones joined me, opening the windows to my right and left. Through the open windows we had a stunning view of the open ocean, nothing but gray-blue waves in all directions, as far as the eye could see. The water churned dark and violent, with bright white caps breaking up the dark blue and greens of the sea. We weren't in a storm, but it was winter, and the air was cold. The wind blew hard in the damp air, making it seem colder. Seagulls floated above and behind us in the streams of air. The only things of note in my view were the ten British warships sailing behind us. Lafayette was right – they seemed to be closing in little by little, but the front two had pulled away from the rest and were closing in on us.

"HMS Defiance and Vigilant," Jones said, tipping his chin to point. "I told you they were fast. Any ideas?"

As if to punctuate his question, four cannons fired at us, two forward cannons from the Defiance and two from the Vigilant. The ships were momentarily hidden in the four billows of dark gray smoke the cannons burped out. Lafayette and I stood straight, muscles tensed up as we waited for the explosions, as four cannonballs ripped through the ship. Jones leaned forward into the window. The explosions never happen, and we relaxed as four cannonballs plunged into the water about three hundred yards behind us.

"What's the range of those things?" I asked.

"They're six pounders," Jones answered. "Fifteen to sixteen hundred yards depending on how good the gunners are."

I let that information sink in. "How long until we are in range?"

"At the rate they are closing in on us," Jones said, looking at the ships and calculating the distance and speed in his head, "I'd say an hour. Maybe a little less."

"You asked if I had any ideas, Captain," I told him. "Follow me."

We walked out of the captain's quarters and onto the main deck. Jones stopped and examined the sails. He nodded in approval, so I guessed he was happy with Lieutenant James' sailing abilities. The speed of a ship depended not on how much wind there was, but on how much wind you were able to capture in the sails. Jones was pleased at the amount of wind James was capturing at the moment.

"How much gunpowder did you find in the ship's magazine?" I asked Lafayette.

"Over twenty barrels," Lafayette answered. "We didn't need to bring any with us."

"Maybe," I said. "But I didn't want to take that chance. If the ship was low on supplies, we'd be wishing we'd brought some. As it is, I wish we'd brought more. Bring up one barrel of gunpowder and five empty barrels. Have one of the carpenters report to me. I need to explain to him what I want done."

Lafayette gave the order, and several men ran below. Jones gave a few orders to James and followed me to the stern of the ship. The men returned with the barrels and with one of the carpenters.

The carpenter, who Lafayette introduced as Mr. Tubs, was about fifty-five or sixty years old. He was completely bald, but a huge, magnificent gray mustache sprouted on his upper lip. He was a little pudgy in the stomach but muscular in the chest and arms – barrel-chested. His face was dark and hard looking, accented by a thick white scar going down the left side.

I explained to Mr. Tubs what I needed from him, and he laughed lightly, then got straight to work. His hands moved on their own while he laughed and shook his head in disbelief. Sometimes he would talk to himself or answer questions no one asked.

"Are you sure this guy is sane?" I whispered to Lafayette.

Lafayette shrugged. "How would I know? I just now met the man."

It only took Mr. Tubs fifteen minutes to secure four of the empty barrels to one of the barrels of gunpowder, with the barrel of gunpowder being in the middle of the tied bundle. He then pulled the cork out of the top of the barrel of gunpowder.

I threw another empty barrel over the side and counted. The empty barrel bobbed in the water behind us. It took to the count of ninety for the ships behind us to reach the barrel. The crew of the British ships didn't seem to notice the barrel as it floated by them.

"Eighteen inches," I told the carpenter. "Make it two feet. It will take time to lower it into the water."

Mr. Tubs measured out three feet of fuse and threaded it into the hole, making sure only the last two feet stuck out. Then, removing the bottom of another empty barrel and drilling several air holes in the top of it, he secured it to the top of the barrel of gun powder. Using a candle, he melted and poured wax around the outside between the gunpowder barrel and the empty one on top of it. When he was sure it was waterproof, he looked up at me and nodded with a smile. Two of our men tied a rope around the whole contraption, and on my order, the fuse was lit and the barrels lowered into the water.

The idea was the four empty barrels tied to the powder would keep it afloat and not allow it to flip over or roll to its side. The fuse was protected from the water by the top barrel. I had no idea if this would work or not, but we'd find out in about ninety seconds.

We watched the barrels bob in the waves. Then it drifted in between the two closest ships behind us, only five or six feet away from one of them and forty feet from the other. The barrels floated halfway down the ships when it exploded. Water and wood burst high into the air, and men on the two ships screeched.

The captains of the two ships steered away from the explosion. The ship to our right, or starboard, veered right, and the ship on our left or port, veered left. Steering a ship, however, is not like steering a car. When they turned, they lost the wind, and their sails went from fully billowed to laying straight and drooping. Without the wind to push them, it would take time for them to steer back. The turn would be slow, and then when they found the wind again, it would take time for them to pick up speed. Meanwhile, we continued to pull forward. They'd get back on track and close in again, but it would take valuable time.

Then, the ship on our port side dropped its sails, slowing the ship more. I didn't see any signs of visible damage, but maybe she was taking on water or the captain wanted to check the water line and make sure the ship was still sound.

"The Vigilant dropped out," Jones yelled with glee. "You bought us six, maybe seven hours with that trick. It will take the Defiance time to find the wind again and get back in the chase."

Jones turned to find our own sails weren't quite as full as they were a few minutes ago and yelled for James to make a course change. The ship listed a few degrees, and the sails filled again. I told Jones I needed a few minutes alone in our quarters to think of a new plan.

Once in the privacy of my quarters, I dug into my satchel and pulled out my cell phone. It was the only phone in the world right now, so I didn't have anyone to call, but it was a smart phone and had a library of information on it that I'd brought with me when I traveled back through time. I kept it in a hardened case to keep it protected, but I hadn't turned it on in weeks, so I could only hope it still worked. I wasn't sure how long the battery might last.

I held my breath and the side button down for about three seconds before the face lit up as the phone came to life. The screen battery icon indicated I had forty-two percent battery life left. I'd brought three portable batteries with me when I first came to the eighteenth century to charge my phone. I had used my phone as little as possible, but still had used up two of the portable batteries already. I had one left, and I was going to have to use it soon. After that, the phone was going to become a paper weight. It wasn't like I had an outlet to plug the charger into, or electricity for that matter. I need to find something quick and turn the phone off, saving as much of the battery as possible.

I searched for ways to make our cannons fire farther, but that was a dead end. Taking what I had already knew and had on hand, I then searched for ways to make a better ocean mine. I found a few things, but we didn't have the time or materials.

I looked up the relationship between weight to speed ratio of the ship, thinking we could throw the few cannons we'd overboard in hopes of making our ship sail faster. Captain Jones would never allow that, and I realized if it would have made enough of a difference, he would have done it already. I then looked up the different types of sails and the next technological leap in sailing.

Sails would soon change to add triangle sails between the main sails. These triangle sails could take better advantage of different wind angles. I read about sails called *jibs* and *staysails* but had a hard time telling the difference.

The person steering the ship had to do what was called *tacking*. I didn't fully understand that either, but basically, we needed to zig zag in the water. By zig zagging, and with the use of the additional triangle sails, we'd kept as much wind in the sails as possible without going too much off target.

I then looked up the HMS Ariel.

"Son of a bitch," I said out loud to myself.

I couldn't believe what I was reading. According to what used to be my history, Captain Jones would command the Ariel a few years from now, after she was given to him by the French. She'd been captured by the French, not by us, originally, but somehow history repeated itself and she still ended up with the same captain. He'd later changed her rigging to improve her sailing and made her faster.

I couldn't exactly show Captain Jones my phone, so I searched the former captain's desk for a pen and paper. I found a few sheets of paper and a quill with an ink bottle. I'd never used a real feather pen before, and it took some getting used to. Though it was a mess of ink blots and drips, I was able to draw a childlike copy of the diagram, but it was a caveman drawing compared to the detailed one on the phone screen.

I switched off my cell phone and put it away in my satchel. Walking out onto the main deck again, I located Jones steering the ship. I walked up to him and handed him the paper with the diagram I drew.

"Is that this ship?" he asked, looking around and comparing the diagram to the Ariel. "The artistry is not very good, and the sails are wrong."

Then he peered again at the diagram, and something caught his eye. He yelled for one of the sailors to take the wheel and marched up and down the ship, comparing the diagram to how the sails were set up now.

"Where did you get this?" he demanded, flapping the parchment in my face.

"Does it help?" I asked.

"Yes. This is a much better design. We could increase our speed by six, maybe nine knots."

I really didn't know how fast a knot was, but I did like the sound of us going faster. I wished I could have told him he was the one who had thought of it, and I had only copied his own sketches.

"You said we had six or seven hours before they catch up to us again?" I asked. "Can you do this in that time, while sailing?"

"I might be able to do most of the work while sailing, but not in six hours," he answered, then leveled his gaze at me. "You'll need to stall for more time."

"How much time?"

"If I start now," he said. "I can have it done by tomorrow morning."

The wind went out of *my* sails. "That long?"

"I could drop sail, and have it done in five hours," he said. "Then the British would sink us twenty minutes after the sails went down. We'll have to do it little by little if we don't want to lose speed or get sunk."

"What if we lose some weight?" I countered.

"If we throw ten of the twenty-six cannons overboard, that might give us another knot or two of speed, and another hour," he said, tapping at the parchment as he considered the idea. "We can also throw overboard whatever cargo is loaded, half our cannonballs. In fact we can lose everything except our food, water, and weapons."

Lafayette eyed us talking and walked up, joining in.

"Okay," I said to Jones. "Wake James. I want him at the wheel of the ship. You start on the reconfiguration of the sails. Lafayette, get some of the men and toss everything we don't need. I'll ask Mr. Tubs to build another set of barrels. Then I need to think up another plan to stall our pursuers."

"We only have five empty barrels left," Lafayette said. "We used the first five on the last contraption."

"Then have him use the rest," I ordered. "This time, have him use three barrels of gunpowder. If we only have one more chance at this, I want it to be big."

"Yes, Thomas," Lafayette answered.

Jones took command and shouted out orders. I walked back into the captain's quarters and looked out the back window again. Eight ships sailed behind us now. One of the ships must have stopped to give assistance to the Vigilant. The last three in line were far back and no longer posed a threat. They might give up and turn around soon, if we were lucky. Five were still trying to catch up to us, and four of them kept pace with us, not gaining but not falling back either. The Defiance had corrected her course and fell in line again. She was no longer in front; she'd lost her advantage when her captain turned her. She was now passing the second ship in line, and would soon pass the front one, taking up the mantle in pursuit.

Watching her gain on the first ship made me think Jones may not have given her enough credit. I didn't think it would take six or seven hours for her to be in range for her cannons. We could drop the barrels again and maybe cause some damage, gaining a little more time again, but then what? They were going to open fire on us soon enough. If the

Defiance was able to slow us down, then we'd have to fight five ships, any one of them capable of sinking us on their own.

I spent the first hour sitting in the chair at the desk, studying the ships out the window, watching the Defiance slowly gain on us. I had no ideas on how to get away. I didn't want to use up my battery life but was forced to turn on my phone reading about the ships of this century. After using up another ten percent of my battery and finding no inspiration, I switched my phone off. Walking out onto the main deck, I glanced around to see what was at our disposal.

Jones was rigging new sails while Lafayette and a dozen men pushed a cannon over the side where it hit the water with a resounding splash. I approached the group to see how much longer they were going to need.

"How is it going?" I asked.

"Good," Lafayette answered. "Did you come up with any more ideas?"

"No," I said. "Not yet."

Lafayette's face fell. "This is the last of the ten cannons. Do you want us to drop the two Jolly boats or keep them?" he asked, pointing at the two row boats.

"Might as well drop them," I said.

"The carpenter has your bundle of barrels ready," Lafayette continued. "If they see us dropping them in the water, they'll avoid the barrels."

I went down into the hull to see if there was anything else we could get rid of. Barrels of water and gun powder that we needed to keep. A pile of wood beams and planks were neatly stacked for normal repairs. We'd need some of that to fix the ship's damage when we had a chance. Several barrels of salted fish and a dozen more labeled *pork biscuits*, whatever pork biscuits were. At least thirty coils of rope stacked on top of one another sat in the corner. A dozen barrels of tobacco and coal oil, along with some lamps, were in a small pile next to barrels of pitch and tar for waterproofing the hull of the ship.

My eyes flicked back to the coal oil, then to the pitch. There was an idea there somewhere, slowly blooming in the back of my head. Fire could be used, but how? I had wood and coal oil for a fire. The pitch might help, but I had to figure out how to put it all together. Fire must be the answer, but how could we use it as a weapon? The British would open up on us as soon as we were within fifteen hundred yards. I could build a catapult out of the wood – okay, that was stupid. I didn't know how to build one and I didn't know how far they'd fire an object. I was grasping at straws.

"How's it going?" Lafayette asked, walking down the steps and bringing me out of my deep thoughts.

"I have an idea," I said. "But not sure how to implement it. How are things going up top?"

"Good," Lafayette said. "The men are getting ready to cut the Jolly boats loose."

My eyes returned to the ropes, then back to Lafayette. An idea lit.

"Shit!" I yelled, as I raced up the steps.

I made it in time to stop the men from cutting the first of the two Jolly boats free. Lafayette had followed me up the steps, trying to figure out what was going on.

"I got it," I said, turning to Lafayette. "Tell the carpenter to get the barrels ready. We are going to drop it in the water."

"Why?" Lafayette asked. "They'll steer away from them."

"Not if they can't see them," I said. "How long is a coil of rope?"

Lafayette squinted at me. "On a naval ship? The normal length is three hundred yards. I know because I asked the captain when I sailed to the colonies. They brought a coil up to repair one of the riggings, and I was surprised at how long a coil was."

"Have the men bring up five coils of rope, some coal oil, pitch, tobacco, and several of the smaller pieces of wood."

"What?" Lafayette asked. "Why? Tobacco?"

"Marie," I said a little louder. "Just do it, and I'll explain while we get it ready."

Shouting for Jones, I ran up towards the prow. He was in the riggings himself, showing his men what he wanted done, but when he saw and heard me yelling for him, he slid down one of the hanging ropes like a man born on a ship.

"My God, man! Now what's wrong?" Jones asked, concern tainting his voice.

I told him my plan and asked if he was able to do what I needed. He nodded his head, but doubt flared in his eyes. I didn't know if the doubt sprung from his doubt in the plan or in his ability to do his part.

We started with the tar. Fire would burn through the tar, but we coated the whole boat, hoping to prevent the bottom from burning through too quickly. We loaded the Jolly boat up with wood and poured pitch on top of the wood. The coal oil went on top of the pitch, and I also threw in a few barrels of tobacco. Sailors were known for tying rope knots, so I had them tie the ropes together to make one long fifteen-hundred-yard-long rope to pull the Jolly boat with.

By the time we were done, the Defiance had closed in, only about eighteen hundred yards behind us. It would still take them another hour to close enough distance to open fire on us, but I didn't want to wait any longer. We lowered the Jolly boat into the water and as it fell back and pulled away from us, I yelled for Lafayette to do the honors.

"Let's hope this works," Jones said tersely as he stood next to me. "Do you want me to take the wheel?"

"That's up to you, Captain," I told him. "But I don't have your knowledge. It might be better if James stayed at the wheel, and you gave commands from the stern with me."

Jones nodded his head, his eyes straight ahead.

Lafayette threw the first of three lit lanterns at the Jolly. He managed to hit the wood in the boat with the first lantern. The lantern broke with a shattering of glass and ignited the coal oil. The crew knew the plan and let out the rope slowly as the Jolly pulled away. They walked the rope back and tied it to the stern of the ship. The fire was burning hot and between the pitch, wood and tobacco, dark thick smoke billowed out and up into the air. The waves tossed the little Jolly boat around. It managed to not tip over and remained afloat. We let the slack out of the rope but slowly, so our ship was still pulling it forward through the waves.

"Captain, if you please," I said when the Jolly reach the end of the rope and fifteen hundred yards behind us.

Jones dictated orders to Lieutenant James. Jones instructed James to turn the wheel a few degrees starboard and then to port, causing the ship to make a snake like movement in the water. It was a long delay, but the small Jolly cut through the water like a baby snake following its mother. The smoke created a thick, hazy wall between us and our pursuers. It didn't take long for us to lose sight of the fleet of ships trying to sink us. I patted Mr. Tubs on the shoulder, and he lit the fuse, then supervised the lowering of the barrels into the water.

The Jolly was fully engulfed in flames as we pulled it past the barrels bobbing in the water. We watched as the bottom of the boat finally gave out and the Jolly dropped into the water and out of sight. We untied the rope and dropped it into the water behind us. My hope was the smoke hid the barrels until it was too late for the ships to turn and avoid them.

The Defiance burst through the dissipating smoke undamaged. A few seconds later, a heinous explosion from somewhere behind the lead ship shook the water. We all leaned far over the railing. As the smoke cleared up, we could see the stern of the second ship and prow of the third ship were on fire. The waves of the ocean were putting out the fire on the lower hull of the ship. Their sails, however, were also burning, and the crew was dropping the engulfed sails to prevent the fire from spreading to their remaining sails. We'd made the fuse too long, but the extra gunpowder and coal oil really did a number on them.

Unfortunately, the Defiance was going too fast and suffered no damage at all. The last ship dropped its sails, most likely to offer aid to the two burning ships. If nothing else, we were only being pursued by two ships now, even if one of them was going to have us in range of its guns soon.

In the movies, this was the part where we would steer the ship into a storm and lose our pursuers. It was cold as heck on the open water, but no winter storm in sight. With a grinding sound, the Defiance fired her cannons at us. The steel balls fell harmlessly into the ocean two hundred yards behind us.

Captain Jones eyed the churning water. "That was a well-placed shot."

"They missed," Lafayette retorted.

"They were two hundred yards short of us," Jones snapped back. "At this distance, they should have shot at least four hundred yards short. They raised their elevation to the max and timed their shot as the ship was rising over a wave, increasing their distance. Her captain has experience."

"Not to mention he's upset with us," I added. "We have whittled their fleet of ten ships down to two. Her captain wants to end this before we pull another miracle out of our hats."

"They're only two hundred yards short of us being in real trouble," Lafayette said, giving me a wry look with one eyebrow raised high on his gallic forehead. "Do you have another miracle for us?"

"No," I sighed. "It's up to you, Captain. Did you get enough of the job done?"

Jones ground his jaw. "Not enough to outrun them."

"Set whatever sails you have, Captain, and pray it's enough to match their speed," I said.

Jones rushed forward, barking orders to the men in the riggings. Two additional sails dropped and filled with the wind. They were small sails, not the larger one he was planning to add. He'd wisely chosen to add the easier, smaller ones first. The ship surged forward under my feet, and it was obvious we'd increased our speed.

"It's not enough," Lafayette yelled from the stern of the ship.

"We're not pulling away," I explained. "But we don't have to. We need to match their speed so they can't close on us."

Jones came back to stand next to me. He pulled out his looking glass and examined the two ships behind us.

"They're dumping cargo over the side now," Jones reported. "They're determined to stop us. I can't read the flags, but the two captains are signaling one another."

The second ship fell farther behind and was no longer able to keep up with us or the Defiance. Suddenly, the second ship behind us turned to her port and veered away from the pursuit.

"The Ajax seems to be giving up," Jones said. "She's turning away. Most likely giving up and going home."

"At least we're only up against one ship now," Lafayette pointed out.

"Only one ship," Jones repeated in a flat tone. "One Intrepid class war ship with sixty-four guns. While we sail with sixteen guns. We can't stand against a single broadside from her."

"If we stay ahead of her, won't she have to give up sooner or later?" Lafayette asked.

"She is dropping cargo," Jones said. "If she lightens her load enough, we'll be right back where we started from. With her gaining on us. The one good news is that as a British war ship, she wouldn't dare to throw over any cannons or military issued equipment. Cargo is the only thing her captain will be willing to lose."

"Then it's a race between them throwing over cargo and you finishing the last of the new sails," I said, directing my words to Jones.

He nodded his head and walked forward with a purpose, bellowing orders again. If we survived a few more hours, we could lose them at night. No one likes to sail in complete darkness, but we would need to tonight.

"Thomas," Lafayette said. "The crew is getting very nervous. They are starting to talk. You need to do something to distract them."

"What do you want me to do? Put on a puppet show for them?"

"I don't know," Lafayette answered. "Don't sailors sing?"

I had no idea if that myth was true or not. I thought about the problem for a minute and of the only sailing song I knew. I didn't know when it was yet written or if the sailors had ever heard it before.

Walking over to the railing, I grabbed a wooden lynchpin from the railing used to help tie ropes in place. I grabbed one that didn't have a rope tied to it, raised it in the air, and brought it down onto the wooden railing with a deep thunk. It got the attention of the surrounding men. I hit the railing again and again in a rhythm of *thunks*, setting a beat of sorts.

As everyone near was looking at me to see what I was doing, I broke out in song as loudly as I could in a bawdy, warbling voice.

"What will we do with a drunken sailor? What will we do with a drunken sailor? What will we do with a drunken sailor? Early in the morning!"

No one joined in, so I wasn't sure if the song had even been written yet. I continued anyway, including stomping my foot in time to the banging and my singing. Maybe someone would eventually join in.

"Way hay and up she rises! Way hay and up she rises! Way hay and up she rises! Early in the morning!"

I dropped the lynchpin and slapped an open-mouthed Lafayette on the back to push him forward, making him walk with me as I kept singing. Captain Jones had stopped what he was doing and was now staring at me wide-eyed.

"Shave his belly with a rusty razor! Shave his belly with a rusty razor! Shave his belly with a rusty razor! Early in the morning!"

On the next chorus, Lafayette and about ten men who must have been familiar with the tune joined in chanting the tune and stomping.

"Way hay and up she rises! Way hay and up she rises! Way hay and up she rises! Early in the morning!"

The whole ship was watching me now. Most kept working, but all were listening.

"Put him in a long boat till he's sober! Put him in a long boat till he's sober! Put him in a long boat till he's sober, early in the morning!"

Before I could belt out the next chorus, Captain Jones pointed at the Defiance and yelled out he wanted the British to hear us. I shouted the next round so they'd know what to sing, and the whole crew joined in this time, and our voices echoed across the water.

"Way hay and up she rises! Way hay and up she rises! Way hay and up she rises!
Early in the morning!"

I whispered to Lafayette that this was the only song I knew, and he'd better think of the next one. Then I started this one over, mainly because I didn't know the rest of it.

The men sang for the next hour. Their spirits were raised and for a time they felt at home, sailing the ocean, and not thinking about the war ship behind us. I hoped the British behind us could hear the men singing. What must they think? The very men they were trying to kill were singing with joy in their voices.

***

As the sun fell in the sky, the Defiance lost weight. She slowly closed in on us, knot after knot. She would reach the apex of the wave, then fire her two forward guns. Predictively, the splashes of the steel balls seemed to get closer and closer.

When the splashes were within twenty yards from us, I ordered the carpenter to build another barrel apparatus. We didn't have any empty barrels left, so he had to empty out a few filled barrels. We began with two tobacco barrels, issuing everyone sacks of tobacco. Then we emptied two barrels of salted fish and instructed the cook to make a meal out of the fish before it went bad. The cook needed to fix the men a meal anyway – we just took away his choice of meals. We opened two barrels of pork biscuits and passed them out as a reward for the men's hard work. Captain Jones protested using up our food so quickly, but then he realized what we were using the empty barrels for and stopped his protest. We only had three fourths of the men we'd planned on taking, so the food was still in good supply.

As one of the cannon balls splashed into the water next to our starboard side, I told the carpenter to make a show of putting the barrels into the water. He made sure the captain of the Defiance saw him light the fuse with a torch and lower the ropes. As expected, the captain turned his ship away from the barrels and the explosion only scared a few fish. He kept his tacking small and managed to only fall back a bit. Enough to buy another ten minutes, but we weren't going to be able to keep this up.

"Why hasn't he fired again?" I asked no one in particular.

"It's getting dark," Lafayette said, stepping up next to me.

I jumped a little at his words. I was so focused on the Defiance and trying to come up with a new idea, I never noticed him walk up. I also never noticed how dark it had become in the last few minutes.

The captain had ordered one lantern lit and had placed it at the stern of the ship for the captain of the Defiance to see. It was like a beacon for them to follow. I wanted to protest, but Jones held up a hand to stop me.

"You're not the only person on board who has ideas," Jones said. "In a few minutes, that lantern will be the only thing they can see of us."

He turned and walked to the middle of the ship with me in tow. The second Jolly boat was ready to be lowered into the water. Mr. Tubs and another carpenter had fastened several poles together and built a mast of sorts for the small boat. The mast wasn't strong enough to hold a sail but was tall enough to hold a lantern at the top of it, about twenty feet in the air.

Jones lit the lantern and yelled for the lantern at the stern of the ship to be blown out before lowering the Jolly into the water, with the lantern twenty feet high. It was still lower than the lantern at the stern of our ship, but being a little lower would look like we were a little farther away. We towed this Jolly boat like we had with the first Jolly boat. Except this time, it was with only one hundred yards of rope. Captain Jones ordered his new sail opened and our ship captured more wind than before. I could feel a brief sensation of our speed increasing as the ship pulled faster through the water. Then he ordered James to turn the wheel hard to port and signaled for the crew to cut the Jolly loose.

As we sailed to the left of the Defiance, the Defiance herself sailed straight for our Jolly boat. It would only take the Defiance a few minutes to collide with and destroy the small boat and discover our deception. Our hopes were that by then, it would be too late. At best, they had to guess if we had continued straight or veered left or right. They had a thirty-three percent chance of being right. If they guessed right, Jones had planned on changing course several more times throughout the night. It was a little unnerving to sail into the dark open water. Yet, as big as the ocean was and how few ships there were in the water in the eighteenth century, our chances of hitting another ship was next to none.

"What now, Captain?" I asked.

"I'll get my sextant," Jones said. "Figure out where we are exactly now that we are not being chased. Then I'll plot the fastest course to France."

The night lit up with a group of flashes and with the thunder of cannons, as the HMS Defiance fired her sixty-four cannons, about a mile away from us.

"The captain realized what we did," Jones explained. "Most likely he's afraid we may have been coming up alongside her. He's making sure we weren't trying to board her."

"If I had thought of that, I might have suggested it," I said.

Chapter Five: The Storm

The next morning, we sailed with a skeleton crew, letting as many sailors sleep as we could. The captain had ordered Lieutenant James to make up a shift roster with the crew divided into two work forces. Captain Jones and I stayed up and took the first watch as James and Lafayette slept.

After everyone rested and the crew fell into a normal working routine, Lafayette and I found ourselves getting bored. We didn't know anything about sailing, and every time we tried to help, we were in the way. I decided to let Captain Jones take full command. I told him I'd stay out of his way, deferring to his judgement for the rest of our voyage. He seemed to appreciate the gesture, and we began to form a real friendship.

With nothing else to do, Lafayette and I honed our fighting skills. We spent our days practicing the sword. We also practiced throwing knives at a dart board-sized target, and I took the time to teach him how to fight with his hands. Captain Jones and Lieutenant James didn't care to practice with the knives or learn how to box, but they did practice the sword with us.

We only had sixteen cannons left on the ship, but Jones made the men run drills until they were proficient at loading and firing the cannons. Some of these men hadn't sailed on a ship in years and needed the practice.

His crew did a fine job at repairing the damage we'd suffered escaping the harbor, and the carpenters worked non-stop until the captain declared the work finished. On the morning of the tenth day, the sails of a larger ship appeared on the horizon. We didn't know what flag they sailed under, so we adjusted course and avoided them altogether. Captain Jones was no coward, but he'd promised General Washington to get me to Paris in six weeks, and he intended to keep that promise.

Three weeks into our voyage, a storm threatened on the horizon. Captain Jones decided it wasn't worth the risk of going through it and tried to sail around it. As hard as the captain, crew, and ship tried, we weren't able to outrun the storm. The wind wasn't in our favor that day. Jones ordered everything tied down, the cannons secured, and turned the ship into the wind. Right before the storm swallowed us, he changed course and sailed the Ariel straight into it, dropping the sails at the last minute.

The crew was sent below as he ordered me and Lafayette into our cabins. The ship was thrown around like a toy in the bathtub as walls of water struck the ship. The waves were like nothing I had ever seen before. One minute the ship was almost standing on its end, going up a wave and the next minute, it was standing on its head, crashing down the wave's back side with bone-shaking force. The constant pounding of the rain hitting the wooden ship sounded like a train going by. Except this train seemed to never end.

I spent the first day in my hammock trying not to throw up. On the second day, I had already eaten what little food I thought to grab before going into the storm and made my way down below deck to get some more food. I was afraid I wouldn't be able to keep any food down, but I needed to check on the crew anyway. If nothing else, I needed to refill my canteens to ensure I didn't dehydrate.

The crew wasn't lying around idle like I had been. They were scrambling around – bailing water out of the ship, sealing leaks with pitch and tar, and constantly looking for any signs of new damage. The carpenters were examining the hull to ensure it was going to hold up to the nightmare storm we were in.

The crew quarters smelled like vomit and until I had gone below, I had managed to hold everything down. One whiff of the putrid smell and I lost what little contents I had in my stomach. The one member of the crew who wasn't a doctor but had some experience doctoring on a ship went around checking on everyone. He moved from one man to another. He made sure everyone drank water while he passed out pork biscuits. He said they were very dry and didn't taste that good but would help settle our stomachs. I grabbed some biscuits for Lafayette, Jones, James, and myself.

Even though I wasn't in any shape to help once I started vomiting, I walked around, talking to the men. If nothing else, it took my mind off my aching stomach. Some men seemed to take comfort in having the Pale Rider on their ship; others thought it was funny to see the boogie man on his knees, puking. Personally, I didn't care who saw. Half the time I wished I was dead, and half the time I was happy I could amuse these poor souls. I carried a bucket around with me, knowing my next internal explosion was always minutes away.

No matter how sick I was, I made sure to go below twice a day to check on the men.

Jones and James took turns at the wheel, not trusting anyone else to the hazardous but equally important job. On the third day of the storm, Jones and I were thrown from our hammocks as the ship was struck from the side. I had learned that if you didn't want to capsize your ship, you needed to sail straight into the waves. As waves continued to hit the ship broadside, our chances of capsizing increased exponentially.

Jones hit the floor next to me and let out a tirade of curses. He ran for the cabin door, and I followed. The wheel was spinning out of control with no one manning it.

"Lieutenant James!" Jones yelled, as he rushed straight for the wheel.

Jones made it halfway to the wheel when he was hit by a wave and thrown to the deck, sliding downward on the wet wood like a water slide. He nearly went over the side, but at the last few feet, the ship shifted and turned. What was down a second ago was now up, and what was up was now down. I was still in the doorway of our cabin, soaked and hanging on to dear life as Jones rode a layer of water my way. I stuck out a hand and grabbed his shirt, stopping him as he swept past.

When I thought we were safe, the ship rotated again, and I was now on the deck, clutching onto the captain with one hand and the door frame with the other.

The door swung wildly back and forth, and the only thing I could think of was if it slammed on my fingers, we were both going to be swept overboard and out to sea. I hadn't realized we were screaming until a green-faced Lafayette opened his door. He reached out for me, but I shouted for him to grab a rope. The ship had no shortage of stashed ropes, and he managed to grab one from his room.

"Tie one end to the ship, then tie it to yourself!" I yelled.

The young man kept his calm and did as I told him.

"Throw some of the rope to us!" I hollered, my voice growing hoarse.

He threw the middle portion of the rope to me and when it hit my chest, I let go of the door frame and grabbed it. Jones and I slid across the deck a few feet before Lafayette yanked on the rope and stopped us. Jones managed to climb up my body and get a hand on the rope as well. Every time I caught my footing, the ship violently shifted, and I stumbled in the opposite direction.

We pulled Lafayette out to us and tied the rope to every part of the ship we could as a safety line as we continued our way to the wheel. When we finally made it to the wheel, Jones howled out orders, and it took all three of us the turn the wheel, directing the ship back into the waves.

I told Lafayette to stay with Jones as I fished out another rope from a nearby locker. Tying the rope to myself and the then to the main mast, I started walking the ship, searching for the Lieutenant.

I worked my way to the front, struggling between thrashing waves and holding on for all I was worth when the swells crashed against our ship. The ship was now in a constant bouncing motion, so my window for movement from one spot to the next was incredibly short. Lafayette fed me rope as I went. I finally made it to the front of the ship, working my way up the port side, then back down to the wheel on the starboard side, yelling James' name the entire time.

When I made it back to Jones, I shook my head to answer his unasked question. James was lost, and there wasn't anything we could do about that. I untied the rope from my body and secured it to the same main mast I'd started from. We now had a safety rope that extended around the whole ship if we needed it again. I prayed we would not.

Lafayette had taken another rope and tied it around Jones and fastened it to the railing of the ship behind the wheel.

"James must have been hit by a rogue wave," Jones shouted in my ear.

"I'm sorry, Captain," I yelled back. "He was a good kid."

"Aya," was all Jones said, his face tight.

Jones untied the rope from his waist and tied it around Lafayette.

"Keep the ship facing into the waves," Jones screamed and pointed. "I have to go below and check for any new damage. Then I'll need to pick my new first mate."

With those words, Jones ran below. What a hard life. A good kid and sailor had been thrown overboard and killed, and we were already looking for his replacement. Now I understood why captains had to be hard men. It wasn't about sailing experience or knowledge; it was also about making the tough decisions quickly.

We suffered through two more days of that watery hell. From that point on, I insisted on standing watch with

Jones in case of another rogue wave. Lafayette stepped up and did his part, standing watch with the new lieutenant and first mate. This sailor was a little older than James had been. I had spoken to him a few times, and he seemed like a competent Navy man.

On the sixth day, we broke from the storm and the seas went calm and the rain stopped, as we watched the storm leave us and continue towards the way we'd come. We all took a moment of a collective sigh of relief before the crew went to work, cleaning the ship of bodily waste and vomit, as well as taking inventory of what was lost.

Other than James, we'd lost three more men in the raging tempest. One from dehydration, one from cargo falling on his head, and the third was missing. The hull was leaking, and men bailed water out of the ship using the bilge force pump as the captain and carpenters supervised repairs. The front and smaller of the three masts had snapped in half, most likely by the same wave that had killed James. I hadn't noticed the damage when I originally searched for the man.

Much of our food had been ruined, and half our barrels of water contaminated when they busted open under the pressure of the waves. Ropes used to tie them down snapped, which happened to be when the crewman died from his head injury.

We spent the whole day adrift, working on repairs on the dripping, water-logged ship. With all we had to do, the captain thought the work would go easier and faster if we dropped sail and drifted in the water. The broken barrels and ruined food were thrown overboard. The carpenters patched or repaired the hull to the captain's satisfaction. The bilge pumps held up and pumped the water out of the hull.

For the most part, the ship and crew were in good working order. The two enormous problems facing us were that we no longer had enough food or water for the voyage, and the broken mast could not be repaired. The broken-off portion of the mast had been lost in the storm, and between the repairs already made after our first battle and the wood used during our chase, the carpenter no longer had enough wood to construct a makeshift mast.

"We have enough food for two weeks if we ration our meals," Jones told me in confidence in our cabin. "It's not my concern, since we only have enough fresh water to last the crew maybe five days. Ten days if we cut water rations as well. But that means cutting the workload as much as possible, or the men will drop from dehydration."

"Can we make shore in ten days?" I asked him.

"I don't know where we are," Jones admitted. "After six days in that storm, I have no idea where it blew us. I'll figure out our location tonight with the stars, but best-case scenario is we are at least two weeks from France, and that is if we had a third mast, which we don't. Call it three weeks to France, if we are anywhere close to on course."

"Where do you think we are?" I asked the captain.

Jones pursed his lips and shrugged. "If we were blown south, we're closer to South America. If we were blown south-east, we're closer to Africa. God forbid we were blown west, because we might be closer to where we started off in the first place. If we kept east, we might be three weeks from Spain. I'll know more tonight when I figure out our location and determine the closest shoreline. We can always pray for a nearby island that has fresh water."

Later that night, using his sextant and the stars, Captain Jones plotted our location on the map. He turned to the table and put a finger on the map on our desk.

"We are here, in the middle of the ocean. The good news is the storm pushed us in the right direction. We're still on course and didn't lose much time. At the slower speed we're now going, we're four weeks from Portugal."

He explained that there were a group of islands halfway between our location and the mainland of Spain, under Spanish control, so we didn't know what kind of assistance we might get. The biggest problem was with our freshwater shortage. Jones wasn't sure if we would live long enough to reach the islands.

"We can capture water if it rains again," Jones added. "If it doesn't rain and we don't come across a French ship for help, we're as good as dead."

Either way, the captain didn't like having an American crew on a stolen British ship, sailing through Spanish waters, heading to France.

"So many things could go wrong," Jones said.

"Like?" I asked.

"For starters, between pirates, the British, and the Spanish, any ship we come across will want to sink us. Otherwise, we'll most likely die of thirst. Those are just the most likely outcomes."

With little to no choice, we set sail for the small group of islands in hopes of living long enough to reach them.

Captain Jones had the remaining freshwater barrels moved to Lafayette and his new lieutenant's room for safekeeping. We put Lafayette in charge of the water. Men lined up and received one cup of water every eight hours. Lafayette had a list of names of the crew and put a check mark next to their names as they received their water to ensure no man tried to get in line twice. I stuck to the same schedule as the men, but insisted Jones drank a cup every four hours. He argued at first, saying he needed to set the example, but I convinced him we needed the captain to be of clear mind for any up-coming problems.

Three days later, the sailor at the top of the main mast yelled down, "Ship ho!"

We scrambled to see which direction he was pointing. Forward, somewhere in front of us, and we were heading right for them.

Jones called for his new lieutenant, Mr. Task, to take the wheel, and we moved to the prow for a better look. He had his spy glass, and I had my range finder. The ship didn't look any bigger than us, and she didn't have too many more guns.

"Pirates?" I asked.

"No," Jones said with a heavy exhale. "Worse. British. But we might be in luck. It's the HMS Liverpool. Coventry class ship. I believe she has twenty-eight guns."

"Fight or run?" I asked.

"We don't have any choice," Jones said. "If we run, she'll chase, and we'll have to fight anyway. We can't outrun her with only two full sails. Plus, we'll die without her water. We've to fight."

Jones spun and shrieked orders to load the cannons. Then he ordered the American flag raised.

"Wait," I said, putting a hand on his arm, stopping him. "Move the cannons. Fill the thirteen cannon ports on one side. Raise the British flag. As far as she knows, the Ariel is still a British ship. Make sail for her and we'll board her. We look damaged and they'll assume correctly we got caught in that storm."

Jones thought about it for a moment, then nodded his head.

"Go put on the captain's uniform in our closet," I said. "Have Task put on the British uniform in the first mate's room. That might buy us some time."

We had thirteen guns on the starboard side of the ship and only three on the port side. Jones was going to have to bring us up with the Liverpool on our starboard side. Then he and Task walked around in plain sight for the British captain to see. They ran up the distress flag as we sailed straight for the Liverpool. Muskets, bayonets, swords, and knives were passed out to the men.

Most of the men stood ready below deck, with only twenty-six men still on deck, laying down and hidden under the railing. Two men per cannon. We didn't want to sink her, so I ordered half the cannons loaded with grapeshot.

I was a big believer in delegating and dividing responsibility, so I put Lafayette in charge of the cannons. On his first command to fire, the cannons with cannonballs would let loose, and the one loaded with grapeshot would fire on his second order to fire. That would give the men below enough time to run up on deck and board the ship.

We opened the last two barrels of water and let the men drink their fill. We needed them strong and not ready to pass out. If we won this battle, we could refill our water supply, and if we lost, we wouldn't need any water, anyway.

Jones and Lafayette complained about flying a British flag and not the American flag. They talked about the dishonor of it and how we were acting like pirates. Jones had agreed with me at first, but with Lafayette's objections, he was worried about his reputation.

I ignored them both. I didn't care what people said. Winning was all I cared about.

"We can't fly the American flag," I explained, giving in to their protesting and explaining why. "My mission is to *not* be associated with the colonies. If these men report I was transported by an American ship, the mission is as good as failed."

Lafayette nodded his head, thinking back to Washington's words. Jones still didn't understand and didn't want to be known for this kind of underhanded deception as opposed to open warfare.

I tried to placate his noble sensibilities. "Okay. As we get close, we'll run up the Jolly Roger and pretend to be pirates. No one will ever know you two were involved. In fact, we'll tell them the Pale Rider is in command. That will please General Washington and keep your good names clean from the stain of the blood we're going to spill."

Neither man liked my plan, but they gave in at the thought that I'd be given the credit, or in this case, blame for sailing under a British flag. Lafayette passed the word to the men we were to act like pirates, with the Pale Rider as captain. This would help separate me from the colonists and therefore separate the colonists from the assassination.

"Once they see the Jolly Roger, how long will it take them to fire their cannons?" I asked.

"Two seconds," Jones answered in his clipped tone, "if they're loaded and ready for us. Sixty seconds if they're not."

"Change flags right before we open fire," I said. "Don't give them more than thirty seconds."

Task stood at the wheel in a British Lieutenant's uniform while Jones stood next to the rigging with the flags.

Task's only job was to get us close. Jones was to order the flag change at the right time, and Lafayette oversaw the cannons.

I was in the captain's quarters with twenty-five volunteers. I would lead the boarding party with my group, and Jones would order some of the men below deck to follow me and some to join Lafayette, firing from our deck, picking their targets. This wasn't the normal way sea warfare was conducted in the eighteen century, and I had hoped the change in tactics might give us an advantage. We were outnumbered by at least fifty to seventy-five men, and I had to rely on shock and awe to take the day.

We came in head on, facing one another. We dropped our two sails about sixty feet away from the Liverpool and drifted forward with them twenty feet to our starboard. They dropped their three sails, and everything appeared nice and friendly. Their captain stood in his formal coat like Jones did.

It was common for ships to pass lines back and forth so they could pull themselves in close enough for captains to transfer over and speak. One of our sailors stood at the prow with a rope in his hand to throw over to his counterpart on the Liverpool.

"Wait until they throw their rope," Lafayette instructed the sailors.

I stood in the dark room waiting for the signal. I held my Tec-9 in my left hand and my sword in my right as I controlled my breathing. The ship's magazine had over twenty-five pistols, so the men with me were issued swords and flintlocks. The men below carried muskets and bayonets. I had taken off my guns and black vest after our first night on the ship, and it felt good to have them back on.

The two forward sailors threw ropes, and Jones yelled, "Now!"

The British flag flapped down, and the Jolly Roger unfurled, taking its place. It took a few more seconds, but men from the British ship calling out in panic. "Pirates!"

From the main deck, Lafayette screamed, "Fire!"

Seven cannons erupted as one as men stood up and fired half of our cannons. I threw open the door and ran out with my men right on my heels. Sailors on our ship pulled the rope that the sailor on the Liverpool had thrown over to us. They knew if they didn't draw the ship close enough or fast enough, this plan would never work.

Our seven cannonballs had ripped through the main deck's railings and killed dozens of men as the nine-pound steel projectiles continued through and out the opposite side of the ship, leaving shards and splinters behind. Lafayette got in several accurate shots, managing to destroy a few of the enemy's cannons. I ran up on the quarterdeck, running for the side of our ship, as Lafayette yelled, "Fire!" a second time.

I jumped over the side of our ship, clearing the four feet of open air between the two ships as grapeshot ripped through more British sailors. Dark billows of smoke filled the air, and the screams of men filled my ears.

The two ships were the same height and now so close together there was no chance of either ship sinking. The cannons were only going to cause damage to human flesh and anything on the main deck.

As I landed on the prow of the Liverpool, her captain was shrieking orders. Seven of her cannons boomed, but not as one – they fired sporadically. Her own nine-pound cannonballs ripped through the Ariel's main deck, destroying our railings and several cannons. There was so much smoke I could not see if Lafayette was injured.

The Liverpool's captain wasn't taking chances, and although his cannons weren't manned, they were already loaded and ready to go. He fell for our trap, but not completely. He was somewhat prepared for deception like what was going on now. He, like us, had his own men standing by ready to fire in case of a trick.

I rushed to the main deck, firing my pistol and swinging my sword. At first, sailors attacked with clubs or knives, and the first six to stand in front of me went down like wheat in front of a scythe.

Twenty-five flintlocks fired in rapid succession as my men scrambled onto the deck, eager to fire their pistols. No one wanted to die with the embarrassment of a loaded pistol in their hands. Between the cannon fire and the first wave of flintlocks, we must have killed at least forty or fifty members of the Liverpool's crew.

Men from below deck on our ship ran up and joined the fight, as men from the Liverpool, who had also been armed and waiting below their decks, ran up and charged us. My men had been ordered to scream, "Surender or die!" while fighting.

As a wave of British sailors charged me, muskets from the Ariel opened up and dropped the front rank. The second rank, to their credit, didn't hesitate to jump over their fallen comrades and come at us screaming. The twenty-five men behind me swarmed around and in front of me, taking me into their circle of safety, not wanting me to stand alone against the next horde of attackers. Muskets and flintlocks fired in all directions, and men fell. I spotted the Liverpool's captain screaming orders and directing his men. I pushed my way towards him, thinking the quickest way to end the fight was to kill him.

The fighting was thick, with over two hundred men in total on the quarterdeck of the main deck, clashing in close combat. No one on deck had room or time to reload their flintlock or muskets, so it was the clanging of swords and knives only. Some of the sailors swung hatchets and axes. My pistol had long since been emptied and holstered, and I now held my sword and knife as I pushed through the throng toward the captain. I could stab with my sword, or if attacked, I could parry with it and step in close with my knife.

For their part, my men had stopped yelling for the enemy crew to surrender and picked up a new war cry: "Pale Rider! Pale Rider! Pale Rider!" I didn't know who had started that ridiculous battle cry, and I didn't know if this crew had ever heard of the Pale Rider, but they pulled back in unison. Muskets from the deck of the Ariel still fired as fast as they could reload, taking out sailors in the back of the enemy's formation. The tip of a sword stabbed me in my left shoulder, sinking in with a shocking throb, but the men were so tightly packed I never saw who'd done it. My arm burned with pain as blood oozed from the deep cut.

I finally made my way to the Liverpool's captain who'd run one of my sailors through the stomach with his sword. As the man slipped off his blade, the captain made eye contact with me, then ran up a set of stairs that lead to the poop deck, the highest deck on a ship. In this case, like the Ariel, it was above the captain's quarters.

He stepped back from the edge, giving me room to follow him, so I did. I spotted Lafayette back on the Ariel, thank goodness. Lafayette's arm shot up and pointed at us. He ordered his muskets to aim for the captain until I held up a hand stopping him. Killing their captain with a musket wouldn't create the fear I wanted. The captain noted the exchange between myself and the men with the muskets and realized I wanted him for myself.

He didn't hesitate but came at me fast, chopping down at my head. His clumsy attack was simple to block, but he didn't give up. He hacked, chopped, and stabbed at me frenetically but never got close to draw blood. Conversely, I slashed low and cut deep into his calf muscle. He screamed and fell to one knee. His sword arm dropped down to his side. I stepped forward, putting my knife to his throat. His hand opened, dropping his sword, and he closed his eyes, waiting for his life to end.

"Order your men to surrender, and I'll not kill you or what's left of your men," I instructed in a hoarse voice.

He nodded, trying not to cut himself on my blade at his neck, and I yanked him to his feet. With my knife still at his throat, he called for his men to cease fighting. It took a few more minutes for his voice to carry over the clashing cacophony, but the fighting stopped, and swords, knives, and empty flintlocks clanged and thumped as they dropped to the deck.

Men separated as our men moved to the outside, circling the beaten crew who were now in a tight group, pushed together. I wanted to slow things down and finish this with no more loss of life. The dead were again thrown overboard without the dignity and respect they deserved. Our wounded were transferred back to our ship while their wounded were separated into one large group. They seemed to have more wounded men than those not wounded. I permitted their surgeon to see to the ship's injured. He went first to his captain and inspected his leg.

"See to the others first," I bellowed with distain dripping in my voice. "Start with those more seriously injured."

The man actually apologized to his captain, before standing up and moving on to those that were in genuine need of his help.

We had lost thirty-five men, half of those from the cannon fire the Liverpool managed to let loose on us. The Liverpool had lost over one hundred. Like our losses, many of theirs were from our cannon fire. Grape shot had also served as a devastating weapon. I had the Liverpool's captain order his men to sit down while my men took turns reloading their flintlocks and muskets.

"I'm the Captain of the Ariel," I yelled to the prisoners. "I'm known as the Pale Rider. If you don't resist, no more of you will have to die. We were blown off course by the storm and will be returning to the colonies once we make repairs," I lied. "We will be taking your food, water, gunpowder, and one of your masts. In exchange, we'll leave you your lives and a ship we'll not scuttle. You can limp back to your king and tell him who did this to you. The point is this, you'll be alive as long as you don't test my patience."

Heads nodded, telling me the crew was more than willing to go along with the trade.

"You'll be doing the work," I continued. "My men will watch. If anyone fights or resists, I'll kill every one of you sons of bitches."

With those last words, I spoke slowly and loudly, and the head nodding stopped. Their eyes suddenly found their feet to be more interesting. Lafayette appeared at my side and gave orders.

"I thought you didn't want to be seen on this ship?" I asked, grateful he lived through the destruction. I really didn't care that he didn't want to be seen. I was glad to see him.

"I didn't," he responded with a casual air. "I had thought our attack was less than honorable. I see now you won the day without either ship being sunk. You could have killed these men but chose not to. What could be more honorable than showing mercy to your enemy?"

As one of my men tied a bandage around my arm, I studied the crew of the Liverpool transferring over most of their food and water. Our carpenters cut down the smallest of the ship's three masts. They needed to tie pulleys to the main mast of both ships to first lift out our broken mast, dropping it in the ocean, then lift the smallest but still long mast from the Liverpool to the Ariel. We again made the crew of the Liverpool do the work. Their carpenters seemed adept and worked quickly, wanting us off their ship.

Mr. Tubs promised he'd be able to attach it while we sailed but didn't promise how long the new mast would last. Better repairs could be made in France. Lastly, we transferred over cannons from their ship to ours. We again had twenty-six cannons. The rest of their cannons we dropped into the ocean to ensure they didn't fire at us as we sailed away. Lafayette wisely thought to collect up the swords, muskets, and flintlocks from the deck and ship's magazine as well.

After a cursory search of the captain's quarters, I found a leather purse with gold and silver coins. I didn't know if it belonged to the captain himself or if it was the property of the Empires, but I did know who that purse belonged to now.

Captain Jones was in a rush to get underway. Even with the additional loss of men, Jones told me he'd be able to finish the voyage to France. We'd lost time because of the storm and this battle. With Task at the wheel, we sailed away from the Liverpool. Her captain and crew wore surprised expressions, as if they thought we were really going to kill them and sink the ship before we finished. It was odd to see smiles on the faces of the British sailors as we sailed farther and farther away. Those who were still alive would live to see their families again.

After returning to the captain's quarters, I dry swallowed some pain killers and used one of the few antibiotic shots I still had. I cleaned and bandaged my arm with a clean dressing and was pleased to see the laceration wasn't as deep as I had feared. The bone wasn't damaged, and the muscle and skin would heal fine if I avoided infection. It would just be another scar to add to my collection.

Chapter Six: The Messenger

We sailed into Bay of Biscay on the morning of January 21st, six and a half weeks after we'd first taken the Ariel. The storm and battles had slowed us down, but Jones had made up some time with his new and improved design and added sails.

From there we turned north and headed for France. We dropped the American flag again, this time raising the French flag as we traveled through the English Channel, hugging the French coastline. So close to England herself, in waters filled with British warships, it felt like we were holding our breath until we made port at the Port of Le Havre.

"It's a good thing the British would never expect someone to capture one of their ships and then sail it all the way here," I told Jones. "Just the same, we may want to paint over her name."

"Marie has many contacts at this port and can help me with repairs and additional crew members," Jones said. "He also said he'd be able to get both of you a carriage to Paris."

"Where is Marie?" I asked.

"Changing. Speaking of changing, I'll be changing myself as soon as James relieves me."

Crew members tied the Ariel to one of the piers at the port as I walked out of the captain's quarters and onto the main deck. Lafayette and Jones stood at the stern of the ship, talking in low tones.

Lafayette looked more comfortable once again dressed in his fine blue uniform. Jones was himself dressed in his American naval uniform. Between the vomiting and horrible food, we'd lost weight, and their uniforms hung on their frames and needed some filling in. They would need to gain a few pounds back or have their uniforms tailored.

Lafayette and Jones were clean-shaven, whereas I hadn't shaved since we left American waters. If England had heard of the Pale Rider, he would have been described as clean-shaven, so I had taken the time during our voyage to grow out my beard again. Annie seemed to like the beard, so I was going to give it another try. It felt good to be out of the linen pants and shirt I had worn for this voyage and back in my well-fitting deer skin pants, white shirt, and black vest. I also wore my black leather triangle hat to cover my forehead scar.

Against Lafayette's advice, I wore my two pistols, three knifes and my sword. I was going to draw eyes, but what were the odds anyone here had ever heard of me?

A man who spoke mild English boarded the ship, and Lafayette introduced him as the Harbor Master. Captain Jones spoke less French than the Harbor Master spoke English, so Jones asked Lafayette to interpret for him.

With Lafayette's help, the Harbor Master agreed to arrange for repairs to the ship and made suggestions on where to find new crewmen. Most of his suggestions were at the local drinking pubs or inns.

I was surprised to learn that quite a few French sailors wanted to sail on an American warship. Americans were known for pirating against the British, and this was seen by the young men of France as a way for a man to make a reputation, and possibly a fortune for himself.

Lafayette hired a carriage to take us to Paris, which I paid for with the money I'd found in the captain's quarters back when we first captured the Ariel. Jones agreed on a price with the Harbor Master for the vital repairs to the ship, and then left his First Mate in charge of recruitment of the much-needed new crew members.

Jones then asked if he might accompany us to Paris. He wanted to speak to Mr. Franklin and inquire what new orders he had now that he'd delivered me to France safe and sound.

Neither Lafayette nor I had any objections about Jones riding with us to Paris. In fact, though it surprised me, I now considered Jones as a friend. If we'd not fought in several battles, gone through the worst storm of my life, and spent six and a half weeks in the same room together, I would probably think of him as another arrogant aristocrat instead of an honorable gentleman who I could trust. But we had, and I did. So, there it was.

Lafayette surprised us when he gave the carriage driver a local address to take us to. The driver grinned slyly, as if he knew the place well. When I asked where we were going, Lafayette said he wanted to send a message to Mr. Franklin ahead of us.

"Madam Fournier's place," Lafayette told me.

"I take it she's not going to ride ahead of us on horseback?" I asked.

"No, not on horseback," Lafayette answered with an odd emphasis. "She delivers messages for certain friends of hers, and I happen to know *Monsieur* Franklin is one of those special friends. He also pays her quite well for the service."

If he expected me to understand what he was talking about, he was mistaken. We rode in what I doubted was the worst part of the city, but not the best part, either. When the carriage stopped, a tall, young black man dressed in a fine shirt, waistcoat, and a white powdered wig opened the carriage door. He stepped back, holding the door open to allow us to exit the carriage. Lafayette held up a hand to Jones to halt him.

"It might be best if you wait in the carriage."

"Why?" Jones asked.

Lafayette eyed him as he reconsidered. "You're right. My apologies. It might be more suspicious if you sat in the carriage."

Lafayette twisted and stepped from the carriage. Jones looked at me and shrugged with a questioning expression on his face, then followed Lafayette. I stepped from the carriage and came face first to a wave of smells and sounds that the carriage had muted. Loud music and singing came from behind the red door right in front of the carriage. Fluttering pigeons flew and cawed from the roof tops. A strong mixture of stale piss and cheap perfume lingered in the air.

At the mouth of the alley, next to the building I assumed we were going into, a woman knelt in front of an overweight sailor, who gripped her head in one hand and a bottle of wine in the other. He actually took the time to take a swig of the wine while she was pleasuring him.

"What the fuck?" I whispered under my breath as I stepped down onto the sidewalk. I had a sudden idea of what this place was.

Lafayette slipped a coin into the elegantly dressed man's hand, and the man tipped his head to Lafayette, then rushed to open the red door.

We walked into what looked like a mixture of the playboy mansion and a 1970's New York City pimp's house, and I tried to look everywhere at once. Half-naked women raced around in filmy clothing while shirtless young men carried silver trays topped with glasses of wine. It looked like some sort of eighteenth-century house party. A man stood in the corner playing a fast-paced tune with the violin. His hand held his bow and moved too fast to keep track of. Everyone not sucking face or busy drinking sang along loudly. I didn't understand the words, but it sounded like a happy, upbeat bar song.

Three beautiful half naked ladies sat on a bright yellow couch in front of us. They only wore high heels and overly cinched, white skirted corsets that left little to the imagination. Enormous white, curly wigs sat on top of their heads and heavy makeup painted their faces in blues and reds. The three ladies smiled at us and lifted their hands, wiggling their fingers to get our attention and wave hello, as if they knew and remembered us. Matching chairs sat against the wall and a low table was in front of them, obscured by half emptied glasses. The outside smells gave way to stronger perfume, sweat, wine, and sex.

"What the fuck?" I asked no one again, the full understanding of where we were penetrating my brain.

"Marie!" Jones yelled over the music. "I don't begrudge you, if you want to visit . . . friends, but can't it wait, man? We do have important business to see to."

This was a brothel, a French brothel. I'd heard of them but never thought to see one. At least not from the inside.

"This is business," Lafayette shouted back.

A woman in her late thirties wearing a blue dress walked in front of us, pulling on the hand a young man of about nineteen behind her. She knocked on a door and when there was no answer, she opened the door and yanked the young man in, shutting the door behind them.

Another woman, who appeared older and in a tight yellow corset that pushed her breasts to her chin, sauntered up to me. Her breath reeked like tobacco and wine, and her makeup was thicker than that of the three triplets on the couch. Before I could say or do anything, she placed her right hand around my neck. Her left hand grabbed my groin, and she spoke something that sounded both sweet and sexy to me in French as I tried to jump back. Then I froze, not knowing what to do and afraid to move, lest her hand grip me any harder.

Lafayette plied me with a wry grin and managed to rescue me. He said something into the woman's ear. Her smile faded, and she took her hand off my member and held it out to Lafayette as if he didn't know where that hand had been a second ago. Lafayette placed a coin in her palm, and she smoothly tucked it into her ample cleavage. She spoke low to Lafayette and pointed up the stairs. The woman then kissed me on the cheek and whispered sultry-sounding French in my ear. I had no idea what she said or how much it would have cost me. She finally turned away and put an arm around another man who walked in behind us.

Lafayette motioned with his head for us to follow and started up the stairs. As we made our way up to the second floor, couples were walking down. Most of the men were still getting redressed as they walked down the steps, with satisfied grins plastered on their faces. The women also smiled, but they were well-practiced fake smiles, betrayed by the fact their eyes scanned the room looking for their next coin.

Lafayette didn't stop at the second floor but turned and headed up to the third. Through the walls, I could both hear and feel headboards slamming against the walls.

The third floor was much quieter. Like the second floor, there were six doors extending down the hall, but the hallway wasn't filled with people waiting their turn. I could hear grunting from the rooms, but I had the sense these were the prime rooms with the youngest and best-looking ladies who charged the most for their services. The only person on this floor not in a bedroom was a large man who stood in front of a door at the end of the hallway.

Lafayette approached the big man, who looked to be about thirty years old. The man stood about three inches taller than I did and had about forty pounds on me. Lafayette bowed politely as he asked for Madame Fournier. The man seemed acquainted with Lafayette and shook his head.

"What's going on, Marie?" I asked.

"We need to talk to Madame Fournier," Lafayette said. "But Luke here says no."

"No what?" Jones asked. "She doesn't want to see you? Or he doesn't want you seeing her?"

Lafayette asked something of Luke in French, and Luke went into a fit. He shouted and waved his arms.

"He says he doesn't like me because I'm friends with the king," Lafayette interpreted. "He says Madame Fournier is too busy for the likes of us. He says for us to leave now, or he'll break our legs."

And with that, and without the slightest warning, I stepped up and punched the big man right in the nose. His head flew back and struck the wall behind him hard and with a loud thump. My stomach tightened when he looked at me like I was crazy and raised his own fist. Instead of waiting to see how hard this guy could hit, I punched him again, not holding back. His head again bounced off the wall but this time he stepped forward to grab at my shirt. I slapped his hand away and gave him a quick one-two jab punch combo, with little effect. Apparently, I wasn't the only bare knuckles boxer in the hallway. Lafayette and Jones had taken several prudent steps back and away from us, giving us plenty of room and staying out of the fight.

He swung a meaty left hand the size of a catcher's mitt at my face, and I ducked under it. I didn't, however, sidestep the right upper cut he followed up with, aiming for my chin. Forced to step back and shake my head, I tried to clear the stars from my vision.

The wall collided into my back, stopping me. I knew better than to get trapped against a rock and a hard place – the man being the rock and my over confidence being the hard place.

"Look out, Thomas!" Lafayette yelled from somewhere to my left.

Two enormous hands grabbed the front of my shirt, and out of reflex, I did what I had never needed to do before, but what my father taught me to do if I was ever in this position. I dropped straight down.

The bigger man was strong, but my dead weight was too much for him to hold up. Since he didn't let go of me, my dead weight pulled his body forward and his face smacked into the wall in front of him. The big man was now bent over, right above me. His hands released my shirt, and I shot straight up to my feet, slamming my head into his nose. Until my skull crushed his nose, I hadn't noticed my hat had been knocked off my head.

He stumbled back into the wall behind him, holding his bloody nose with both his hands. I kicked hard, bringing my foot up into his balls. As he doubled over, I put my full power into an upper cut into his jaw. His head flew back, and he stood straight against the wall for a second before his eyes rolled into the back of his head, and he slid to the floor.

Jones clapped his hands, hollering "Bravo!" as I doubled over panting as I tried to catch my breath.

"That was a fine showing, Thomas," Lafayette told me. "But I think he was fishing for a bribe. I could have gotten us in for a few coins."

"Oh," I said between breaths, giving the sly Frenchman a side glare, "you couldn't have said that sooner?"

Ignoring my comment, Lafayette walked past me and knocked on the door the big man had been guarding. Before his knuckles could tap on the door a second time, the door shot open. An angry lady, no doubt wanting to know what the commotion outside of her room was, stormed out the door and glared at us. She was in her fifties but was trying to look younger with a full face of makeup. She had shoved Lafayette backwards with one strong left hand and held a pistol, steady and level, in her right hand.

She wore large gold and silver rings on every finger and her thumbs. Her white wig was slightly taller but a lot more expensive than what the girls downstairs had on their heads. A set of pearls encircled her pudgy neck and wrapped around her wig and a tan dress, which expanded wide at the waist as if she were a walking umbrella. Her dress had brushed against the sides of the doorframe as she had walked through it and appeared to be several layers thick. The last layer against her skin had to be a corset, because her breasts were pushing up and out, spilling out with the intention of drawing the eye. For a woman her age, the corset made her breasts look large and firm.

As Luke had done, her first reaction was to shout at us in French. There was no doubt she oversaw this place and was accustomed to doing the yelling. Most of her harsher words were directed towards Lafayette – she and Lafayette had obviously met before. She gestured to the boxer on the floor with her pistol and asked Lafayette a harsh question. Lafayette shook his head in denial and pointed at me, ratting me out.

Thanks, friend.

I raised my empty hands in a "don't shoot" move, not wanting to have to kill this woman and wanting her to kill me even less.

She stopped talking and peered at me hard with narrowed eyes, and she now directed her pistol at me.

Lafayette and she exchanged a flurry of French back and forth. She was speaking to Lafayette, but her eyes and pistol were trained on me. Her eyes went up and down my bruised form. They stopped on my pistols, and then again at the top of my head. I assumed she was studying my scar – she was a woman accustomed to taking in the full measure of a person quickly.

Lafayette introduced Jones and, at the mention of his name, Jones bowed formally at the waist. Not sure what title to use for me, Lafayette introduced me as "*mon ami.*" She finally shifted her gaze off me and onto Lafayette. Her eyebrows raised up in a question.

An awkward silence filled the hall, then she glanced back down at the boxer.

"Is he dead?" she asked in perfect English. I'm sure my face showed my surprise. *Really, she spoke English now, after the pistol was off me?*

"No," the three of us answered at the same time. God forbid what she might do if she thought we'd slain her man.

"Leave him there," she instructed. "It might teach him to win next time. Please, let's talk in my office."

I almost expected her to spit on the unconscious man. She lowered the pistol as she turned and walked into her office, the three of us on her heels. Jones handed me my fallen hat, and I flopped it back on my head.

"Why are you up here and not downstairs with my girls?" she asked Lafayette, her lips tight with a hint of a smile.

"Your girls are beautiful, Madame Fournier," Lafayette responded politely.

"Lafayette," she interrupted him. "I have told you before to call me Lille."

"Your girls are most beautiful, Lille," Lafayette tried again, this time dipping his head. "But it's your services we need tonight, not theirs."

Her eyebrows climbed, and she smiled at him.

"I'm afraid I've not offered my personal services in many years."

"As pleasant as your personal touch would be, Lille," Lafayette said, after clearing his throat, "it's your additional service we are in need of tonight."

That's how I met Madame Fournier, the madam of one of the best-known whore houses in Le Havre. She also ran a side business of messengering, with hundreds of pigeons on the roof of the brothel. Each pigeon flew different prescribed destinations. Mr. Franklin had learned of this service during – well, I can guess how he learned of it – but she had several pigeons and a large cage on a rooftop of a house belonging to a friend of Franklin's. This Mr. Franklin was starting to sound more like a spy than an ambassador.

"My additional services?" Her smile dissipated slowly as her lips pursed together.

Her words held a razor's edge. She still gripped her pistol in her right hand as she eyed us, trying to determine if we were a threat to her business or not. I'm sure the king of France would be upset if he knew a messenger service, one that was passing secrets, and wasn't under the Royal control, operated inside his country.

"We need to get a message to *Monsieur* Benjamin Franklin," Lafayette explained.

"He's in Paris," she said, adjusting her skirts as she perched on the edge of an ornate, padded chair. She dipped her fingers into a carved tobacco jar and sniffed the brown powder off her finger in a flourish, then breathed heavily at Lafayette. "You could be there by tomorrow if you leave tonight."

"Yes," Lafayette agreed, clearing his throat again. He actually seemed *uncomfortable.* I had to bite back an inappropriate smile. "You know I'm an acquaintance of his. I wish him to know I'm back in France and to arrange a meeting."

She didn't respond, but her head tilted up a bit, peering down her nose at us. The silence was designed to encourage

Lafayette to continue speaking without her acknowledging anything he'd said so far. I could see how her skills, brothel Madame or otherwise, were in high demand. Madame Fournier was good at what she did.

"I wish to have a meeting with him before the king or anyone else learns I've returned to France," Lafayette continued.

"And what makes you think I can get a message to him?" she asked.

"He told me to contact you if I ever needed to get word to him," Lafayette explained.

She stared hard at Lafayette, weighing his words, deciding whether to believe him or not. She kept glancing my way. There was a question for me in her eyes. The wrinkles around the corners of her mouth twitched a bit every time she looked at me. She was good at hiding her expressions, but something was wrong, and she didn't want us to know what it was.

After a minute, she turned to her desk and slid a quill and a small pot of ink over to Lafayette. Then she handed him a small piece of parchment, the same size as you might find in a fortune cookie. When he finished writing, I took the paper and read it to myself. Lafayette had written in tiny letters that he'd returned to France with a new friend of GW and asked to meet tomorrow at noon, an address below that.

"Why did you pick this place?" I asked Lafayette as I pointed to the note, making sure I didn't say anything loud enough for Madame Fournier to overhear.

"It's private, and it's where he and I first met. This way he will know the message really is from me."

"Then write that," I told him as I placed the note in my pocket.

"Write what?"

"For him to meet us where you two first met," I answered. "If the note falls in the wrong hands, they won't have an address and we won't be walking into an ambush, because no one else should know where that location is."

Lafayette rewrote the note and handed the paper to Madame Fournier, who then yelled something in French. A young boy opened the door behind her desk and entered the room. Through the open door, I could see stairs leading up to the roof.

"This is my grandson," Madame Fournier said.

She handed the paper to the boy who appeared to be in his early teens. She never looked at the paper or tried to read it – maybe because she saw me watching her every move, or maybe she prided herself on confidentiality. A messenger service that didn't keep one's message secret wouldn't be in business for very long.

"Send this to Monsieur Franklin," she said in English to the boy.

I assumed she spoke in English for our benefit. The boy took the note and left the room, shutting the door behind him.

With that done and gold removed from my purse and placed into the hands of Madame Fournier, we turned to leave. Madame Fournier placed a hand on Lafayette's arm, stopping him.

"*Où l'avez-vous rencontré*?" Madame Fournier said softly to Lafayette.

Her dark eyes flashed back on me. Lafayette shook his head in some sort of denial or refusal to answer. Though I didn't understand it, my chest tightened at her question.

"English, if you please," I said.

"She asked me where you and I had met," Lafayette answered in a tight voice.

I locked eyes with Madame Fournier and saw her fear. She was a woman who dealt in information. I doubted there was much she didn't know, including the bounty on a man wanted by the English. Tension between us changed and not for the better. The hairs on the back of my neck stood up.

"What's the reward up to?" I asked, hardening my stare.

She burst out in a laugh, and I could hear the protest in her tone before she spoke a single word. Her left hand moved up to her neck, in a movement some might mistake as being insulted. I interpreted it as subconsciously putting up a barrier between us. A shield to protect herself from the boogie man.

She was going to say she didn't know what I was talking about, but I held up the first finger of my right hand, stopping her from talking. My arm went back down until the cool metal of my pistol pressed against my skin. I didn't grab my pistol, but I could feel it with my wrist.

"How much is it up to?" I asked again, but this time in a low, threatening voice.

As I continued to eye Madame Fournier, I knew I was staring down a woman who knew who I was, a woman who looked for profit in any situation. She was thinking about how much she could get for turning me in.

I also knew this woman made a life not only from sex but from knowledge, from being able to read people and finding weakness. As she had looked at Lafayette's eyes and realized he was telling the truth about his needed message, she now looked into my eyes and didn't like what she saw. She had locked eyes with a killer who was wondering if this woman had now become too much of a liability to leave alive.

She seemed to understand what kind of man stood behind the eyes she was looking into. I don't know how my face looked at that moment, but the blood ran from hers. Even with makeup covering her skin, her face turned a pale white. She glanced down at my hands and then at hers. Her pistol was still in her own hand, and she quickly dropped it on her desk as if it was a snake ready to bite. Her right hand shook, and she quickly grabbed it with her left. She held her hands in front of her stomach, knuckles of her left hand turning white from squeezing her right so hard.

"How much?" I asked a third time, but with more force.

She sputtered her words, then taking a deep breath, she paused and composed herself. She was trying to remind herself she was a woman of power and wealth, and she spoke slowly in her second language.

"I have it on good authority the king is raising it to sixty-five thousand pieces of gold," she said, her voice cracking on the last word.

Lafayette and Jones looked like someone had pissed in their Cheerios. Not at the reward, but in realizing who I was.

"Is *your* life worth sixty-five thousand pieces of gold?" I asked in a lower voice.

Would I have killed her in that moment? I don't like to think so, but there was an entire revolution to consider.

Madame Fournier tried to speak, but her sense of authority fled and she seemed overwhelmed and afraid and reverted to her native language. She spoke rapidly to Lafayette in French. Her voice went up and down between anger and fear as her gaze skipped back and forth from Lafayette to me. Lafayette tried to keep up with her, translating for me.

"She assures me that she's a loyal French citizen and would never help the British," Lafayette interpreted. "She says her pigeons and her girls are at your disposal. She would never betray you."

Okay, black vest, white shirt, dear skin pants, two pistols and let's not forget the scar on my head. I get it – I was an easy mark and needed to change clothes. Briefly, I pondered exactly when she had figured it out. Yet, if a whorehouse madam from an entirely different continent could quickly figure out I was the Pale Rider, then I was in a bit of a dangerous situation. What kind of rumors had been going around about me to make this tougher than nails, whorehouse madam who had worked her way up the food chain from the very bottom to the very top, so afraid of me?

I took a deep breath and blew it out through my nose as I shifted my gaze to Jones and Lafayette, trying to figure out my next move.

"Well, Thomas," Jones said, "you do stick out like a sore thumb. Maybe a disguise would be fitting."

"I can help with that," Madame Fournier belted out quickly in English.

She was trying to make me see her as an ally and not a threat. Smart woman.

"How?" I asked her.

She raced to the door and out to the hallway, leaving the door open behind her. Luke was back on his feet, still in the hallway and giving me the stink eye. Madame Fournier banged on the door across the hall. A young topless girl wearing only a type of frilly under-bloomers answered the door, not bothering to cover her breasts. The young lady listened carefully as Madame Fournier gave her a series of commands. Luke screamed in protest until Madame Fournier slapped him hard, and then, bringing her face inches from his, she whispered something quickly.

The young lady ran from her room without taking any time to put on a shirt. Luke slowly turned around, glaring at us again. The stink eye was gone, replaced with something different. Not fear. Respect? No, not respect. *Caution.*

Dipping his head to us, he walked down the hall and into a different room.

"Marie?" I asked, my nerves on fire.

"I'm not sure what's going on," the Frenchman answered.

***

Twenty minutes later, I was laying naked in a cloth-covered bathtub filled with hot water. The once naked and beautiful young woman was now in a loose-fitting man's shirt and sitting behind me, shaving my face.

I had argued against shaving my face. I had grown fond of the beard, and it felt like it hid who I was. Madame Fournier pointed out it wasn't in fashion here in France and would only draw attention to me.

Luke brought in some clothes for me to try on, and one of Madame Fournier's girls carried in a man's wig. Madame Fournier had several boxes of clothes that had been left behind by men too drunk to remember everything when they left, a lost and found of sorts. The wig was a short, white wig with a single curl above the ears and a small, thin ponytail dangling in the back. The young lady shaving my face also insisted on cutting my shaggy hair. I objected to that as well, but Jones said it was necessary for the wig to fit properly.

After my hot bath, shave, and haircut, the first I'd had in a very long time, I dressed in my newish clothes. Madame Fournier agreed to keep my current clothes for me until I return for them. I was used to seeing men of the century in the clothing of the time, but I still felt funny putting on the knee-high socks. I kept my calf-high boots, and they blended in well with my new, thin brown pants. I then put on another white shirt, one that was cleaner and fancier than mine, with ruffles in the front. I topped it off with a functional and dressy black waistcoat, which was not very warm at all. I was going to miss my warm waterproof coat.

My shoulder holster fit under my new dress coat fine, so I kept it. My cowboy style holster was never going to work, so I had to leave it with Madame Fournier as well. My Tec-9 fit into a red sash I had tied around my waist and didn't look out of the ordinary. I tucked one of my knives into the small of my back under my coat and put one in my satchel. I folded my black vest into my satchel for now. I wasn't going to leave it behind. Adding the wig and my sword for the final touches, my look was complete.

My cheeks were hot, burning with the knowledge I looked like a complete idiot. Lafayette and Jones both said it was the first time since they had known me that I looked and dressed like a true gentleman. I grumbled at the compliments.

I gave Madame Fournier another handful of gold coins and a promise to be back with more gold coins if she kept my clothes and secrets safe, or with my knife if she didn't. Then I slipped Luke a few coins to make sure there were no hard feelings. Finally, I gave the young lady whose name I never learned several coins for the shave and haircut. The coins were leaving my purse more quickly than I cared for.

I investigated my reflection in the mirror and didn't recognize the jackass looking back at me. The wig really did a good job of hiding my scar. However, the man in the mirror looking back at me was anyone but the Pale Rider. I sighed heavily at my reflection before we walked back down the stairs. The house party was still going strong. Climbing back into the carriage, Lafayette gave more instructions to our driver.

The carriage departed the city and headed out into the greener countryside. Lafayette said we wouldn't make it to Paris until tomorrow. I thought we'd make camp somewhere on the way, but the driver didn't want to stop. Since we were going to travel all night, we made ourselves comfortable and slept.

Chapter Seven: The Meeting

The next morning, we woke in the early hours as the carriage rolled down a cobblestone road. The steady clacking of horseshoes against the brick had a steady rhythm to it. Sitting up and looking out the carriage window, I could see we were indeed in Paris.

Lafayette popped up and looked out the opposite window, smiling widely.

"*Vive la Paris*!" Lafayette called out the wooden-framed open window.

I didn't speak French, but even I understood what that meant. The young man loved his country, and Paris, with over six hundred thousand people, stood as the jewel of France.

He stuck his head out the window and yelled something to the driver.

"We have a few hours, so we can get something to eat while we wait," Lafayette said.

It turned out Lafayette's meeting place with Mr. Franklin was the restaurant we were eating at. We sat for three hours, eating, drinking, and talking. The crepes were excellent, and I ate enough for three people. I couldn't believe they had an orange juice drink. Lafayette claimed the drink, which he called *shrub*, was a favorite of Franklin's. It was heavy with syrup and sweet with a shot of rum, but still exceptional. After our six and a half weeks on the ship, I needed some good vitamin C, or I might have started losing some teeth.

Even after a night's sleep and decent food, I still felt like a clown with my long socks and wig. It was around eleven thirty when Lafayette stood up and waved to two men who had walked into the cafe. At this time of the day, only half the tables had patrons, so the two men spotted us easily. One of the two men was older, maybe seventy years old. That had to be Franklin. His companion was younger, but not young. Mid-forties if I had to guess and going bald on top but still had brown hair on the sides. That would be John Adams. They were overweight by my standards, and I could see by their soft hands that neither had ever put in a hard day's work that didn't involve reading, writing, or arguing.

Franklin, I had to admit, was better at this political game they were playing. He walked in smiling, as if he was here to have lunch with some old friends. He was a cool customer for an old man. He made a point of shaking hands and saying *bonjour* to people as if he had nothing to hide and wanted everyone to know he was there.

Adams, for his part, seemed to be trying to make himself small. He didn't move or duck down, but I could see him trying to be invisible. He refused to make eye contact with anyone, but at the same time, his eyes shot back and forth, trying to take in the faces of everyone there. He looked uncomfortable and nervous, like someone who had something to hide.

Adams walked straight over to our table and sat down as if he hadn't noticed the three of us standing there to greet him. Lafayette bowed his head slightly while Jones stuck out his hand. I watched as Adams sat down and grabbed my water, drinking it down in one long gulp. He set the glass down, and ignoring Lafayette and Jones, stared at me.

"Are you him?" Adams asked, eyeing my ostentatious wig. "I thought you would look different. Bigger. Meaner, and without a silly wig."

Gee, thanks.

Jones's hand slowly went back down to his side, rejected as he realized there was no handshake to come. Lafayette coughed into his closed hand, clearing his throat.

"You should know I was against this plan from the beginning," Adams said to me, ignoring them.

Franklin finally made it over to the table and placed his left hand on Adams's shoulder to calm him and stop him from talking. I could see Franklin's fingers squeezing Adams's shoulder, not hard but enough to wrinkle Adams's coat and turn his own knuckles white. Franklin stuck his right hand out to shake Jones's neglected hand.

"Captain Jones," Franklin started with niceties, "how was the voyage over here?"

"Eventful," Jones answered. "Very eventful. But we made it."

"Marie, my boy," Franklin continued, smiling warmly. "Seeing you is both unexpected and wonderful. Did the great General Washington send you? Did you come straight here, or did you have a chance to see your magnificent family?"

"I volunteered to help Thomas," Lafayette said, motioning his head toward me. "And we came straight here. *Monsieur* Franklin, *Monsieur* Adams, may I introduce Major Nelson."

Franklin offered his hand to me.

"I had expected you to look more like a mountain man," Franklin admitted, with disappointment in his voice.

So did I.

He then raised his hand in the air, motioning for two glasses of wine.

"Major?" Adams asked, one eyebrow raising high on his balding forehead.

"Yes," Jones responded. "He was given the rank by General Washington himself, before we left."

Everyone took to their seats, and I sat dumbfounded, watching these men fidget and shift around, adjusting themselves in their chairs. They were planning on being here for a while and were getting comfortable for a long discussion.

"Captain," Franklin said, bringing his attention back around to the Naval officer. "We need to talk, but unless you've already been informed about what this is about, I think we'll have to ask you to give us a minute."

Jones still didn't know why I was here, so he stood up to go. I put out a hand to stop him.

"Captain Jones doesn't know why I'm here," I told the man. "But he needs to know."

"We will decide who needs to know about this," Adams countered, protesting.

I stared him down. "I don't know what your plan is to get me out of France and back to America, but if you want Captain Jones to sail me back, then he needs to know. If you don't plan on him sailing me back, I still want him to know and to stand by on the ship as a backup plan. Either way, it's my ass on the line, and I'll decide who knows. I've only waited to tell him out of respect for you two gentlemen."

I was lying about the last part, but it sounded better than I didn't give a crap about what they wanted. In truth, it was only in the last few weeks I trusted Jones enough to tell him at all, and only in the last two days I'd decided I might need him. I had promised Annie I would do whatever it took to come back to her alive. Captain Jones might improve my odds of survival, so he got to be in the know.

Adams and Jones's mouths hung open in surprise, Adams more out of anger and Jones more out of appreciation. Franklin stepped in to calm things down.

"Very well, Major," Franklin said, speaking over whatever Adams tried to say, and putting a little volume on the title *Major* for Adams's benefit. "If that is what you want, we can include Captain Jones in on our plans."

General Washington had been right, the cunning fox. If he'd sent a civilian over here, these two sharks would be dictating every aspect of this operation.

"Thank you," I said, waiting for the other shoe to drop. With men like these, there was always something else.

Franklin turned to Captain Jones and opened his mouth, when Jones held up a hand, stopping him. Jones pulled out a folded piece of paper from his pocket and slid it over to Franklin.

"Before you start with that," Jones told him, "I have a request."

"What's this?" Franklin asked.

"My first mate, Lieutenant James, died on the voyage," Jones said, pointing at the paper. "That's the date and details of his death. I would appreciate letters from you, if you may, telling his parents he was a good man who died bravely. Plus, any words you think might bring comfort to them. He died bringing Thomas here for you, so it's the least you can do for him."

Franklin tucked the paper into his jacket. Again, Adams started to open his mouth to protest, and again, Franklin spoke over him.

"Consider it done, Captain," Franklin said. He really was quite the diplomat. I could see why Washington employed him here in France. "We will have them written before you leave France."

"Can we move forward now?" Adams said.

Franklin looked at Adams with an air of irritated sadness, then turned back to Jones.

"We're going to kill Lord North, the Prime Minister of England," Franklin said plainly, as if he'd said it was raining outside.

To Jones's credit, he didn't react to the news, only nodded his head in acknowledgement, and his eyes turned to the right as if he was thinking about what he heard.

"Then I'll be wanting you to write a letter to my wife as well," Jones said. "Just in case."

"Before we talk about the mission," Franklin continued, ignoring Jones's comment as his smile melted away and facing me, "we need to know you're the right man for this job. We've heard some rumors of you, all the way across the ocean, but are they merely rumors?"

"That depends on what you have heard," I said honestly. "I've found most rumors get twisted or exaggerated but are still based on some truth."

"Any rumors you heard, *monsieur*, are true," Lafayette broke in. "If anything, they were watered down. Thomas is being modest."

"We'll see about that," Adams stated flatly.

"The plan is for a French spy to get you in close to Lord North in England," Franklin said. "But we hit a snag. The spy's help is not exactly free, as it comes with a catch."

"A catch?" I asked.

Franklin nodded. "Minister Charles Gravier has a spy who can not only get you into the castle, but get you alone with Lord North. He is, however, refusing to involve a French citizen. To do so would go against the king's commands."

"And?" I asked.

"The minister happens to have an altogether different problem that we'd thought you could help him with."

"Gaining his favor, as it were," Adams finished. "You help him, and he'll go against the king's commands and help us."

"He'll go against the king if we help him?" I asked. "But if we don't help him, he won't go against the king?"

"It's complicated," Franklin admitted.

"Charles's wife, Anne Duvivier. Her first husband was Francesco Testa. He was a merchant and belonged to one of the oldest and most distinguished families of Pera, Turkey. Her husband died when she was only twenty-four years old, before she ever met Charles," Adams explained.

"I have met Anne Duvivier," Lafayette said. "She is a fine woman."

"Yes, well," Adams broke in. "After her husband died, she became Charles's mistress before he was a minister, back when he was the king's ambassador. She lived with Charles for a time. It was somewhat a scandal back then, you see. Charles did end up marrying her, but without the king's blessing."

"French Ambassadors are not allowed to marry without the king's blessing," Lafayette clarified for me.

"She's a sore spot between the king and the minister?" I guessed.

Franklin held up a hand to stop the conversation as a waiter came over to the table with two glasses and a bottle of red wine. The young man set down the two glasses and filled them both. He asked something in French, and Lafayette answered, shaking his head. The man walked away, and Franklin turned his attention back to me.

"Yes. A very sore spot indeed."

"Anne's first husband's family has come to France," Adams said. "Francesco's nephew Marco has been spreading foul rumors that the minister and Anne started their romance while she was still married to Francesco. Because, as you say, it's a sore spot. If the king hears of these rumors, Charles will be replaced as minister, and we lose this opportunity."

"Three months ago, when Marco first came to Paris and started spreading rumors, the plan was to have you kill Marco," Franklin told me, "solving all our problems."

Franklin's face had hardened as he spoke. He no longer looked like a kindly grandfather. He now resembled a predator.

"You said the plan *was*, not is. Has the plan changed?" Jones observed.

"Yes, well," Franklin said between drinks of his wine. "Two days ago, Marco found and insulted Charles in public."

Lafayette let out a deep groan, as if he heard something I had not.

"So what?" I asked, looking from Franklin to Lafayette, then back to Franklin.

"Charles challenged Marco to a duel," Adams said. "We can't let them duel."

"When is the duel?" Jones asked before I could.

"In two days," Franklin answered.

"Why can't we let them duel?" I asked.

"If Charles wins the duel, he's safe from the rumors and no longer needs our help," Lafayette answered. "Then he shan't take the chance of going against the king. If he loses the duel, he'll be dead and again, we lose his help."

Lafayette truly understood the politics of these matters.

"So, I only have two days to kill this Marco before the duel?" I asked.

"Thomas," Lafayette said in a low voice, resting his hand on my wrist. "You can't kill Marco now."

Adams nodded his head in agreement.

"I don't understand," Jones said, again taking the words out of my mouth. "Why not?"

"If he's killed before the duel, everyone will assume Charles had him killed out of fear. They'll assume the rumors were true, and the king will hear of them," Lafayette explained.

I rubbed my forehead just below the itchy wig. "What is the plan now?"

"We don't have one," Franklin said, matter of fact. "I was told you were resourceful in these kinds of situations."

Adams nodded at Franklin's words. "If Charles goes through with the duel, win or lose, we lose his help and we can't get near Lord North. If you kill Marco, you make the minister look poorly, and we again lose Charles's help, and again, you'll not get close to Lord North."

The table grew quiet and all of us took a drink of wine at the same time.

"You need to think like the Pale Rider," Lafayette commented, trying to sound encouraging.

"First off, you guys are wrong about one fact," I told them.

"What?" Franklin asked.

"I can, and will, kill this Marco. What I can't do is murder him."

"What is the difference?" Jones asked.

"If I murder him, everyone will think Charles was behind it," I said. "But, what if Marco challenged me to a duel? If I kill him in a duel that he himself challenged me to, Charles could not be blamed for that, correct?"

The table went silent again as they all considered what I had said. They were working it out, looking for the pros and cons.

"Ingenious," Franklin said with a note of awe. "But he would have to challenge you. If you challenge him, Charles could still be blamed."

"That would work and solve all our problems. Charles would have to risk defying the king and help us, if for no other reason than to keep his own secrets," Adams said.

"You have tonight and tomorrow to get him to challenge you and kill him," Jones said. "Will he not want to fight Thomas *after* his duel with the minister?"

"Yes," Lafayette said. "He will insist on it."

I tapped my fingers on the tabletop. "Are duels ever fought on the spot?"

Lafayette shook his head. "It is possible, but rare. We French like to make sure we've an audience. Civilized men have rules about duels that we almost never disregard. It's a question of honor."

"He's not French," I interjected. "He's Turkish."

"The Turks are hot-blooded," Franklin agreed. "It's possible."

I leaned my elbows on the table. "We need to find out where he is. I need to know as much as I can about him. I need to know how to make him mad enough to challenge me and know what weapon gives me the best chances of winning."

"If he challenges Thomas, then Thomas chooses the weapons?" Jones confirmed as he shifted in his seat. He knew what I could do with a choice of weapon.

"*Oui*," Lafayette said. "As for angering him, I've no doubt you'll do that by being yourself." He waggled his eyebrows at me.

"With regards to weapons, Thomas. You'll have to use pistols," Jones told me.

"Why? I'm good with the sword and great with the knife."

"I don't think knives are allowed," Jones said, flicking his eyes to Lafayette and Franklin for confirmation. "And if you choose swords, he can always yield if he's injured, before you can kill him."

Franklin leaned back, gripping the lapel of his waistcoat and nodding at Jones's explanation. "Captain Jones is right. You'll have to choose pistols and kill him with the first shot. As for where he is right now, I've a man following him. He'll send word to me every few hours."

Now that we'd a plan of action, we needed to bide our time until Franklin's man reported Marco's whereabouts. While we waited, Lafayette went over the rules of a duel with me.

Chapter Eight: A Walk in the Park

We only had to wait two hours before a young man of about sixteen rushed into the restaurant. The *maître d'* grabbed the young man by his coat and yanked him out the front door. He undoubtingly thought the boy was going to steal some food and run. Franklin stood up and waved his arms. The boy saw Franklin and pointed while being dragged backwards. When the attendant saw Franklin, he stopped. Franklin motioned with his waving hands that he wanted to speak to the boy. As soon as the attendant let go of the young man, he ran to our table.

The boy was out of breath and couldn't talk. Instead, he panted as Adams handed him a glass of water and told him to drink. Adams called the boy Tuck, which I guessed was short for Tucker or maybe a nick name. The young man was dressed more like a commoner than a diplomat's aide. His baggy trousers were old and had holes in the knees. His shirt was dirty, but on closer inspection, I could see it was a fine enough shirt, with fresh dirt rubbed into it, to make it look more old and worn than it was.

Franklin pulled out the chair next to him and told the boy to sit down and catch his breath. The kid must have run the whole way here, from wherever he was coming from.

"I take it you were able to follow Marco?" Franklin asked in his grandfatherly voice.

The young man nodded his head quickly, then took another drink.

"Tuck, where is Mr. Testa right now?" Adams asked.

"Down by the river," Tuck answered, his panting making his words breathless.

"The River Seine," Adams clarified.

"Yes, sir," the young man said, nodding his head.

"It's a big river, Tuck," Adams said. "Where on the river?"

"Pont . . . Pont . . ." The boy kept saying.

"The Pont Neuf Bridge?" Lafayette asked.

"Yes, sir. That's the one."

"What is Mr. Testa doing at the bridge?" Adams asked.

"Flying kites, sir," the boy answered.

"What?" Franklin asked before anyone else could.

"He and another man are flying kites with two ladies," Tuck answered. "In the grass, next to the bridge."

That wasn't what I had expected to hear. I thought he'd be practicing for his upcoming duel or the like. Kite flying seemed surprisingly casual in preparation for a duel.

"How far is that from here?" I asked the table.

"A five-minute walk," Lafayette answered.

"You two wait here," I told Franklin and Adams as I pointed at them. "I don't want anyone seeing you with us."

As I stood up, so did Jones and Lafayette. Tuck rose without being told and led us out of the restaurant. He tensed to run again until I grabbed his shoulder, hauling him by my side.

"Let's walk," I said to Tuck. "I want this to look natural, not like we were rushing to get there."

We walked for about a few minutes and then turned left through the city. When we got close to the river, Tuck pointed up into the air. I followed his finger and saw four kites flying in the wind. They were of different, colorful, teardrop-shaped, thick pieces of paper. They danced in the air, falling to the earth, then changing directions, going back up.

As we got closer, I followed the strings down to the grass and saw two Turkish men. There were two ladies who I assumed were Turkish standing next to them. Trying to guess which of the two men Marco was, I peered closer at them. One of the men wore draping red robes, and the other had on blue robes. Matching white scarves wrapped around their heads, leaving the tops bare. Long, raven black hair went down to the middle of their backs. They were of the same age, or close enough that I could not guess which was older. They appeared to be of similar height and weight. Matching thick, full beards and mustaches covered their faces.

"Shit," I said under my breath.

Twins. They were identical twins.

I glanced down at Tuck. "Which one is Marco?"

Tuck turned his face up at me and shrugged.

"I can't tell them apart," Tuck said, his face a mask of confusion.

"So, do I ask them which one of them is Marco?" I asked Lafayette.

"Does it matter?" Jones asked. "How do we know it was Marco who challenged the minister to a duel and not his brother? Maybe the minister assumed it was Marco. He might not know Marco has a twin."

"Even if you kill Marco," Lafayette added. "His twin brother might show up to duel the minister in his brother's place. For the honor of his families, and because that's why his family sent them here in the first place."

"Well, this is problematic," I said aloud to no one in particular.

Why did life have to be so complicated and never easy? Twins, really?

We continued to watch from a distance as the two twin brothers and their female companions laughed and flew kites. Neither of the twins seemed nervous, like a man facing a duel in two days. Neither of the two ladies behaved as though they may be without their man soon. Either they weren't thinking about the duel, or they were so confident in Marco's ability to kill the minister that it wasn't worth worrying about.

When the two couples tired of flying kites, they sat down on a blanket and opened what I guessed was a picnic basket. I wanted to find a spot to sit down and observe the two couples for a while.

"John," I said, turning to him, "I need you to go back to the ship and make sure she's repaired and ready to sail at a moment's notice. I don't know if I'll be coming to you or if I'll need you to pick me up somewhere off the coast of England. They may not know about her being captured yet, so make the crew look as English as possible."

"My ship and crew will be ready whenever and wherever you need her," Jones responded.

Jones wore a hard look on his face, like a man who truly understood what was at stake and took his part in this seriously. He locked eyes with me to shake my hand, eyes furled, and I realized I'd made the right choice about letting him in on our secret. Jones shook hands with Lafayette while grasping Lafayette's right arm with his left hand.

Jones then turned around and headed back to inform Franklin and Adams about the twins and our new problems.

"The first thing we need to do is figure out which one of those two twins is Marco," I said to Lafayette. "Any ideas?"

"I have a Turkish contact who is a merchant," Lafayette said. "Not so much a friend, but I've done business with him before, and he may know something."

"Go see what you can find out," I said. "I'll stick with the twins and see where they go."

"Keep Tuck with you. He knows his way around. I'll meet you back at the restaurant." Lafayette then turned and walked away behind me.

I didn't know how long we were going to be here, so I handed Tuck two silver pennies and told him to go get something to eat and come back. The boy's face lit up as he took the two pennies and ran off.

I lounged on a bench about fifty yards away from the two couples. I didn't see any reason to get closer. I was willing to bet they'd be speaking Turkish anyway, and the last time I checked, I didn't speak Turkish.

The two ladies wore beautiful, multicolor, multilayered dresses. Their dresses appeared to be of fine quality and expensive looking. Their clothes also covered most of their bodies, only showing their hands and the neck up. The women served the men from the basket as Tuck returned, gnawing on a chicken leg.

A carriage pulled up, and the ladies packed everything back into the basket. The four of them climbed into the carriage, and the driver tied the basket onto the top of the carriage. As the carriage pulled away, Tuck and I stood. We were able to keep the carriage in sight thanks to the crowds of people the driver had to work his way through. When the crowd thinned out, the carriage sped up. I stuck out like a sore thumb as it was and running through Paris would only make things worse. A boy running through Paris, on the other hand, was commonplace and not unusual.

"Stay with them," I instructed and gave Tuck a slight push on his back.

Tuck took off running, following the carriage. I had to jog a few times to keep Tuck in sight, but the carriage was too far ahead to have noticed me. Poor Tuck had to run two miles down river to keep up with the carriage. When I caught up, I located Tuck standing behind a tree, his gaze fixed on a three-story brick house. The window frames, like the picket fence, were white. The carriage wasn't in sight, but a barn stood behind the house, so it might have been in there. Lamps illuminated every floor of the house, even at midday.

I walked up and stood behind Tuck, peeking around the tree.

"In there?" I asked him.

"Yes sir," Tuck answered.

"Now that we know where they are staying, let's go back to the restaurant."

"Yes, sir."

We returned to the restaurant, but Lafayette wasn't there. Franklin and Adams were also gone. They must have tired of waiting for us and went back to their residence. The waiter understood enough English for me to order food and wine. I bought Tuck dinner and sent him back to Franklin with a few more pennies in his pocket. Lafayette made it back to the restaurant well after sunset. He had two horses with him, and I wondered where he'd picked them up at.

"Find your friend?" I asked as he sat down.

"*Oui*," Lafayette answered, "but you're not going to be happy."

"What's the bad news?"

"They are known in the Turkish community as the Testa Twins," Lafayette said. "Adams was right when he said oldest and most distinguished family of Pera. He forgot to mention richest and most vengeful. Marco and Jacob Testa are wild cards. Their grandfather most likely sent them here to make a point to the French."

"What point?" I asked.

"Don't mess with the Testa family," Lafayette said.

"They think they can take on the French government?" I asked.

"No," Lafayette said. "But they don't have to. They can spread rumors and kill the minister in a fair duel."

"What else?"

"Although they are twins, they are very different," Lafayette said, leaning in toward me. "Marco is the smarter one. They say he's a good tactician. He'll be the one making the decisions. Jacob is the hot blooded one. He's exceptionally good with the sword and pistol. He won't make a move without his brother's permission, but when he gets permission, it's usually followed by violence. My friend says Jacob will certainly be standing in for Marco in the duel."

"What if I was to kill Jacob?" I asked. "Will Marco still want to fight the duel?"

"No," Lafayette answered. "Marco, as I said, is the smart one. Typically, he leaves the violence to his brother."

"So that's the plan. I kill Jacob, and we see if Marco still wants to duel or not."

"One more thing," Lafayette said, a sly smile catching his mouth. "I know how to tell them apart."

That was information I needed. "How?"

"Jacob has a scar on his right hand, a cut that goes across the top. It was given to him during his first duel. He was only fifteen years old at the time. He won that duel and killed the man."

"You have a way of turning good news into bad news, my friend," I commented dryly, taking a sip of my wine.

"Don't fight him with swords, Thomas," Lafayette commanded.

"Are you sure this information is good?"

"The merchants in Paris don't like the Testa twins," Lafayette said. "They fear them but don't like them."

"Did you learn anything else?"

Lafayette nodded. "*Oui.* They were invited to a party tomorrow night. One of the merchants is throwing a big party and has invited all the merchants to his house. I was able to get us two invitations. With that wig on, and a little white powder, we might pass you off as a merchant."

"How did you get us two invitations at the last minute, like this?" I asked.

"The merchant throwing the party is my friend who gave me the information," Lafayette answered, his smile widening. "I told you that you needed me."

"No face powder," I said.

He huffed. "Fine. Let's go get some rest and plan this out tomorrow."

"Is there a hotel nearby?"

"*Oui*," Lafayette said. "Several hotels in fact, but we're staying at my friend's house tonight."

"Same friend who is throwing this party, and gave you this information?"

"*Oui*. Like I said, the merchants don't like the twins. He doesn't know what we are planning or why, but if it's not good for the twins, he's willing to help."

"Who is this friend?" I asked.

"His name is Oliver," Lafayette said. "He is a very wealthy businessman. He has investments in a dozen merchant ships. The twins killed one of his captains a few months ago. He can't do anything about it without fear of retaliation from the Testa family."

"Can we trust him?" I asked.

Lafayette shook his head. "No. He's a friend, but he's only interested in his own best interest. I trust in the fact helping us removes an enemy for him."

Late that night after we finished our supper and wine, Lafayette took me to the merchant's home, which was more of a mansion than a house. A successful merchant, evidently.

The front yard alone was the size of a football field. Servants took the two horses Oliver had lent Lafayette and led them back to the stables. Large tents, tables, and chairs were being set out for tomorrow's party. The weather was still cold, but the tents were designed to hold in the heat. Lafayette explained the main party would be inside the house; this area was in case the people wanted fresh air or if the party inside became too crowded. This wasn't Oliver's first party, and they were known for going throughout the night and into the morning.

"You said the twins killed one of Oliver's captains?" I asked Lafayette before we entered.

"*Oui.*"

"Find out the man's name for me," I told him.

"Why?"

"I think that might be something I can use."

***

After a night of hard sleeping in a modest room I shared with Lafayette, I finally met Oliver later the next day.

He seemed very dismissive of me, but with this pompous wig on my head, who could blame him? Oliver was nice enough to lend Lafayette and me some new clothes, but I kept my weapons, boots, and the sash for my Tec-9. Lafayette had sent a messenger to Franklin telling him where we were, and that he might not want to miss the party.

Oliver had told Lafayette his dead captain's name was Captain Crombie, Jack Crombie, from Scotland.

Lafayette and I spent most of the day practicing the sword and pistol. I didn't know the best way to handle this situation, so Lafayette and I discussed our options while we practiced. I found it distracting, but Lafayette insisted it would help me to move naturally and without thought. In my century, we called it muscle memory.

The whole plan revolved around me killing Jacob tonight, so he couldn't stand in for his brother tomorrow night. If I was able to get him to challenge me to a duel tonight, he might not want to go through with it until a week from now. According to Lafayette, one of the unofficial rules to a duel was to conduct the duel a week or so later; that way both parties had time to cool off. The first party could apologize to the second party, ending the whole matter and preventing loss of life. I needed Jacob to break that rule and fight me on the spot.

I had come up with a basic idea of separating the two brothers and challenging Jacob to fight me then and there but was basically going to wing the details.

Chapter Nine: The Duel

The party began at six o'clock, but everyone wanted to be fashionably late, so people started arriving around seven. I walked around with a bottle of champagne, introducing myself as Thomas Crombie.

I had emptied the bottle of champagne and refilled it with water. By nine o'clock, I was stumbling around and slurring my words. I made a point of talking ill about the twins and how they had killed my brother. Word would get back to them soon enough.

Lafayette didn't want his family or the king to know he was in Paris, so he wisely chose to remove his beautiful and eye-catchingly blue French military uniform. He had replaced it with a servant's uniform, making him utterly invisible, better than any camouflage I had ever seen. With his red uniform, heavy white makeup on his face, a white wig on his head, and a large rectangle silver tray of wine and champagne glasses in his hands, he was able to walk freely with no one looking twice at him.

Mr. Franklin and Mr. Adams had also arrived at the party. Little Tuck was always a few steps away from Mr. Franklin, while Franklin and Adams tended to stick near me, watching the night unfold with hawk-like eyes. Neither was foolish enough to be seen talking to me, but they were never far off. Franklin had his cane in one hand and a glass of wine in the other. He kept putting the glass up to his lips, but the wine level never seemed to go down. The old fox, like me, was only pretending to drink.

The twins showed up a bit later with an entourage of six others. His six cronies were all well-dressed but rough-looking men. The twins both carried swords, but I didn't see any flintlocks on them. Their men carried swords and flintlocks. Unlike the last time I saw them, this time they didn't have on vibrant, multicolored robes. This time, they both wore white robes with what looked like black wrappings underneath.

Lafayette watched and waited until the twins had quaffed a few drinks to loosen them up. When the twins finally separated into different parts of the house, Lafayette sent one of the servants to deliver a message to Jacob, telling him Oliver wanted to speak to him about some business. Lafayette had placed my sword and Tec-9 on one of the nearby tables, wrapped in paper. He also kept my Thompson on him, under his coat. I wanted to be unarmed, so no one would suspect any of this was being planned out. The knife in the small of my back was the only weapon I carried. As I was pretending to be a sailor, having a knife wasn't unusual.

I was outside under the tent, talking to a lady in her forties named Evelyn, who seemed to be fond of my company. She'd been recently widowed and appeared to be looking for her next husband. I spoke to her in loud slobbering words, making sure the whole room heard me, and stumbled a few times. I made a show of drinking straight from the bottle, passing as a sloppy drunk.

Jacob and one of his cronies entered the tent like a peacock followed by a wolf. When Jacob was close enough to see me, I tripped and fell on one of the tables. I yanked the tablecloth off the table as I stumbled to the ground. Wine and champagne glasses flew to the ground, with many of them shattering against each other. Several people around me laughed and pointed while others cringed at my performance. Poor Evelyn reddened with embarrassment but pulled on my arm in a kindly attempt to help me up. Acting like a man who was trying to keep my dignity, I got to my feet and straightened my disheveled wig.

From the corner of my eye, I watched as Oliver pointed me out to Jacob and spoke in his ear, telling him I'd been slandering his good name. Jacob walked over to me, eyes narrow and his mouth a snarl. He wanted to extract his pound of flesh.

One thing I had learned about the Testa family was they didn't tolerate disrespect. Anyone slandering their good name was quickly and violently addressed.

He came up to me from behind, and I pretended not to see him standing behind me. I groped at Evelyn, who was holding me up with both hands. As I whispered in her ear, Jacob tapped me on my shoulder. I turned around with a drunken, shit-eating grin on my face.

Jacob didn't say a word to me. I started to ask what he wanted when he slapped me across the face. I let myself fall to the ground. The hardest part about being slapped wasn't blocking his hand, it was that I had to stand there and take it. Lying on the grass, I rubbed at my face, feigning injury. I climbed to my feet again and demanded his name as if I had no idea who he was.

"I'm Monsieur Testa," he said in a haughty tone.

"Testa!" I yelled. "Testa. You killed my brother, you son of a whore."

I was trying to speak in my best Sean Connery imitation. I sounded more like Scotty from Star Trek. It would have to do. I was not one for impersonations. His henchman lunged forward, but Testa held up a hand to halt him.

"I've killed many men," Jacob bragged. "You'll have to be more specific."

"Captain Jack Crombie," I clarified. "You murdered him when he refused to sail for you and your brother."

I then threw a right punch, telegraphing my movement as best I could so he could duck it. I missed his face by a mile and followed through, practically throwing myself to the ground again. Jacob laughed at me and as I struggled to stand, he kicked me in the ass, pushing me forward and back onto my face into the cool grass.

Nice, just what I needed to start this show. I moved slowly, like a man not sure of his movements, and used a table to stand back up.

"Your brother was a pig," Jacob spat out, walking up to me.

This time I didn't telegraph my movements and slapped him hard with my right hand. A red palm print burned on his left cheek like a brand. The crowd around us had been laughing and making jokes at my expense until my blow struck Jacob's face. The tent fell silent, except for the gasps of air from everyone in the audience.

His head had spun to the right and came back to face me. He opened his mouth to speak, and I slapped him with my left hand before he got a word out, leaving a matching red handprint on the right side of his face. This time, I let him turn on me. I wanted to kick him behind the knee and drop him to the ground. But beating him wasn't my goal, and scaring him was the opposite of what I needed to have happen.

Being slapped twice in the face by a drunk Scotsman in front of his peers was too much for him to handle.

"You killed my brother!" I yelled again in a slur of words, holding my fists in front of my chin. "Fight me, you coward."

The anger on his face blazed as bright as his two matching handprints. He wouldn't tolerate being embarrassed in front of the competing merchants. Then, realizing every eye in the tent was on him, his expression changed, like someone flipped a light switch. He laughed.

"A duel?" he asked the crowd in a loud voice, intending to mock me.

"Yes. I accept," I said.

I had challenged him to a fight, but he was the one who said the word *duel.* Even though it was my idea, by bellowing out I accepted his challenge, I had made it sound as if he was challenging me.

"Fine," he said. "In five days' time."

"No, now," I countered.

Doubt filled his eyes. "You're drunk," he spat out, disgust dripping from his words.

"Maybe, but I can still beat the likes of you," I taunted. "Now, sir. I want satisfaction now."

He laughed again but cast his eyes around the tent in a worried way. He knew he was being judged by the crowd around us. For Testa to say no to a falling down drunk in front of these people wasn't going to happen. Their mouths were open, and their eyes fixed on us. Some of the women breathed hard, chests heaving fast with anticipation. Even his crony didn't move, frozen by his employer's behavior and command to stay back. Their laughter had stopped, and the tent was quiet. No one wanted to miss his reply. The scene was like a soap opera playing out in front of them.

"Here and now!" he yelled, asserting himself.

The surrounding crowd cheered like a blood-thirsty mob.

"Choose your weapon, sir," he told me. His words were directed at me but spoken for his peers.

"Pistols!" I responded, except I really said *pestols*, trying to sound drunk.

I stumbled out of the tent, grabbing tables for balance as I moved forward to the open grass. Jacob hollered for pistols as he followed, strutting like a peacock. Oliver ordered two servants to bring and load two pistols.

Only this part had been worked out ahead of time, and Lafayette brought me my Thompson on a silver tray, while another real servant brought Jacob a fully loaded pistol on a matching tray.

"Fetch my brother, to stand in as my second," Jacob directed the man walking with him.

The man standing next to Jacob moved to leave.

"Is the little man afraid to fight without his brother?" I mocked, swinging my arms around for the crowd. "Someone call for his mommy and daddy, too."

"Fine," Jacob yelled. "Let's get this over with. Robert, you'll stand in as my second."

The crony standing next to Jacob didn't say a word but nodded his head. People from the house heard about what was going on and made their way out to the field to catch the excitement. As convention dictated, we pressed our backs together, and Oliver counted aloud. A voice from the house yelled for us to stop. Jacob's back was to the house, but from my position, I could see Marco running our way.

"One!" Oliver yelled.

I wondered what the crowd thought went I stood up straight and walked in a straight line.

"Two."

In a perfect world, we would be twenty paces apart when we turned and fired.

"Three."

But this wasn't a perfect world, and distance was my friend, so I was taking extra-long steps with every count.

"Four."

In the corner of my eye, I could see Franklin leaning on his cane, watching us without expression.

"Five."

Lafayette stood in front of me and to the side.

"Six."

Lafayette wasn't watching me; his gaze was on Jacob. Lafayette's hand rested lightly on his own pistol by his side. He intended to shoot Jacob if Jacob cheated and turned too soon.

"Seven."

I focused on my breathing, trying to slow it down, as I my mind when through the motions.

"Eight."

The pistol was in my right hand, so I was going to turn to my right, not my left. Only a quarter turn, so I bladed him with my body, giving him less of a target.

"Nine."

Marco was only twenty yards away, running fast to stop the duel.

"Ten."

The world went quiet as I shut out the external noises. I turned while thumbing back the hammer of my Thompson. As quiet as it was, I could hear Jacob's hammer clicking as he also cocked his hammer back. I raised my pistol in front of my face. Jacob was doing the same with his pistol. He'd made a full turn, giving me a much larger target than I was giving him. Cocky bastard. My eye focused in on my front sight of my pistol. The sight was clear, and my target, Jacob, wasn't. Front sight picture was everything at this distance.

In the police academy, our firearms instructor had a saying. *Slow is smooth and smooth is fast.* It meant don't rush. Be smooth and you'll find that you're fast. That went for drawing our pistol, aiming, and firing.

My shot was smooth. The gun kicked in my hand. The wooden grip pushed back against my palm as if it had jumped, trying to leap free of my grip.

Jacob's shot was rushed. He turned and fired as fast as he could, not wanting me to get off the first shot.

This wasn't a man who was known for fighting duels. He wasn't calm or smooth. In this moment, he was out of his element. In that microsecond, that blink of an eye, I knew the messenger had delivered the message to the wrong brother. The man who stood over twenty paces in front of me wasn't Jacob, but Marco.

Two shots rang out so close together they could almost have been one. A cloud of smoke billowed out from my opponent's pistol, straight at me, obscuring Marco's face. I waited for the large steel ball to rip through me and tear its way through skin, muscle, and organs.

The impact never came. I was alive and exhaled heavily. He had rushed his shot and missed. Marco was now on his back, not moving.

My mind reeled as people rushed toward Marco. How did this change things? The plan was for me to kill Jacob, not Marco. The real Jacob could still stand in for his brother in the duel against the minister. Now that I had killed Marco, would that make the minister look bad? It was the day before the minister was supposed to fight his duel.

The real Jacob pushed his way through the crowd, yelling for people to move out of his way. Jacob's voice was the only voice I could hear, the only one I could focus on. The crowd of people around us watched in stunned silence. One of the ladies off to the side dropped her glass of champagne, and the glass shattered, breaking the silence. The observers couldn't believe their eyes. One of the Testa twins laid dead, while a sotted Scotsman who had been falling down drunk and stumbling still lived.

Jacob fell to his knees next to his brother. He ripped open his brother's shirt, right where his heart laid in a fleshy, bloody mess. Jacob pulled his head back and screamed a horrible cry into the night. He bent forward and kissed his brother on the forehead, then slowly sat up straight. His head turned my way, and we locked eyes.

Oh yeah, this was the *real* Jacob. This was a man who really had killed many times. A man who was going to avenge his brother and kill any man who got in the way.

Including me.

He rose in a smooth movement and turned his body towards me. His hand flew of its own accord to his sword. His steel leaped from its scabbard like a snake striking out. The blade sliced through the air and from twenty long paces away, I could hear a *swoosh*.

Lafayette's voice reached my ears, and I shifted to look at him. He ripped the wrapping paper off my sword and threw it in the scabbard high into the air to me. I caught the leather scabbard out of the air with left hand and tossed my Thompson back to him underhanded with my right. Gripping the handle of my sword, I swung the blade in a wide arc, letting the scabbard fly off my steel to land where it may on the grass.

Jacob marched towards me with his arm extended, the tip of his sword aimed at me and murder blazing in his eyes. There it was, on the top of his hand. A thin scar about four inches long. The whiteness of the scar clashed with his duskier skin around it.

Normally in a duel, if someone tried to interfere or avenge the loser, the seconds would jump in and put a stop to it. His second was a crony who feared him, and my second was one of the servants ordered to be here but not to interfere. Our seconds and everyone in the crowd took a few more steps back and away from us. I was on my own. I'd told Lafayette not to interfere, no matter what. He was a French citizen, and if he were involved, that would only hurt our efforts with the king.

Jacob's sword was longer than mine but had an exaggerated curve to it. A scimitar. It looked worthless for stabbing and was made for slashing and cutting. It most likely had originally been designed for fighting on horseback, hacking down on a person on the ground.

Jacob stopped halfway to me and stabbed his sword into the ground. He shrugged out of his thick, multilayer robes and waved his arms in a circle. He wore the tight black wrapping cloths under his robe, and they looked like effective clothes for fighting. They'd not snag, get caught on anything, or get in his way.

Marco had been the one to see my act of pretending to be drunk. Jacob had no misunderstandings of believing I was impaired. He wasn't going to make the same fatal mistake his brother had made.

Imitating him, I stabbed my sword in the ground and pulled off my own fancy blue coat, dropping it on the ground. There was no need to act the fool anymore, nor could I afford to. I pulled off my itchy, askew wig and dropped it on my coat.

Jacob grabbed the handle of his sword and yanked it free from the ground. I did the same with my sword. A small clump of mud caught my eye near the tip of my sword, and I wiped it off, scraping the blade against my boot. I was hopefully going to kill him with this sword, and here I was, wiping it clean, as if killing him with a dirty blade was somehow wrong.

He swished the sword in the air twice, then headed it up in front of his face in some sort of salute or "get ready," signal.

I copied the act. A random thought coursed through my mind: *Thank God I didn't have any of that white face make up on.* If I was going to die, I didn't want to die looking as foolish as Lafayette presently did.

I could see sick smiles on the pasty white faces of the blood-thirsty crowd. Not only the men, but the ladies wanted to see another fight. The duel with pistols was too quick and clean for them. They wanted to see real men fight for their lives. No help was coming my way. No one would lift a finger to try to put a stop to it. The only people I could count on to try had been ordered not to.

Jacob stepped into range and slashed at my face. I stepped back, and he missed, and pressing forward, he slashed again but lower. I blocked his swing and went on the offensive. I went for the stab, and he blocked it easily, almost contemptuously. I stabbed again, but he expected it and this time, when he parried my blade, he slid his blade along mine, pushing both blades out of the way. Stepping into my personal space, Jacob head butted me in the nose.

So, not just sword fight then.

I fell back, blinking tears from my eyes, in time to see him hack at my neck. I ducked under his blade and raised my own sword in time to block his back feint with a clang and drowned out the gasps of the crowd. I was still blinking tears and my vision was blurry, and I needed to focus. One misstep . . .

Raising my sword, pointing the tip of my blade at him, in hopes of keeping him back, I side stepped towards the tables.

I had been practicing with the sword for months, and was better than the average Joe, but Jacob had been practicing since he was a child. He was an expert with his weapon.

He stepped in closer and slashed at my right leg. I shifted backward, and he missed but was already slashing again. I blocked his second swing and then his third. When he swung for a fourth, instead of blocking directly, I moved and stabbed at his face. He lunged back and, rather than following through with his swing, he turned it into a parry, deflecting my sword.

Before either of us could get our swords back in front of us, he kicked out at my stomach. I spun in a circle, dodging his kick and then delivered one of my own. My foot hit him low, directly behind the left knee, and his leg buckled. His left knee sunk to the ground and his right was half bent. There it was – my moment. I moved in and slashed for his throat, but he brought his sword up in time to stop mine. I pressed the attack, feigning another swing, but then I kicked him in the shoulder. He knocked over but didn't stop. He went with the force of my kick and rolled away. I ran at him and slashed down wildly for his head.

He came up from his roll, mechanically swinging his sword upward in front of himself, blocking my swing. He turned his back to me to run and as I followed, he turned his move into a spin, blade extended. Too late I realized what he was doing, and his sword sliced through my shirt, right under my raised arm.

Not stopping or letting him swing again, I continued my momentum and barreled into him like a runaway train. He went down under my weight, and my knee collided into his face as we both tumbled to the ground.

I rolled first and came up, sword raised in front of me. He was getting to his feet, and like me, he had his sword raised high.

His left eye had swollen closed from the impact of my knee. I was panting hard and risked a glance at my side. The cut was shallow along my ribs. Blood seeped through my shirt, but his sword had cut only a thin layer of muscle, missing the important parts. I would need a few stitches later, if I was still alive.

He feinted forward again, and I stabbed for his chest. He slapped my sword aside with the flat of his sword. This time I stepped in close before he could swing again, and my left hand exploded out towards his face. I heard more than felt his nose break under my knuckles, and his head whipped back from the force.

A scream of surprise came from the on lookers, no doubt a female who also heard the gory snap of Jacob's nose.

I thought Jacob was stumbling backwards, but he was wisely going with the punch to distance himself from me while he swung his sword in front of him out of instinct. When he saw I hadn't followed through and continued after him, he raised his sword high as he backed away a few more steps. Wiping a finger under his nose, his left hand came away covered with blood. He smiled a bloody-lipped smile as if he was looking forward to whatever was coming next.

I knew that look. He'd enough of this fight and was going to put an end to it.

This wasn't a duel; it was more like a cage fight with swords. A mad fight to the death. The only difference between the two was there were no rules this time. He passed his sword into his left hand and, reaching into his shirt, he pulled out a small flintlock pistol. He brought his pistol up as he thumbed back the hammer.

I threw my sword in a desperate act of survival. I was hoping to impale him on the shoulder, but I missed. My blade did slice across his forearm, slicing deep through muscle and tendons like a spear. His arm dropped down uselessly, and the flintlock fired. Dirt kicked up where the lead ball dug into the earth. A few feet behind Jacob, my sword was sticking into the ground blade point first. His arm bled profusely and uncontrollably, and he now held the useless limb tight to his chest. His arm was flayed wide to the bone with a huge flap of skin hanging open, exposing sliced muscles and tendons.

A few of the ladies screamed at the violent action and grisly result. More than a few men yelled, "Huzzah," to me, or jeered at Jacob. At least, I told myself that's how it was. Or they could have been disappointed in me for throwing my sword.

Jacob tried to place his sword in his right hand, but it was no longer able to hold the weapon. He moved forward towards me like he was closing on an easy kill, ignoring the fact blood poured in a flood from the deep gash in his arm. He may have been holding his sword with his left hand and not his right hand, but he, unlike me, at least *had* a sword.

Reaching behind my back, I pulled out my knife. Not an equal weapon but better than nothing.

I thought about throwing my knife. I could kill him without having to get any closer, but if he knocked my knife out of the air, I'd have given up my only weapon. His arm was still bleeding badly, and his shirt was soaked with his own blood. The blood loss had to be affecting him.

He circled to my right. He held the bigger advantage but wasn't going to charge with the sword in his left hand. He was wary of my knife, which was wise of him. Most people would have charged me since I only had a knife against his sword. However, his self-preservation had kicked in, recognizing I did in fact hold a foot long piece of highly sharpened steel, and I had managed to do quite a bit of damage to him already.

His eyes, though, were still clear and kept going up to my head. I finally figured out he was marking my scar in his mind.

Not having the strength to slash and hack at me, he tried to keep his distance and stabbed. I deflected his stabs with my knife. I was waiting for the right moment when he raised his sword for a slash. My plan was to step in and cut him with my knife. I needed this to be an up-close fight. He'd a three-foot-long sword, and I had a one-foot-long knife. Unlike with the pistols, distance was no longer my friend.

He stepped back, increasing the distance between us. He stumbled but caught his balance and held his sword straight and level with my chest. His upper body swayed in a small circle, and he stopped in place. His arm lowered, pointing his blade towards the earth. I moved in for the kill. On my first step, I decided I was going to go for his throat. On my second step, his eyes rolled up into his head and his knees buckled, dropping him to his knees, then forward straight down to the ground and onto his face, all from his blood loss.

Several of his friends and cronies rushed to his side, checking to see if he was still alive. One of the cronies flung champagne glasses into the air as he ripped a tablecloth off one of the tables to wrap it around Jacob's arm.

"Is there a doctor here?" the crony, whom someone called Robert, yelled into the crowd.

Jacob was still alive but dying fast from blood loss. I stood back and watched as several men picked him up and carried him to a carriage. Men screamed in high-pitched panicked voices, and a whip cracked against the air. The horse screeched and bolted. They were gone before I realized what was going on.

I jumped when the crowd of blood-thirsty savages cheered as one and pushed toward me. Lafayette walked up and handed me my sword and scabbard. I fastened the belt on as people I didn't know slapped me on my back and told me what a good showing I had given. Lafayette then handed me my wig. Tugging the wig on as fast as possible, I realized I had made a mistake in taking it off in the first place. My Tec-9 was next and then my Thompson.

"Let's get out of here before people realize you're with me," I said to Lafayette.

"I tied a horse up for you in front of the barn," Lafayette answered in a low voice that was almost lost in the noise of the crowd. "But let's get a look at your ribs first."

"Is my satchel with the horse?" I asked.

"*Oui.*"

"The cut's not deep," I told him. "I'll doctor it myself. I need to get out of here."

"I'll meet up with you at the bridge where we first saw the twins," he answered, knowing by now that arguing with me wasn't going to help.

Looking over to where the carriage with Jacob had been, I noticed Robert still standing there. Why hadn't he left with Jacob? Why was he still here? Maybe he planned to follow me. I'd need to keep an eye on him.

As if he read my mind, he turned his back on me and walked away with a slow gait, disappearing into the crowd.

I pushed past the crowd and towards the barn. The crowd seemed upset I was leaving, calling out for me to stop and celebrate. They followed me to the horse, and some even ran behind me until I rode off the property.

Chapter Ten: The Spy

I waited at the bridge for about two hours before the clattering of horseshoes on cobblestones made me turn and peer up the road. A carriage pulled by two brown horses rode up and stopped next to me. I hadn't been idle at the bridge. While I'd waited, I had used my first aid kit to clean the laceration across my ribs. Then I attached a few butterfly stitches, followed by a clean bandage and covered it with some good old fashion duct tape to hold the bandage in place. The cut wasn't as deep or long as it had felt, so I didn't bother with the pain killers this time. I was down to three antibiotic shots, but didn't use one, wanting to save them for worse injuries.

The curtain blocking one of the windows of the carriage moved, revealing the sharp lines of Lafayette's face.

He grinned at me and waved for me to get in. Walking around, I tied my horse to the back of the carriage and climbed in. Without a word, the driver flicked the reins, and with a sudden jerk, the horses hauled the carriage forward. Lafayette sat next to the door, holding a lamp. He had wiped the white powder off his face and had redressed in his military uniform.

Mr. Franklin sat across from Lafayette, with both his hands resting atop his black wooden cane. The tip of his cane rested on the floor of the carriage between his feet. Franklin wore his disarming grandfatherly smile on his face. The man really was a wolf in sheep's clothing. Mr. Adams sat next to Franklin with what I had come to recognize as his normal, discontented expression. Another man, one I'd never seen before, sat next to Lafayette.

"Minister Gravier, may I introduce Thomas," Mr. Franklin said. "Thomas, may I introduce Minister Gravier."

I couldn't help but notice Mr. Franklin didn't give my last name, and Minister Gravier didn't seem surprised by this rude formality. After this mission, I'd likely be one of the most wanted men in the world, or at least the most wanted man in the English-controlled parts of the world. It served no purpose for any of us to reveal my last name or identity any further. Minister Gravier appeared to understand what was at stake. Then again, he had a spy of his own, so maybe he was used to these kinds of informal meetings.

"How are the ribs?" Lafayette asked me.

"Not bad at all," I said, shifting in my seat. "I already took care of them."

"You did well tonight Mr. – Thomas," Adams said. He almost gave up my name but corrected himself mid-sentence.

"Not really," I responded. "I killed the wrong twin. The messenger gave the note to Marco, thinking he was Jacob. The plan was to kill Jacob."

"Yes, yes, but it worked out in the end," Franklin reassured me. "Now that Marco has been killed by Captain Crombie's brother, a well-known fact by now, thanks to myself and Mr. Adams here, I assure you, Jacob can't stand in and pretend to be the now dead Marco. Everyone at the party was fooled like you and thought you shot Jacob."

"When the truth came out that Marco was the one in the duel, not Jacob," Adams said, "it was apparent to everyone Marco died because he was pretending to be his brother."

"The minister's reputation is safe," Lafayette said. "No one will think this was planned out since fifty witnesses watched him challenge you to the duel."

"What about Jacob?" I asked.

"Last we heard, he was alive," Franklin answered. "The muscles in his arm were sliced deep. If they were able to stop the bleeding, he'll most likely live, but I don't know how much use he will have of his right arm."

"He will want revenge, Thomas," Lafayette warned. "He won't be able to let this go."

"A problem for a later day," I commented with a sigh.

But not a problem for me, I thought to myself. I'd be back in America soon enough and living with Annie and her daughters under a different name. The little fuck can seek revenge until the cows came home, if he wants. I knew how to hide, and America was a big place, getting bigger every day, and he didn't know my real name. Neither he, nor his family, would ever find me.

"What now?" I asked.

"Now, you do what you came here to do," Franklin instructed. "You go to Windsor Castle and kill Lord North."

The minister handed me a piece of paper and said, "You will meet my contact in three night's time, in this tavern. They'll walk you through the front gate and into the castle."

"How will I know your contact?" I asked.

He handed me a pair of white gloves with a red stripe sewn on the top of them.

"They'll know you when they see these," the minister informed me. "They'll have a matching pair on, so you'll know them."

"Does your contact know what the mission is?" I asked him. The less anyone knew about this, the better.

"No," the minister said. "Nor can they. They are to get you in the castle and close to Lord North, nothing more. They'll figure it out soon after it's done, but by then, it will be too late for them to give warning if they chose to betray us. And they know it will mean their death if they betrayed us after the deed is done. Until the job has been completed, trust no one."

That didn't give me a lot of faith in his contact, whoever the guy was. I was so on my own for this mission.

"The deed, the job, the mission," I commented. "Why can't you guys say what you mean? The assassination."

"*Oui*," the minister said. "The assassination."

"I'll ride tonight, but how will I get across the English Channel?" I asked.

"Captain Jones is waiting for you," Franklin told me. "He'll drop you off nearby and sail back. You'll be on your own from there."

The carriage came to a stop and the opposite side door opened. The minister was the first out, followed by Adams. Franklin shifted to exit but paused and turned back to me.

"Marie will go with you to the ship," Franklin said. "He is not to leave the ship with you. He cannot be involved in this. Too much is at stake to risk it all by involving a French citizen. Especially one who is a friend of the king."

I nodded. "I understand."

He was pressing the point because he knew Lafayette was going to want to come with me. Franklin offered his hand, and I took it.

"Find your way back to France, and Jones will sail you back to the United States," Franklin instructed as he stepped out of the carriage.

***

The horses ran and the carriage wheels rolled all night and into the next morning. Lafayette and I slept most of the way, the jouncing lulling me into an uneasy sleep. We made a quick stop at Madame Fournier's place and picked up my clothes, then made it to the Ariel a few hours before sunset. We were met by Captain Jones at the gangplank, and to my surprise, a handshake followed by a manly hug.

"How'd it go?" he asked.

"Cast off as soon as you can, and I'll tell you about it, I promise," I said. "Please tell me you kept the British Captain's uniform."

Jones grinned. "Yes. The ship's not fully repaired, but she's ready to go."

Lafayette brought the horse up to the ship for loading, and I ducked into the captain's quarters and changed. The thick, itchy, red uniform hung a little loose on me, but it would do. The fact it was a little big made it easier to hide my Thompson shoulder holster. The white wig went well with the over-the-top uniform. I couldn't believe how much brass these uniforms had. I was the picture of perfection, as far as overdressed British officers went. I buckled on my sword and put one of the knives behind my back, under my coat. The original captain had a leather belt with a loop in the front, meant to hold a flintlock pistol, so my Tec-9 fit in it nicely. I placed several extra magazines for the pistol in a side pocket of the coat, and the rest I put in my satchel with my vest and deer skin pants.

Lafayette and Jones came in, and we discussed possible escape routes on the coast. With only one ship, there was no need to come up with more than one coastal pickup point. I also wanted a backup plan in case I missed the pickup point or was forced to run in a different direction. If I had to, Jones explained I could travel to a place called Dover and buy passage to France.

Jones brought me as close to Windsor Castle as he could, taking me to the entrance of the River Thames. Jones sailed the ship right up to a small fishing pier. The crew knew to pretend to be English and immediately pulled away from the dock as soon as my horse was off loaded. Jones gave some old man who may or may not have supervised the dock a small purse of coins.

I rode throughout the night and most of the next two days, stopping only to rest the horse and eat pork biscuits. The British were nice enough to put markers on the road, like signposts, telling me which way to go. I had to go slow as to not run into a company of British soldiers, or something worse.

The town of Windsor rose up on the road right before sunset the night of my meeting. I rode into town, looking for the inn called The Little Piglet. It was a small inn made of timber and not brick like many of the other buildings, and I tethered the horse outside. I walked in, relieved to not see any soldiers. The civilians appeared happy to see a captain of the

British Navy walk into their inn. With my satchel on, I must have looked like an important messenger on the king's business.

I sat down at a table in the back of the room and took off the silly British hat from my head. To my dissatisfaction, I left the even sillier white wig on as seemed appropriate, given the other patrons in the room. A smoky haze hung in the room, and sweet pipe tobacco filled the air. The owner rushed over and asked if I'd like some food or drink. I said I would, and moving as fast as he could, he made a line for the kitchen. He never asked me what I wanted to eat but returned a few minutes later with a big serving of roasted duck with mushrooms and freshly baked bread on a plate.

He made a second trip, this time bringing me a hot bowl of potato soup. He also brought me a large stein of dark beer. After eating one of the best meals I'd had in months, I reluctantly pushed my plate and bowl away. The owner saw this and was quick to bring out a bowl of thick black pudding for dessert.

The owner's name was Jasper, and he turned out to be a real chatty guy. He was in his seventies and seemed like a sweet old man. His wife Alice still cooked in the kitchen. His two sons, their wives, and his three grandkids worked and lived at the inn. I wanted to invite him to sit down and have a drink with me, but I was afraid he might ask a question I didn't want to answer.

After I ate the pudding and as it started getting dark outside, I tugged on the white gloves the minister had given me. I motioned for another beer and reclined in my seat, nursing it. A half a dozen town folks sat in the inn, eating, drinking, and talking.

After an hour of sitting there, the front door opened again. I was hoping this would be my contact. I was disappointed when a taller woman walked in, wrapped in a common brown cloak. She didn't wear any gloves. Rather, she had the hands of a woman used to a hard day's work.

Bringing my attention back to my half-finished beer, I didn't notice the woman walk my way until she was standing right in front of me. I glanced back up at her, and she reached into her cloak pocket to withdraw a matching pair of white gloves. She tossed the pair on the table in front of me with a casual air.

"They're too small for my hands," she stated.

She wasn't a small woman. Her broad shoulders and muscular arms nearly matched my own. She opened her cloak and threw back the hood. She had brown hair and brown eyes. Her yellow dress had a wide opening at the neck that showed off her generous cleavage.

Forcing myself to shift my eyes from her chest, I looked back up to her face, then down at the table where the gloves laid.

"You're my contact?" I asked.

“Come on, then,” she ordered. “We need to get to the castle before the gates are locked.”

She picked up her gloves, and wrapping her cloak back around her, she walked away without another word. Fishing out a few coins, I tossed them on the table. I grabbed two more coins and stacked them next to the first two. I was sure I was overpaying, but damn, that duck was good. Grabbing my hat off the table, I rushed to follow the lady out the door, waving goodbye to Jasper as I went.

“Who are you?” I whispered.

She ignored me and walked away in the direction of the castle. I untied my horse and yanked on his reins for him to follow me. I jogged to catch up to her, leading my horse the whole way.

“I’m a chambermaid in the castle,” she said. “My name is Esther. I was born and raised in France but have lived here for the last eight years. My family is still in France. But now we must hurry. Lord North is expecting me to come to his bed before he falls asleep.” Her lips twitched in a moue of a grimace. “The pig fancies me. Instead of going home and spending time with his own poor wife in his own damn house, he prefers to stay at the castle and call me to his bed most nights. I may feel bad for his wife, but she was dumb enough to marry the fat bastard. She should have to take care of that particular burden. I’ve spent the last three months laying on my back with my eyes closed, pretending to enjoy his attentions, as the wanker climbs on top of me with his small prick, groaning like a brute."

That was a lot of information, and I'm sure my eyebrows were lost in the edge of my wig. She stopped walking and turned on me, finger extended as if it were a weapon and my face was the target.

"Don't dare judge me," she said, with fire in her eyes and scorn in her voice. "I just need you to know that everything I've done, I've done for France. I was asked to stay close to him and learn what I could, and I've done just that."

"Not judging," I said, hands held high in surrender.

She turned back and marched off again. We walked down a long, straight road leading to the front gate of Windsor Castle. Large trees and beautiful green grass laid around the walkway to the left and right. I don't really know what I had expected, but it was an honest to God castle, straight from the history books, with towers about six stories high, and the entire structure was made of stone or brick. It was impressive to look at, even by twenty-first century standards.

I stopped halfway down the road and tied my horse off in a clump of trees next to a stream. If no one stole him, he'd be fine here. As we started back down the road, Esther stared at the steel roll-down gate that was slowly lowering. She shook her head.

"We didn't make it," she said. "The gates are closing. The guards will not let us in. You'll have to try again tomorrow, and I need to come up with a reason why I didn't come to Lord North's bed tonight."

I didn't want to hang around the town tonight, hoping to try again tomorrow.

"I need to get in tonight," I urged her.

"The gate is closing," she repeated flatly.

"Esther," I said sharply, trying to get her full attention. "I'm here to kill Lord North."

Her eyes went wide, then a thin smile formed on her face.

"Truly?" she asked, sounding hopeful.

"You wouldn't need to stay here any longer," I told her. "You could go back to France."

Esther swept the hood off her head and opened her cloak to show off the girls. Grabbing my hand, she pulled me along as she broke into a run. As we got close to the gate, Esther moved my right hand, putting it on the upper curve of her own butt, then wrapped her left arm around my waist. She tugged the opening of her dress to show off a little more cleavage to the guards.

The two guards who stood at the entrance in front of the portcullis gate recognized Ester right away.

"Sorry, Esther, the gate just closed," one of the guards said.

"I'm sorry we were late, but we really need to get in," Esther pleaded, her chest heaving from our short run.

In the torch light, I could see the guard staring at her chest. After a few seconds, he waved an arm upward, and the gate rolled back up.

"Last time," the guard said.

He waved us in as the gate was rising. Esther kissed him briefly on the cheek as we walked by him. The guards smirked at me with their own knowing looks of what we would be doing, until the light from their torches identified my rank. Then the two guards snapped to attention and saluted me.

The gate rolled back down as soon as we walked through it. We found ourselves entering the main courtyard, which was large enough to place several football fields in without them ever touching. A gravel walkway extended around a remarkable field of grass.

Two soldiers marched towards us, and my hand automatically reached for my pistol when Esther pushed me against the wall and kissed me. She held the back of my head, pulling me forward into her. When the two soldiers got closer, she pushed my face down into her cleavage and giggled as if I were tickling her.

The soldiers chuckled but kept walking. Next thing I knew, she was off again, pulling me by my hand down the gravel path. Man, she could walk fast. She took me through a side servant's door and down several hallways. Then she let go of my hand and slowed her walk and her breathing. She straightened her dress and removed her cloak, hanging it on a peg. She led me through a dining room that housed a thirty-foot dinner table in the center flanked by at least thirty ornate chairs. We left the dining room through a door at the far end of the room and headed down a bigger hallway. The hallway alone was amazing, nearly fifteen feet wide and covered from one end to another with a crimson red rug. We then went up a set of stairs to the second floor.

Esther stopped in front of a bedroom door and knocked on it. No answer came, so she swung open the door and pulled me into a huge blue room. Oversize paintings of people I didn't know decorated the blue walls. A desk sat in the middle of the room with a headless and armless mannequin next to it. A giant four-poster bed, big enough for three people, was against the back wall, with heavy drapes tied to the round wooden post. A massive blue rug covered the entire floor, and gigantic windows lined the whole far wall.

"Lord North is in the room next door," Esther whispered. "I'll go over there and distract him. Give me ten minutes, then sneak in. I'll make sure the door is unlocked."

"Ten minutes," I repeated.

"Are you fine with cutting his throat while he's mounting me, grunting like the beast he is?" she asked with a straight face.

She seemed a woman serious about her business. I wasn't sure if she was joking or not.

"He will be naked and defenseless," she explained. "Plus, I'll make sure he never notices you until it's too late."

"Are you sure you want me to do it with him on top of you?" I asked, raising one eyebrow. To say such a task was untoward was putting it lightly. Even the Pale Rider had some standards.

"Don't worry about getting blood on me," she assured me. "I'll give you fifteen minutes to run, then start screaming. I'm not going to lie there with his dead body on me for any longer than that. You have to be out of the castle before they start searching."

Oh, this buxom mistress was heartless. She stepped out of the door, and I looked at my watch. Seven minutes in, the hallway filled with a man yelling and screaming. It sounded like a chair being thrown against the wall. I opened the door and stuck my head out.

A barefooted man in long underwear with a white fur-shouldered coat over his shoulders stood in the hallway banging on Lord North's door. Four soldiers and two servants hovered behind the upset man. A slender hallway chair laid on its side.

I recognized the man immediately. I had seen his picture several times on my phone. I had also seen two large paintings of him as Esther walked me through the palace. This screaming man was King George himself. My first thought was, *fuck Lord North, I could step out and kill the king himself.* One step past the door, and one shot right where he stood.

I had no idea what that would do to the timeline. I could end the war tonight with that shot, or I might turn the king into a martyr, ensuring the colonists lose their revolution.

The king turned his head and saw me.

"Who are you?" the king screamed.

"Captain Thomas," I answered quickly, in a panic. "Of your highness's Royal Navy."

"What are you doing here, Captain?" he yelled, his fist still resting on the door.

"I just arrived here tonight, your highness," I told him, making it up as I went. "I was ordered to report to Lord North tomorrow."

The king took a wobbly step towards me, mouth open, ready to yell something else, when the door to Lord North's room opened. The king turned toward Lord North's door and roared at Lord North, who wore nothing more than a robe. The king seemed to have forgotten about me for the minute. I slipped back into my room before the king remembered me again and closed the door as quietly as I could.

Putting my ear against the door, I listened to the king scream about one of his ships being captured in America and another being boarded closer to home. Lord North spoke in a tranquil voice, trying to calm the king down, talking about how ships are captured from time to time, that these weren't the first ships lost in war. The king lost his mind at those words, and resumed screaming so loud and fast, sputtering really, I had a hard time understanding him. It seemed like he was upset about the fact the reports had indicated the colonial criminal known as Pale Rider had captured the first ship and molested the second.

My cheeks ached as I tried not to smile to myself.

Lord North continued trying to calm the king. Their voices seemed to be getting farther away as they talked.

A minute later, a soft knock came at the door. I answered the door, pistol in hand. Esther appeared in the doorway, a bed sheet loosely wrapped around her. She didn't wait for me to say come in and pushed past me.

"What the hell was that?" I asked, closing the door behind her.

"The king is upset about some news he received," Esther explained. "He gets like this sometimes. Lord North will be with him throughout the whole night."

"What now? We have to sneak out and sneak back in tomorrow night?"

"No," she responded. "No one is staying in this room for the next four days. You can sleep here tonight. So many new people come and go, no one will notice, least of all the king. I'll sneak some food up to you in the morning, and we can continue our plan from there."

I looked over at the bed and had to admit it was calling to me.

"The piss pot's in the corner," she said, pointing to a fancy large bowl in the far corner. "Hang your uniform on the mannequin. I'll return in the morning."

Esther slipped back out the door, presumably headed for Lord North's room.

Stripping down, I hung my clothes on the mannequin, used the piss pot, and slipped my Tec-9 under my pillow. You would think it would be nerve racking sleeping in the castle, knowing the king was offering a fortune for my head. Surprisingly, it wasn't. This place was a mad house; no one knew what anyone else was doing. I slept like a baby.

The next morning, I woke up with the sun breaking through the window. After using the piss pot again, I dressed and planned out how I would escape the castle after I killed the man. Twenty minutes later, the door opened, and Esther walked in, fully dressed this time and carrying a tray of food and a pitcher of water. She set the food and pitcher down on the desk. Bacon, eggs, and brown bread sat on a plain silver-colored plate.

"Thank you. Looks great," I told her.

"Lord North never returned last night," she said, getting straight to business. "I checked, and he's still with the king, going over military reports. I've never seen the king this angry. I think Lord North is afraid to leave him alone."

"Let me know if anything changes. I can't stay in this room forever."

"I'll be back around noon," she said.

Without another word, she left the room. I went to the window and peered out beyond the courtyard. The trees started about fifty feet from the castle. That was my goal – I'd have to make it to the tree line when the time came for me to escape. I was dead if I got trapped in the castle. The room was on the second floor, so the drop wasn't too bad, but I didn't want to risk a sprained ankle or broken foot if I landed wrong. I'd need to think of something to help me escape.

Noon came around, and Esther was good to her word. She came in with another tray of food and a pitcher of water.

"Lord North?" I asked. We had to get this show on the road.

"The king finally tired out," she said, setting the tray gently on the table. "He's asleep in his room. The queen is worried about him and won't let anyone in his room. Not the servants, not Lord North, no one. Lord North decided to go home for some peace and quiet. He told the Queen he'd return in the morning."

I groaned at that news. "I need you to do something for me."

She came over to the window to stand next to me. I pointed out the window to a group of trees.

"Tomorrow morning, go get my horse and tie him up in that group of trees," I instructed. "Leave a bucket of water and some grain with him. I don't know how long he'll be there."

"I can do that," she said, eyeing the trees. "I'll put some food in the saddle bags for you, too."

"Thank you. Then, let me know as soon as Lord North returns. You should avoid coming back until then. I don't want you seen coming to my room."

"I'll be careful," she told me in a sure voice. The woman was unflappable. "I'll bring you some dinner later, then stay away until the pig returns."

"Thank you," I said. "Can you bring me some more bed sheets, too?"

"Yes. You need your bed changed already? You've only been here one night."

I laughed and asked her to do one more thing for me as I walked her to the door.

I spent the rest of the day hiding in the room, cleaning my guns and sharpening my knives. I wanted to work on a plan but that wasn't possible since Lord North wasn't in the castle, and I had no idea when he would get there.

Later, as the sun started to tuck itself in for the night, Esther brought me a bowl of cold lamb stew and bread. The stew was okay, but would have been better if it was hot. She also brought me clean sheets that I had requested. She unmade my bed, thinking I wanted her to change my sheets for me. I stopped her by putting my hand on her arm.

"I'll take care of that," I told her. "You should leave."

After she left, I picked at dinner while trying to think of ways to increase my chances of escape. I glanced over at the door leading to the hallway. The door was made of solid hardwood, about three inches thick, a strong English oak door.

The hinges were constructed of good, thick steel. The weak point of the door was the lock. It was designed to provide privacy and look elegant for the castle, but not for security. It would take a tank to break down that door but only a few hard kicks with my foot to break the lock.

Looking around the room, I located what I was searching for. I got up and walked over to one of the fancy chairs. Tipping the chair on its side, I stomped down hard on one of the legs, breaking it off. I did the same to the remaining top leg. Taking my knife, I whittled down the two broken chair legs. It took me a few hours to carve them the way I wanted. By the time I was done, I was ready for sleep again.

Chapter Eleven: The Hit

The next morning, I woke early to a brightening room as the sun broke the horizon. I got up and stretched, then peed in the corner piss pot. I wasn't expecting Esther or breakfast today – I didn't expect her until Lord North returned to the castle. My piss pot was starting to stink, but I didn't want to have one of the chambermaids come up and replace it, so I went to the window onto the back side of the castle to dump it out. I opened the window and dumped out my urine as I checked out the rear courtyard. The horse Lafayette had given me was tethered where I had asked Esther to tie him. So that part of my plan was done. Now I needed to get the rest of my half-baked plan completed.

I turned around to face the room. My crimson red British uniform hung on the mannequin, while my deer skin pants and black vest laid on the bed. The uniform gave me a better chance of getting close and killing Lord North. But how would they know *I* was the one who had done it? General Washington wanted the Pale Rider to take the blame, but if I couldn't get close to him, how would I kill him? The deer skin and vest were more maneuverable and would blend into the forest better during my escape. Bright red didn't really blend in well with the forest. Camouflage was my best chance for escape.

Captain Jones and Lafayette would sail by the fishing village for four nights, starting the previous night. They'd anchor offshore until they saw my signal, then sail in and pick me up. After the fourth night, we'd agreed they'd assume I was dead or making my way own way back. If I took care of Lord North tonight, I was going to be hard pressed to make the pickup. Any time after tonight meant I was on my own for at least a day. I didn't like that idea, but what I liked didn't seem to matter much. I planned on having to make my own way back anyway, in case Lord North didn't return to the castle until tomorrow.

It was still morning when Esther knocked on my door. I had decided to wear my deer skin pants and black vest. My weapons and satchel were packed in case I needed to move fast. I crammed my wig and British coat and pants into my satchel, in case I needed them later. It wasn't the full uniform but might fool someone from a distance. I unlocked my door and cracked it open. I put my foot a few inches behind the door in the event it wasn't Esther. I flushed with relief when I saw it was Esther, and she had her back to me.

"He's on his way up," she whispered over her shoulder, then walked away.

I shut the door and grabbed my gear, moving to the window. Climbing out the large window, I cautiously made my way across the six-inch wide stone ledge to Lord North's room I had noted my first day here. Esther had already opened one of Lord North's windows for me the night before, just as I had asked her to do. Exhaling after that precarious walk, I climbed into North's room and pulled out the makeshift rope I'd made by ripping the sheets into strips, and then braiding them together. *That* idea came from a prison break movie my dad had taken me to see when I was a kid. Not a great plan, but not a bad one either.

I tied one end of the sheet rope to the heavy, oversized, well-crafted bed. I threw the rest of the tied-together sheets out the window where they dropped to the ground.

The door handle jiggled, and I drew my Tec-9 as I spun to face the door. I held the pistol out in front of me in a two-handed grip. I aimed dead center at the door and walked forward, towards my target. I was four feet from the door when it opened.

"I need to wash up, and I'll be right down to talk to the king," Lord North said before fully entering the room.

He was talking to three soldiers standing behind him as the door opened fully inward. The four men remained where they were, frozen in place as I held my pistol steady on Lord North. Front sight covered the center of his forehead, above his nose. My suppressor wasn't attached to my pistol, so the shot was going to be loud and heard throughout the castle. I made sure the soldiers got a good look at me, black vest, scar, and all. Then as Lord North lifted a pasty-white hand and opened his mouth to speak words that he was sure were going to be all-inspiring and or terrifying and cause me to drop my pistol and beg his forgiveness, I squeezed the trigger,

As my bullet exited the back of his head, spraying blood and gray matter onto the wall and poor soldier behind him who blinked at the shock of the gunshot. Lord North's body fell back into the three soldiers, who scrambled to catch him. The shot surprised everyone, and in their moment of failing to act, I stepped forward, kicking the door closed, and turned the lock.

Well, that was anti-climactic.

As I holstered my pistol, I reflected on what happened. You'd think the assassination of one of the world's most powerful men would have been more difficult, or at least more dramatic. No large conspiracies, no fanfare. No sniper shot from a bell tower or bomb hidden in his carriage. No, I did it with little thought, one bullet, and the help of an abused and vengeful chambermaid. I was almost disappointed in the spectacular lack of planning and effort that I used.

Thump, thump, thump. The soldiers threw themselves at the door, trying to force it open. Well, I wasn't out of hot water yet. The lock wasn't going to hold for long. The men yelled for more soldiers. I pulled out one of the wooden wedges I'd carved from the leg of the chair and jammed it under the door. Kicking the wedge twice to make sure it was good and tight, I then pulled out the second one and jammed it between the door and door frame above the lock. The door wasn't going to open, no matter how many times they crashed into it.

They'd need an axe to get in here now.

I rushed to the window and climbed down the torn sheets. Running for the tree line, my shoulders tightened up and scrunched together as I waited for the bullet that never came.

I mounted onto the horse's back and settled into the saddle. I pulled hard on the reins to spin the horse around and heard him snort in protest. The smell of horse shit and the creaking of the leather saddle made me suddenly miss Little Joe. He was a coward, to be sure, but he was my coward, and he was fast. I hoped Annie's girls were taking good care of him.

Pressing my luck, I decided to ride for the pickup spot thirty miles away. It was early enough in the day that I might make it if we rode hard.

"Ok, horse," I said to the animal. "No rest for the wicked. I hope you're ready to run."

Kicking the horse's sides, he bolted forward, streaking through the trees. I needed to head due east and find the River

Thames. Following the river was the fastest and easiest way to find my way back to the fishing village. First, I need to head south, in case the soldiers picked up my trail. I didn't want them to know which way I was really heading. The dirt was soft, and the horse was going to rip up the grass, making it easy to track me. In the distance behind me, a bell rang from inside the castle, and it urged me on. The whole countryside was going to be up in an uproar and searching for the Pale Rider.

I couldn't help but wonder if I had done it. Did killing Lord North balance the damage I had done at Saratoga? Would the king's new advisors now advise him not to send seventy-five thousand soldiers across the ocean? If his advisors were able to convince him not to send so many troops, would France join in the war? I had no idea what effects my action would cause or if I'd even live long enough to find out. I only hoped I had not made things worse. For now, I needed to focus my attention on getting back to France and then to America.

I rode for about a mile before I came to the River Thames. A bridge continuing south extended across the river. The water looked churned too deep and swift to cross without using the bridge. The bridge was long, wooden, and exposed to gunfire from either side. Some local villagers crossed the bridge from the far side, who surely heard the palace alarm that had spread to the church bells in the town behind me. They'd be sending out patrols any minute now, if they haven't already.

Urging the horse on, we started across the bridge at a slow walk. The *clunk, clunk, clunk* of the horse's steel shoes impacting with the wood seemed overly loud. The villagers who were crossing towards me had been looking down until they heard me coming. They flicked their heads up to see who was coming from the other direction. They moved to the side, yielding to this odd stranger who, for all they knew, may have been a lord or something.

None of them were armed with a sword or flintlock, so I waved to them as we passed each other in the middle of the bridge. They'd remember me when questioned. When I made it to the opposite side of the bridge, I again broke the horse into a full run. We continued south for a bit then came across a shallow stream. I dismounted and led the horse east, walking in the freezing cold water. It was my hope the British soldiers who were coming wouldn't be able to follow me through the water.

The horse and I kicked up a lot of loose sediment, making the water murky. The swiftly flowing water carried the sediment away, so I also hoped there would be no sign of us by the time the soldiers came across the stream. The small, loose rocks we walked on and knocked over were covered in algae. The bottoms of the rocks were clean and algae free. Some of the rocks even looked shiny once upturned. If any of the patrols had a tracker worth his salt with them, he might notice this. It was like leaving a trail of breadcrumbs, but it couldn't be helped. I had to hope that any patrols coming this way didn't have a tracker with them or wouldn't think to look.

After a half mile, I began losing the feeling in my feet and was forced to wade out of the ice-cold water. The stream had taken me into a low depression, with the land extending upward on either side of me. It'd be hard for anyone to see me here, but the land was going to flatten out up ahead. Despite the chill, I took the time to change out of my clothes and back into the red British captain's uniform. I hid my deer skin pants under a bush, and not being able to depart with my vest, I tucked it in my satchel. I climbed into the itchy red pants and threw the coat over my white shirt. It wasn't the full uniform, but it'd have to do. With the wig back on my head and covering my scar, I rode across land again in a north-east direction. I needed to find and stay close to the river.

The thrum of horses echoed from the north of me on the far side of a rise. I trotted the horse up the hill, high enough to look over the crest. A group of about thirty soldiers on horseback rode east. I was willing to bet more soldiers rode in four different directions, hoping to find me. I pushed over the rise and fell in at the back of the group of soldiers, trying to blend in.

I stayed with the troop of soldiers for about five miles until we neared a town. I figured they'd stop there and asked if anyone saw me. They might have orders to leave a few soldiers behind to keep an eye out for the mysterious assassin. I reined in on my horse, slowing and falling farther behind.

When the thick cloud of dust kicked up by their horses obscured them from my sight, I turned north and broke away, kicking the horse and demanding more speed.

I made it another five miles east without seeing anyone except a few local farmers. Then a group of three soldiers rode down the road towards me. If they were coming from the east, they most likely hadn't heard about Lord North yet.

The three riders slowed their horses as we neared each other, to be polite and not kick up a dust cloud over me. I did the same, intending to not appear rude or gain their attention and scrutiny. My uniform was a mess from being stuffed into the satchel, and I only had the pants and coat, so I hoped they didn't look too closely.

My heart dropped, and my hopes were crushed when the three riders turned out to be a major and two lieutenants. They were no doubt riding to the castle on official military business.

The major stopped his horse in front of me, making it apparent he expected me to stop and speak to him. I tugged on the reins, halting my horse in front of the three men.

"Captain," the major greeted, his voice hard and official.

"Sir," I said. "Good day to you."

"Where are you coming from?" the major inquired.

His eyes flicked from my face to my shoddy uniform and back.

"Windsor Castle," I answered, keeping as close to the truth as possible.

"And where are you heading?" he asked.

I'd been a cop too long not to recognize when I was being interrogated.

"East, sir," I answered, maintaining my own clipped answers.

"I can see you're heading east, Captain," the major snapped. "Where east? And why are you out of uniform? You look like you slept in a barn. You're an officer in the king's Navy, and you look disgraceful."

"Yes, sir," I said. "There was an attack on the castle."

His eyes widened, and the two lieutenants brought their horses closer to hear what had happened.

"An attack?" he asked. "Don't be daft. Who could attack the castle?"

"An outlaw called the Pale Rider," I told them. Time to see what they knew about me. "They say he's from America. He killed Lord North himself and fifty soldiers."

Okay, so not as close to the truth as I wanted.

"Impossible!" the major yelled. His horse reacted to his shouting, flinching under the major who yanked on the reins to control his beast.

The major may have had his doubts, but my lie had the desired effect on the two lieutenants. One was licking his lips while trying to swallow, and his counterpart searched the road as if he thought we were about to find ourselves in an ambush.

"Sir," the lieutenant on the right interrupted, "they say two of our ships were sacked by a pirate called the Pale Rider. He's known to be in these waters, sir."

"Yes, lieutenant," the major responded slowly, his voice heavy with frustration. "I've heard the same reports. You're suggesting he sailed his ship thirty miles inland, and attacked the heart of England?"

"No, sir," the timid lieutenant responded. "Sorry, sir. It's just…."

The major lifted a hand, cutting the Lieutenant off mid-sentence. Then he swung his attention back to me.

"You still haven't answered my questions," the major pressed. "Why are you out of uniform and where are you going?"

I had no idea of the names of the villages or towns around here. That second question was going to be a tough one.

"I was asleep when the attack occurred," I lied. "I rushed out the door with orders to ride as fast as I could to the coast, passing the word to be on the lookout to every town on the way, sir."

The major slowly looked me up and down again, his gaze full of doubt. His eyes stopped on my boots, examining them, then his scanning orbs moved up to my non-British issue saddle.

He squinted at me. "Your accent, Captain? Where are you from?"

"Sorry, sir," I said. "I was assigned to the Americas for the last eighteen months. I may have picked up a little of their rough, common tongue."

"Who is your commanding officer?" he pried. The guy would not give up! "I know the officers at the castle."

I kept my eyes on the major, but in my peripheral vision, the lieutenant on the left moved his hand to his pistol. He didn't grab the pistol; he merely rested his hand on top of it. He was trying to act casual, but his point was clear. He sensed his officer's demeanor and was prepared to attack.

"Your commanding officer, Captain?"

The lieutenant on the right was slower, but he finally caught on as to what was happening and moved his hand upward. Unlike his counterpart, he didn't just rest his hand on his pistol. No, he wrapped his finger around the smooth, solid English oak grip.

"Captain?" the Major yelled, demanding an answer.

"Your mama," I answered.

I drew my Tec-9 and fired in one smooth move. The dumb one was my target, and he drew when I did. I was faster on the draw, and he was dead and falling off his horse. I shifted to fire at the second lieutenant. A second shot echoed in the open field, but it wasn't from my pistol. It was from the pistol being held by the smarter lieutenant.

Before I could blink, I was on the ground, sprawled in the wet grass on my left side. Pain shot down my right arm, starting from my shoulder. My horse jumped forward and sprinted between the major and the lieutenant's horse. The major pulled on his reins, backing his mount up a few feet for safety while the Lieutenant who'd shot me climbed down from his horse and drew his sword, intent on finishing the job he started.

My right hand didn't want to move, and my pistol laid uselessly on the ground next to me with my satchel at my backside. I sat up before he got close and snatched up my pistol with my left hand. He, of course, didn't think I had anything more to give with my pistol and took another step toward me, sword high. I fired twice into his chest.

My shots were off a bit, shooting with my left hand and all, but he was just as dead. The major reacted instantly and kicked his horse and charged me. I rolled backwards, out of the way of the sharp hooves. I sat up as he rode past me, firing my last three shots into his back. He flew off the side of his horse, arms out wide, and collapsed in a heap.

Tentatively poking at the bullet hole in my shoulder, I knew I was going to have to do something about it fast, or I'd bleed to death.

"Well, that's the last time I take off my vest," I griped to myself.

I manage to holster my pistol awkwardly with my left hand, then looked around. My horse was a hundred yards down the road and still running hard.

I peeled off the thick red coat and dropped it to the ground. My shirt was soaked with blood. I needed to get off the road and find a safe place to take care of my injury. Grabbing the wig off my head, I threw more than dropped it to the ground on top of the red coat, grateful to be rid of the thing. Grabbing the lieutenant's horse, I pulled myself up with my left hand. I turned the horse, left the road, and rode deep into the trees.

I found a safe place under a group of trees and tied the horse off. Taking off my satchel, I found a log to sit on and pulled out my first aid kit. The air had grown far too cold to take off my shirt completely – I could see my breath – and I didn't know if I'd have the strength to put it back on if I did. I pulled at the hole in the shirt, widening it to reveal my gunshot wound.

The wide, jagged hole in my shoulder coursed with blood, and I yelped in pain as I stuck my finger into the hole. I could see a small piece of my white shirt in the wound.

In the eighteenth century, most people who were shot either died of blood loss or infection. My kit had a set of forceps and I grabbed them. Using the forceps and a small mirror as best I could with my left hand, I dug the piece of cloth out.

The wound was hot and tender, and the searing pain shot through my body. My mind spun wildly, greying out, and I wobbled on the log. I needed to search for the slug, but if I passed out, I'd probably bleed to death. Sweat poured from my forehead, and I wiped my brow with the sleeve of my left arm.

I managed to pour a packet of blood clotting powder into the hole, and it only took a few minutes for the bleeding to stop.

Taking a deep breath, I stuck the forceps back into the hole and jumped when the metal touched the slug. Based on the location of the hole, if I had to guess, and I did, I'd say the bullet went through the subscapular muscles and tendons. The fact I felt the bullet meant it didn't go through the scapula bone itself. Holding my breath, I clipped the forceps around the small piece of lead and pulled. The bullet *was* embedded in the bone.

It didn't move, but I went blind with pain. I opened my eyes and found myself on the ground again, on my back, breathing hard. The pain was too much. I didn't remember even falling off the log. I didn't realize I had let go of the forceps until I looked over and saw them sticking out of my shoulder.

I desperately wanted to give myself a morphine shot, but I needed to keep my wits about me. Instead, I dry-swallowed two of the powerful narcotic pain killers and tried again. I pulled on the forceps once more, but my fingers lacked the strength to dislodge the bullet. I laid there breathing and waiting for the pills to kick in enough for me to get the bullet out.

There was a water bag on the horse's saddle horn, and I needed a drink badly. My mouth was parched, and I was pain-sweating out my fluids. I was also risking dehydration among everything else, but the water wasn't worth the effort of trying to stand to get it, so it'd have to wait.

On my third try, I took three quick breaths, holding in the last one as I put a small stick in my mouth. Then I pulled hard on the forceps and tried to block out the pain that shot through my entire body. I squeezed my eyelids shut and kept pulling. I clenched down with my teeth, biting into the stick, but kept pulling. I kept pulling as my mouth opened, letting the stick fall to my chest, and I screamed. I screamed loud enough for the world to hear. I screamed like a wounded animal and kept screaming. Stars filled my vision, and I kept pulling. My head spun, and I was going to pass out, but I kept pulling.

I either heard or imagined a loud snap as the bullet broke free, and the forceps slipped out of my shoulder, still clamped around the round marble size piece of lead. The forceps dropped from my shaking hands as tears ran down my face.

That was the last thing I remembered, before God showed mercy on me and let the blackness overtake me in its sweet caress, like a blanket freeing the pain from my thoughts.

I opened my eyes, not knowing how much time had gone by and more than a little surprised to still be alive. The only good news was I was able to wiggle my fingers on my right hand, but lifting my arm was asking too much. I needed stitches, but with only my left arm working, that wasn't going to happen anytime soon.

Reaching into my first aid kit, I grabbed a tube of combat wound seal, the size of a small tube of toothpaste. Once applied, it expanded the way installation foam did. I squeezed the whole tube into the gaping hole in my shoulder. It would pack the wound tight, prevent infection and stop blood loss at the same time. Then I used a large, square bandage and sealed the entire injury. Finally, and as much as it pained me, I used one of the three antibiotic shots I had left. Between my dirty fingers and the possibility of any tiny scraps of cloth still embedded in the wound, infection was most certainly guaranteed.

I took a moment to study my handiwork. If I lived through this, I'd have a matching scar to the bayonet wound on my left shoulder.

Looking at my watch and the fact the sun was going down, I guessed I had been out for about two hours. The British had to have found the dead bodies by now and would be searching the area. I climbed to my feet and, despite my shaking and weakened state, managed to get back into the saddle. Thank God I had a horse. I sure as hell wouldn't be able to walk far. I drank down half the water, saying a silent thank you to the lieutenant whom I had killed. It was his water, after all.

I remembered to reload my pistol and put my vest back on. There was no reason to try to hide who I was anymore. With this much blood on my shirt, no one was going to be fooled into thinking I was anyone except the man the whole country was searching for. Patting the horse on the neck, I rode deeper into the woods. I wouldn't be making camp tonight. I had to keep going, not only because I was running out of time, but because if I did fall asleep, I might wake up with a musket aimed at my face.

Keeping the horse at a steady gait, I made my way back towards the river. Once I located the river, I followed it east again. I came across a few British patrols, but they were easy to spot and avoid, mainly because they had torches that could be seen from far off. Those who had made camp built large campfires to keep animals and monsters like me away. I figured I'd make it to the pickup stop tomorrow morning but needed to find a spot to hide until nighttime.

I was going heavy on the pain killers but that couldn't be avoided. I denied myself sleep and kept pressing on. I could rest when I was back in France or dead. The night dragged on, and I struggled to stay awake. I had to stop a couple of times and splash cold water on my face and neck to wake me up. My bloodied bandage needed changing, but I wasn't going to risk passing out again.

The fishing village came into my view the next morning. Since I couldn't risk being seen, I stayed on the outskirts. Before reaching the village proper, I unsaddled the horse and set him free. Getting as close to the village as I dared, I found a spot where I might hide under some loose dirt and leaves and watch the town. Five soldiers marched around the village, and I was willing to bet the British had at least five soldiers in every village and town within a hundred miles of the castle, searching for me.

I'd have to deal with the soldiers before I signaled for Captain Jones, but that would be a problem for later tonight. If I killed them now, one of the villagers might run for help. Feeling safe buried in dirt, leaves, and branches, I settled down, saving my strength. I was still afraid to fall asleep, so I forced myself to stay wake. When I did let myself fall asleep, I'd sleep for days, and if I did that now, I would miss my ride off this island.

The village didn't have much outside of small homes, a fishing dock with small boats, and a church. The soldiers entered and exited the church, so I knew that was where they'd be sleeping.

Tonight was my last chance to be picked up by Captain Jones. If I didn't signal him tonight, I'd have to find my own way back. And it wasn't like I could grab a rowboat and cross the English Channel. No, I'd have to signal them tonight, and that meant I might have to kill the soldiers. I didn't want to kill the king's men, and then sit around hoping the villagers didn't work up the nerve to capture me, which meant waiting until right before I wanted to signal, then attack. One hour after sunset should be the right time.

When night did finally come, I made my way down to the village. It was a frigid night, but I was burning up. I was still sweating, and my shirt clung to my sweaty back and chest. I felt feverish. Dizziness overcame me and I stumbled, both from the fever and lack of sleep. I knew one thing for certain – if I didn't make it off this island tonight, I was never leaving alive.

The villagers were sleeping, eating, or whatever they were doing, but they were at least doing it in their small wooden shacks they called their homes. With my suppressor screwed onto my Tec-9, I quietly made my way around to the church.

I came around from the back of the church, my hand against the wall for balance. I found one of the soldiers standing guard at the base of the steps leading up to the church's double doors. I wanted to wait and see if he'd fall asleep on duty, but I was surely more tired than he was, so that wasn't a good plan.

A pack of dogs ran through the village barking, most likely chasing a cat or other small animal. The dogs drew the guard's attention away from where I was, but also heightened his senses. Voices followed by laughter came from inside the church. The others weren't asleep yet, nor did I think they'd be anytime soon.

Better get this over with.

I moved past the corner of the church, outside of the ring of light the soldier's lantern put out. Pulling out my Tec-9 with my left hand, I stepped out from the shadow. I planned on pistol whipping him, knocking him out. My fourth step landed on a twig I didn't see. A snap came from under my foot, and I froze in place. In my sick and tired state, I was getting careless and making mistakes.

The soldier's head spun around towards me as his musket rose at me. I fired two quick shots into his chest. He fell back without a word, but the clatter of his musket on the ground was deafening.

Keeping my pistol up, left arm extended, I spun around in a full circle, searching for any threats. I stopped, my pistol aimed at the church doors, ready to fire again if they opened. Spinning around had made me dizzy. Laughter broke out again from inside.

My shoulder was on fire. I glanced down and saw my skin was bright red under my shirt. My vision blurred suddenly, and I dropped to my knees, retching. Acid burned my throat and bile coated the back of my mouth, as I lost what food had been in my stomach. I remained on my knees for a few moments, holding myself up with my left hand.

The nausea relented, and my vision cleared. I gathered my strength and push myself back up to my feet. I wiped the vomit and saliva from my chin and looked up at the church double doors. Four more soldiers were still in the church, and I wasn't sure if my vision or strength was going to hold out much longer.

Desperate times called for desperate measures. I holstered my pistol and dug into my satchel, extracting out one of my three remaining grenades. I placed the grenade in my right hand. I couldn't lift my arm, but I was able to close my finger and hold the little ball of death.

The night went still and quiet again. An English owl broke the silence with his screeching into the night. I didn't know if he was announcing his kill of a field mouse, or if the limy bastard was trying to warn the soldiers inside the church of the death coming their way. If it was the former, well, good for him. If it was the latter, then he didn't know how right he was.

I made my way up the steps as quietly as I could. Grabbing the cold brass doorknob, I slowly turned it. The knob rotated under my direction, and the click of the lock moving, freeing itself from its sister door, vibrated through the knob. Pulling the door open an inch, I peeked through the crack.

The four soldiers sat around a table playing cards and drinking from a brown bottle of what might have been whisky. The table was about ten feet from me, and the soldiers perched on small wooden stools.

Reaching down with my left hand, I grabbed the grenade pin and pulled it out. Throwing with my right hand wasn't an option, so I took the grenade in my left. Pulling the door open with the toe of my right foot, I rolled the grenade into the room straight at them. Then I kicked the door shut and listened to the sound of a metal ball rolling on a wooden floor, as I shifted quickly to the side of the doors.

"What the fuck is that?" one of the soldiers asked, still laughing.

I could picture him pointing to the grenade, and the other three following his finger to look straight at the metal ball as it exploded.

Then the church doors burst open, and the windows blew outward, showering the ground with glass from the over-pressure of the explosion in the room. I peered into the now open doorway and saw four bodies lying on the floor. The table had been blown into several pieces, and blood covered the debris. There was no need to see if they were alive. I was sure they weren't, but if any of them were, they weren't getting up.

I half ran, half stumbled to the water's edge. If Captain Jones was close, then he heard the explosion. I needn't worry about any signal – I had a feeling he'd assume I had something to do with it.

Front doors of the small homes wrenched open as villagers stuck their head out to investigate the explosion.

"Who's there?" one villager yelled, raising his musket at me.

I fired my pistol, aiming for his chest but hitting him in the leg. He fell to the ground, musket firing off on accident.

I wasn't going to be able to wait for Jones to come to me – too many people heard the explosion. I was going to have to go to him. Running down the length of the dock, I more fell than climbed into the small boat at the end. It took me a few tries, but I was able to untie the boat from its mooring.

Shots rang out in the night as the villagers now shot at the man stealing one of their boats. I couldn't row the boat with only one arm, so I pushed off as hard as I could. The boat glided through the water easily, then slowed and came to a stop about ten feet from the dock.

Fuck. Really?

Half a dozen men ran down the dock, armed with axes, spears, and torches. Two of them carried muskets and tried to reload them as they ran. The little boat was pushed back towards the dock as small waves bouncing to shore broke against it. The men noted the poor state I was in and laughed. I wrestled with my holster, trying to get my pistol out but had trouble cross drawing it with my left hand. Even if I was able to pull my pistol out, I no longer had any strength to hold it up.

I was done.

I dropped my chin to my chest just as several cannons exploded behind me, lighting up the darkness. The water off to my right erupted as plumes of water sprayed into the air. The men on the dock had no idea who was shooting at them, nor did they care. Their meager weapons were useless against cannon fire, and they turned and ran back down the dock as fast as they could.

I fell back onto the bottom of the boat and laid there. A few minutes later, a Jolly boat rowed up next to me, and Lafayette's concerned face came into sight above me as he leaned over and into my boat.

“Thomas?” he called to me, his eyes wide. “You made it?”

The only person more surprised than Lafayette right then was me.

“Oh, hey,” I answered with a dry, scratchy throat. “Lafayette, nice to see you. I could use a little help.”

Hands grabbed at me and roughly pulled me over the side of my stolen boat, and I flopped, or rather dropped, into the Jolly boat, every part of my body in pain and on fire.

“Water?” I pleaded.

Someone held a water bag up to my lips, and water poured into my mouth. I drank deeply, feeling the cold liquid wet my mouth and cooled my fiery throat.

Then blackness overtook me.

Chapter Twelve: Conquering Hero

I woke up on the Ariel, in my own hammock, rocking gently with the sway of the ship, and it took me a moment to realize I was still alive.

The fact I was rocking slowly meant that we were back in France, docked, and not out on the open sea. My arm was covered with a thick canvas sling. I looked down at my hand and was able to move my fingers. I could also bend my arm at the elbow with no problems. But when I lifted my arm, pain stabbed me like a knife in my shoulder. A new clean bandage was wrapped around my shoulder and chest. My vision seemed normal and lifting my left hand to my forehead, I felt that my forehead was cool, my fever gone. My antibiotic shot must have stopped the infection.

Lafayette came in a few minutes after I woke up to check on me.

"You're awake. How're you feeling, Thomas?"

"Better," I answered honestly. "How long was I out?"

"About ten hours," he said. "You were exhausted. Madame Fournier sent her own doctor to the ship, and he said you would be fine. He cleaned your wound and redressed it."

"Any pus?" I asked.

"He said it was red, but your body fought off the fever and swelling."

"Where's my satchel?" I asked.

Lafayette walked over to the corner where my weapons and satchel laid, and picked up my leather bag, walking it over to me. I pulled out two more pain killers and asked for some water. Lafayette grabbed a jug of water from the desk and poured me a glass. Taking the two pills and downing the water, I laid back and closed my eyes.

His bright eyes studied my every movement. "Did you do it?" Lafayette finally asked. "Did you kill Lord North?"

I exhaled heavily. "Yes."

"I'll send a message to Monsieur Franklin and let him know," Lafayette said, his tone rising with excitement. "Madame Fournier will send off one of her pigeons for us. She's been asking about your health."

"Why?"

"I think you scare her," Lafayette said. "She's hoping for you to die, and she no longer has to fear you, but she wants you to know she sent her own doctor over to help you, in case you recover."

"Smart woman. She's covering her bases," I said.

Jones entered the room, shutting the door behind him.

"The conquering hero is awake," Jones said, smiling. "Lord North?"

"Dead," I responded.

"I'll go to Madame Fournier's place and send a message to Monsieur Franklin," Lafayette told Jones.

"That will not be necessary," Jones told him.

"We need to send a message *now*. Thomas has confirmed his success."

"You don't need to go to Madame Fournier," Jones said. "She is here, on the ship, now."

That intrigued me. "Why?"

"She is asking to speak to you."

Lafayette looked over at me, eyebrows furrowed in question.

"Does she know about my mission?" I asked.

"She knows about everything that happens around here," Lafayette admitted.

"Hand me my pistol," I told Lafayette, then flicked my eyes to Jones. "Send her in, Captain."

Lafayette handed me my Tec-9, and I slipped it under my blanket while Jones opened the cabin door. He held it open and motioned with his head for Madame Fournier to enter. She came in, and I almost didn't recognize her. Unlike our last meeting, this time she dressed modestly in a simple blue dress, little makeup, and no wig. She had short brown hair, with something between a hat and a bonnet on her head. She also held a bundle of clothes in her hands. She came towards me, handing Lafayette the clothes as she walked past him.

"Madame Fournier," I greeted her. "You're more beautiful today in your natural state, without those accessories and bobbles to distract the eye."

"You're as dangerous with your words as you are with your weapons," Madame Fournier retorted, as she walked over and placed a hand on my thigh. "And I've asked you before to call me Lille."

"So you did, Lille," I said, smiling weakly at her. "To what do I owe this pleasant surprise?"

"I've come to check on you and see if I might be of any assistance," she said.

"It's my understanding you've already been of great help. Do I not owe you my thanks for sending me your own physician?"

"Yes, well, that was a minor thing," she answered with a shrug. "In truth, I've come to warn you."

Lafayette leaned in toward Madame Fournier. "Warn us of what?"

"First, I've received word Lord North was killed two days ago in Windsor Castle. The British are blaming the Pale Rider for the murder. This has nothing to do with you, of course, but I thought you should know the news has reached France. Probably even Paris by now."

"Thank you for that information," I told her. "But you could have sent one of your girls to tell us that. Why have you come here yourself?"

She straightened slightly. "As you know, I've many customers come to me, not only for my girls but for my pigeons. This morning, after I had sent word for my physician to come here, one of the local merchants came to me. He had a message he needed to send to one of my wealthier and more powerful customers. The message was cryptic but spoke of locating *en voulait un*."

I looked over at Lafayette for help.

"The wanted one," Lafayette translated. "Or one you're angry with, depending on the context."

"That could be bad for someone," I responded, shifting my gaze back to the madam.

"Who was this message sent to?" Jones asked.

Madame Fournier was talking to the room, but she was brave enough to look me in the eye as she spoke. Her smile fled her face, replaced with a downward turn at the corners.

"You have to understand. I don't wish to make enemies of powerful people. I had to send the message. The merchant insisted on seeing the pigeon off himself. If word got back I refused to send it ..."

"Who did the bird fly to?" Jones pressed. "Who is your customer?"

"Messieurs Marco and Jacob Testa," she answered. "Or I should say *Monsieur* Jacob Testa, now that his brother Marco is dead."

Lafayette and Jones looked as if they were going to explode into screaming tirades.

"Thank you, Lille," I said, cutting them off. "We know you had no choice in sending the message. You did, however, have a choice in whether or not you came here to warn us. You have risked much in coming here."

Most of what I said was meant for Lafayette and Jones. They thought she had betrayed us, but she hadn't. It also explained why she came here looking the way she did. She didn't want to be recognized.

"I don't know what you thought was going to happen when you came here to tell me this," I told her, "but you have gained my trust. I'll not forget this favor."

She let out a breath of air, which I had not realized she was holding in. She appeared deflated, like an empty balloon.

"How did this merchant know I was here?" I asked.

"Two of the new crew members went to shore and haven't returned," Jones admitted. "I suppose they could have been spies, planted by the Testa family."

"More likely they were grabbed and questioned," Madame Fournier said. "The Testa family owns several ships in this port. Your missing crewmen are probably already dead."

"I knew that little shit was going to be a problem," Jones spat out.

"While you were gone, we got word he lost the use of his right hand," Lafayette said to me. "He was close to dying of blood loss. They stopped the bleeding with a hot iron. It stopped the bleeding, but the tendons were cauterized apart. He can use his arm but not his hand."

"The good news is the Testa family has forgotten about the minister," Jones added. "He is thrilled about how the whole thing turned out."

"You mean because the family is now obsessed with me and not him?" I asked in a harder tone.

Jones nodded. "Exactly."

"What do we do?" Lafayette asked.

I wanted to change the conversation until Madame Fournier left.

"May I ask two more favors of you before you go?" I asked her.

"*Mais oui*," she said, smiling.

"Can you send a message to Mr. Franklin for us?" I asked. "And can you let me know if Jacob Testa sends back a reply?"

"*Bien sûr, mon ami*," she said.

I gave her a message to send for me. This time, I told her what I wanted the message to say instead of writing it, showing her that I did trust her.

Before leaving, she bent over me and kissed me on my cheek.

She whispered in my ear, "If I were twenty years younger, I would tell these two to leave the room for a few hours."

I smiled and whispered back into her ear, "If I weren't injured, I would have already told them myself."

She laughed at my joke and kissed me on the other cheek.

"The clouds are getting dark. A storm is coming this way. I should get back to my place before the rain comes."

Jones opened the door again for her, then barked for his first mate to see Madame Fournier off the ship. The heated tension in the air increased as Jones closed the door.

"How long do you think we have?" I asked the two men.

"Jacob would have the message by now," Lafayette answered. "He will not come alone. He'll need to gather more men, if he comes at all. Twelve to fourteen hours, if he rides non-stop."

"He'll come," I said. "I looked into his eyes when we fought. I killed his brother and wounded his pride. The only reason he's still alive is because he passed out from blood loss during the fight, and he knows it. He wants me dead. No, not want. He *needs* me dead. I don't think he can go back home while I live."

"Then we have two clear choices," Jones announced. "We ride for Paris as he rides here. It's a big country and there are many roads to Paris."

"Or?" Lafayette asked.

"We make sail and leave now. We can sail for another port, or for America itself."

America wasn't an option, yet. I had to stay and make sure all this wasn't for nothing. If the French didn't join the war after Lord North's death, I'd have to come up with a new plan. My insides cringed at the thought.

"We have a third option," I said. "We sail north. Somewhere on the coast, Lafayette and I jump ship and make for Paris. Forty miles, should do."

Jones nodded eagerly at the idea. "I'll pass the word for the crew to get ready. In your absence, we finished the much-needed repairs to the ship, restocked our supplies, and brought the number of crew up to one hundred and forty-five."

"Forty-three now," Lafayette said in a clipped tone.

"We have plenty of time to make sail," Jones continued. "I'd like to give the men a few hours to say goodbye to any family."

I nodded my head to him as I strained to get out of my hammock, then dressed in the clothes Madame Fournier brought me. Long white socks, short black pants that stopped at the knees, a long-sleeved black cotton shirt, and a black coat with gold buttons. I had to admit, without the coat, the outfit was functional for fighting, and with the coat, it was very fashionable. My black vest would blend in with the shirt. Lafayette had to help buckle on my gun belt, shoulder holsters, and sword belt. Only having use of one arm was really starting to suck.

My two friends left the room to ready the ship and men, leaving me alone with my thoughts. Though I had full use of my right hand, I couldn't lift my arm. I took the time to clean and oil my pistols as best I could. I wanted to sharpen my knives, but after cleaning my pistols, my right shoulder gave up the ghost. It throbbed and made me weak with pain, so I slipped it back into the sling to prevent myself from using it anymore.

When the ship and crew were ready, Jones ordered the lines cast off and sails unfurled. We pulled away and sailed out of the harbor and into the wind. It was the middle of the day, but dim outside, sun hidden somewhere behind the thick gray clouds. We stayed close to the shoreline as we made our way north.

I studied the horizon and laughed to myself as I thought about Jacob riding into town eight to ten hours from now, to learn we were already gone. He was going to blow a gasket.

None of this changed the fact that, before I sailed back to America, I was going to have to kill that bastard. I wasn't going to live my life wondering when he'd find me. And I had to make sure the French joined the war before I did anything else. I needed to stay focused. This time, running made sense. I didn't know how many men he was bringing with him, but he had the crews of several ships already here.

As we sailed towards the storm, ships were returning to the harbor, wanting to dock before the storm's full force landed on shore. It didn't take long for us to notice the three ships following us. Besides the Ariel, they were the only ships sailing away from the harbor and not into it. Standing at the aft of the ship with Jones, we watched as they kept their distance, not trying to close on us, but not falling back, either.

"Jacob's ships?" I asked Jones.

"His father's or grandfather's, but yes," Jones answered. "I'm sure they left one or two ships behind to inform Jacob that we left. These three are following, waiting for Jacob to catch up."

"We will be long off the ship and heading to Paris before Jacob catches up," I said.

"Do you have any idea where you plan to disembark?" Jones asked.

"Yes," I said. "Marie says we should be able to locate some pig farmers near the beach farther up the coastline. We're hoping they'll have horses we can buy. Once we leave the ship, you need to sail back to the harbor in a day or two. This should be over by then. Not even the Testa family would move against you while you're moored at a French harbor."

Jones nodded his head, then after thinking about it, I added, "Set up a guard around the ship, in case they are dumb enough to attack you in the harbor. Maybe keep a few of the cannons loaded and aimed at the dock itself."

Jones glanced up at the dark sky, at the heavy clouds ready to burst. The wind was blowing hard, pushing us along at a fast clip. Lightning flashed in the dark skies, striking the ocean out in the open water.

"One, two..." I counted out loud.

The clap of thunder struck our ears before I said three.

"That was a half mile away," I commented, keeping my eyes fixed on the storm. I'd already experienced one – I didn't need to endure another.

"It's getting closer," Jones responded. "If you're going to take a Jolly boat, you should do so soon. The water's getting rough."

The waves were getting bigger, crashing hard against the hull of the ship. The ocean was dark, roaring with white-capped waves.

"How far do you think we've gone?" I asked.

"Thirty or thirty-five miles, maybe," Jones answered.

"Get a boat ready. I'll ask Marie to find a spot he wants to row for."

The captain sailed parallel to the coastline, trying to stay as close as he dared even as the waves battered against the side of the ship. Larger waves pummeled against the rocks on shore. After the last storm we'd sailed through together, one thing I'd learned was you sailed perpendicular to the waves, not parallel with them. After the ship had nearly sunk last the time we'd sailed parallel to the waves, I learned a lesson I'd not soon forget. The fact that Jones was doing this for me showed his commitment to the mission.

The crew, on the other hand, thought we were crazy and cursed us under their breaths. The three ships following us must have thought the same thing, because they sailed in deeper waters, but still behind us.

Lafayette was at the bow of the ship with his spy glass, examining the shoreline. He pointed to a spot up ahead on the beach that was covered with sand and not large rocks.

"That's our best chance," Lafayette indicated as I walked up next to him.

"Okay, the Jolly boat is ready," I said. "Let's get going before we come to our senses."

I had brought about twenty rounds for my Thompson in one pocket and five extra magazines for my Tec-9 in the other. If our Jolly boat tipped over, we'd be swimming to shore, so I left my coat and satchel in the captain's quarters. I'd considered leaving my bullet-proof vest. Without exception, every single time I had taken that thing off, I regretted it and was left with another ugly scar. But again, if I went into the water, the vest was only going to weigh me down and I'd sink like a stone. In the end, after all my hesitation, I decided to put the vest on.

The captain ordered the first mate to turn into the wind and waves, so our little Jolly boat wouldn't be flipped over when we were lowered into the ocean. We were on the north side of the ship, out of sight of our pursuers on the south side.

Our little boat hit the water and was immediately tossed around. Waves crashed into the Jolly, soaking us and tangling the line. The ropes wrapped under the boat wouldn't dislodge from the Jolly. The small boat kept colliding with the much larger ship, and I feared the Jolly was going to be smashed into pieces before we'd a chance to pull away. Lafayette worked frantically to unhook the rope but wasn't having any success. I pulled one of my knives with my left hand and cut the front rope from our little boat. Lafayette stuck out his hand, and I handed him the knife. He cut the remaining rope, freeing our boat. Lafayette dropped my knife and grabbed the oars, setting them in the oar locks, while I pushed us away from the Ariel.

The Ariel pulled away, heading out to sea as Lafayette rowed our boat towards shore. He had to work hard at keeping us straight on, his face grimacing with the effort, but not at moving us to the beach. The waves did that for us.

Looking over my shoulder at the three ships following us, I noticed they had turned towards shore. Their crews scrambled to ready their own Jolly boats for launch. Our little boat was being thrown forward in the surf as their boats were lowering into the water. Lafayette and I jumped into the waist high surf and pulled our boat to shore. Before we left the boat, Lafayette reached in and grabbed my knife that he'd dropped.

"I know you're fond of your toys," Lafayette said, full of his dry French humor.

"I didn't think we were going to make it," I admitted, wiping water from my face.

"You're the only person I know who would say they didn't think they were going to survive something but did it anyway."

I huffed out a laugh as I took my knife, slipping it back into its sheath. Lafayette pointed to the three rowboats coming our way, six men to a boat, eighteen men in total. Armed with muskets and swords, no doubt.

The beach was surrounded by cliffs that, for the most part, would be impossible to climb. Lafayette ran for the one trail winding upward to the top of the embankment. Running in the sand, in wet boots, took a lot out of us. Or at least me. My legs burned as the muscles released lactic acid. I was already working at less than one hundred percent, and this only ran me more ragged.

We were halfway up the snaking sandy trail when thunder exploded behind us. Lafayette and I stopped and looked back the way we'd come. What I first took as thunder was really the Ariel firing a full broadside of cannons at the three Jolly boats now entering the surf. Thirteen cannons fired, and twelves splashes of water kicked up in the already virulent ocean. The thirteenth cannonball managed to hit one of the small boats, ripping it to pieces. The men were thrown into the water, floundered, and were taken under by the white foaming surf. Two of the men popped up, floating face down. I didn't see any signs of the other four.

Captain Jones had turned our eighteen pursuers into twelve in the blink of an eye. Jones had risked the Ariel and her crew by turning her to get off one broadside. As we watched, the Ariel slanted once again, heading out to sea. One of the three ships turned to chase her, while the closest two tried to stay in the area without beaching their ships. I guess they feared Jacob more than they feared the storm.

As we reached the top of the crest, we glanced back again and tried to catch our breath. The sailors stomped in the water, pulling their boats up onto the sand, as Lafayette and I had done.

"Look!" Lafayette yelled over the wind, pointing.

My gaze followed his finger. A farm of some sort appeared in the distance, about half a mile away. Smoke poured out of a chimney on one end of the home. It was dark, but I thought I saw a corral with a horse in it. Reaching into my leather purse tied to my sword belt, I pulled out six or seven gold coins.

"Here," I said, handing over the coins. "Take these and go buy that horse. I'll hold them off."

Lafayette pursed his lips but took the money and sprinted for the stone, shack-like farmhouse. Shots rang out, and sand was kicked up around me as the men at the bottom of the hill fired their muskets at me.

With a painful movement, I pulled out my Thompson with my right hand and placed it in my left. I aimed for the first man who was starting up the pathway. Pulling the trigger, the gun bucked in my hand, but the man didn't fall. Firing my Thompson in overcast light against high winds, at a down angle with my left hand, weren't the optimal shooting conditions.

Placing the pistol back in my right hand, I broke the Thompson open, ejecting the spent cartridge. I loaded a new cartridge into the chamber and snapped the pistol closed, taking it back up in my left.

Taking extra time aiming, I fired again and this time the front man did collapse. Straight onto his face, sliding backwards in the loose sand, tripping the next three men in line.

Loading the Thompson took five times longer than normal, so I was going to need to make every shot count.

The sky lit up with a thousand spotlights right before the thunderclap caused me to duck down. The clouds opened, and the gods cried. They cried buckets. It poured down hard. Down didn't feel like the right word. With the wind blowing as hard as it was, the rain seemed to be coming at me sideways.

I couldn't help myself – I barked out a laugh for two reasons. The first being loading traditional muskets in high wind or in the rain was extremely hard, but in wind *and* rain was near impossible. The second reason was my Thompson and its watertight sealed cartridges didn't give a crap about wind or rain.

Now, instead of being in a gunfight with eleven men bearing primitive and ancient firearms, I was in a gunfight with eleven men who couldn't shoot back at all. I had a sudden liking of my odds. The sad part of it was the sailors kept bravely running up the hill, thinking I couldn't reload any more than they could.

The second man fell to my pistol, but the rest kept coming. They were almost to the top when the third man fell. That's when they realized I wasn't having the same problem they were. They didn't run back down the hill, but they did dive to the ground, trying to hide behind any bush or rock they could find. They laid in the sand, praying to God, hoping my next bullet would kill one of their shipmates or one of their friends and not them.

I didn't see the need to keep killing my assailants, so I only shot the ones who worked up the courage to stand. Two more died before Lafayette returned, riding what I assumed was a horse. It was huge, fat, and old, but it was a horse.

"I gave you enough gold to buy two horses and you bring back that?" I asked incredulously.

"It's the only horse they had," he explained. "But they threw in the saddle."

I shook my head at his poor attempt at humor. He stuck out his hand and pulled me up onto the giant beast's back.

"You bought a Clydesdale?" I asked, realizing the horse was more thick than fat.

"It's not a Clydesdale," Lafayette explained. "It's a Shire."

It sure *looked* like a Clydesdale. I slipped my arm back into the discarded sling still hanging around my neck as Lafayette nudged the huge horse, and we slowly rode away, kicking up huge clumps of mud behind us.

Chapter Thirteen: Paris Again

Two days later, it was still raining when we rode into Paris. Lafayette took me to the house where Mr. Franklin had been staying. The lady who ran the house stated she had not seen Mr. Franklin in two days. She'd assumed he was at the Palace, working with the minister.

We turned around in the rain and rode to the Palace, and although the minister was happy to see us, he too had not seen Mr. Franklin in two days.

"Although we've never discussed any details or admitted any involvement," Minister Gravier stated, looking around in a conspiratorial manner, "the king has mentioned he would like to meet you."

"He mentioned me by name?" I asked, wiping my dripping hair from my eyes.

"No," the minister said as he shook his head. "He heard the Prime Minister's assassination and asked me if Mr. Franklin and Mr. Adams had any new visitors recently. When I told him they had, he insisted upon meeting their new companion. The king never asked for your name, and unless he does, you should *not* give it."

"It would be an honor," I said.

Looking down at my dripping wet self, I added, "I hope he didn't want to meet today?"

"No, no," Charles Gravier said. "Not today. But perhaps we could set aside some time later. Tomorrow or the next day?"

"Sounds fine. I'm at your disposal. But first we need to find Mr. Franklin."

"Have you tried Mr. Adams's house?" the minister asked. "He has been spending a lot of time there."

The minister arranged for a carriage to take us to the Adams residence. We said goodbye to the farmer's Shire and enjoyed the covered and dry carriage. I would have felt bad for the driver if I hadn't already ridden two days straight in the rain on the back of that horse. I was soaked to the bone, which did nothing to help my pounding shoulder.

At the Adams's residence, we were met by the delightful and welcoming Mrs. Adams. She invited us in and called to her husband, who was in the study.

"Oh, thank God," Adams bellowed when he stepped out into the hallway and saw us. "You got my message."

I squinted at him "What message?"

"I sent word to Madam Fournier," Adams said. "For you to return right away. That's why you're here, correct?"

"*Pas assez*," Lafayette said. "We came looking for *Monsieur* Franklin."

"That's why I sent for you. He was taken."

"Taken?" I asked, my chest clenching. "What do you mean, taken?"

"Jacob Testa has him," Adams answered in a low voice as he leaned in to me. "Benjamin was grabbed leaving one of his female friend's residences. I believe her name is Isabella. The poor girl is frantic."

"Jacob should be on the high seas looking for us right now," I told him.

"He somehow learned you were an acquaintance of Benjamin's," Adams explained. "He sent a messenger here. The message was simple. He's not coming to you; you need to go to him."

"Why didn't you go to the king with this?" I asked. Really, I was at the point where it felt like I had to do everything to get it done at all. Lafayette was sagely keeping quiet.

"The king can't know about any of it," Adams answered. "He'd be forced to take action, and that would make us look weak."

I rubbed at the scar on my head with my left hand. I could feel a headache forming. "Where are they holding Franklin?"

"The Testa family has a three-story residence near the river," Adams said.

"I know where it is. Does he expect me to let him kill me or does he want to fight me in another duel?" I asked

"I think he'll want another duel," Adams said. "He'll choose a champion to fight for him. He doesn't have any use of his right arm. In truth, he seems more upset about that, than of you killing his brother."

"Can you send a message for me asking him when and where? But no champions. I don't have use of my right arm, either."

I held up my elbow showing off the sling on my arm. "Have the messenger tell him, left arms only. It might be the first time two right-handed fighters dueled with left hands only. I would prefer knives but will fight him with pistols or swords."

"I'll deliver your message myself in the morning," Adams said with a curt nod. He didn't appear convinced of my idea. "I can explain you were injured and how it will be a fair fight."

After sending the carriage driver back to the palace and asking him to return in the morning, we bedded down on the floor in front of the fireplace of the Adams residence that night. Mrs. Adams was nice enough to have brought us some blankets. We draped our clothes over chairs near the fire and watched the steam roll off them as the water dried by the heat of the open flame. It was the first time I'd felt warm in what seemed like a lifetime.

"How do you think tomorrow will go?" I asked Lafayette.

"He will agree," Lafayette assured me. "He can't expect you to fight someone he chooses with your left hand. He may never regain the use of his right hand, so he can't put the duel off. And he can't go home until you're dead. His family will shame him if he tries. No, my guess is he will want to fight you either tomorrow or the next day."

"Why would he put it off until the next day?"

"You're challenging him to the duel. He gets to choose the weapons. He will want time to choose and practice. He knows you'll need to practice as well, but until you know what weapon he chooses, you're forced to split your time practicing the sword and pistol. The longer he puts off the duel, the better it is for him."

"He'll choose the sword," I said with certainty.

"Because of the rain?"

"Yes," I said. "That, and because I already beat him once with the sword. He needs his honor back. He'll choose the sword."

"Then we'll practice the sword, left-handed, tomorrow," Lafayette said. "You'll need to wear a wig again. Your scar may draw attention. I'm sure word has traveled by now about the Pale Rider killing Lord North. They know you can always hide your vest and pistols, but the scar is what they'll focus on."

"I'll wear a hat," I said, rolling so my back was to the fire. "Not the wig."

***

The next morning, our carriage had not yet returned, so John Adams bravely rode out in the rain on horseback to speak to Jacob Testa. He returned a few hours later, and in the time he was gone, the carriage returned from the palace, the rain had stopped, and the sun weakly peeked out from the clouds. Finally.

Adams was breathless when he returned. "He wants to meet at the Pont Neuf Bridge. He chose swords."

I was surprised he revealed to us what weapon he'd chosen.

"Fine," I said. "When?"

"Now," Adams answered.

"Now?" No wonder the man was exhausted. He'd probably ridden like the devil was on his heels.

"Right now," Adams confirmed. "Jacob will have Benjamin with him. He'll let Benjamin go when he sees you."

"Fine. Let's get going."

"He had one last condition," Adams added. "He wishes to keep this a private matter. He doesn't want people seeing he no longer has the use of his right arm. He has made many enemies in his life. It is to be you, me, and Lafayette only. You may use me or Lafayette as your second. He will have two men with him. No one else is permitted to be there."

"Fine," I said again.

This time I put my bullet-proof vest back on. It wasn't made to stop swords, but it was better protection than nothing.

We arrived at the park two hours before sunset. Lafayette, Adams, and I stepped out of the carriage and checked out our surroundings. Jacob and two of his men stood behind Mr. Franklin at the far end of the bridge. When Jacob saw me, they walked our way.

My satchel was still on the Ariel, so I handed Lafayette my two pistols. Jacob's right arm hung at his side, covered with a wooden splint and clean, white linen wrappings.

"Let Franklin go so we can get on with this shit," I snapped at him.

He pushed Franklin forward, straight into me, and I grabbed the older man to prevent him from falling. I guided Franklin over to Lafayette who gently placed both hands under Franklin's arm.

As Lafayette walked Franklin to the carriage, I turned to face Jacob.

"I'm surprised you came," Jacob said in his haughty tone.

"You wanted swords, right?" I asked.

“There has been a change of plans,” Jacob answered with a sneer.

With that said, both the men with him pulled flintlock pistols. Lafayette rushed to my side, his own pistol in his hand. Footsteps on the cobblestones behind us made me turn to see four more men walking up to us, flintlock pistols in their hands.

“Lower your pistol, Marie,” I told my friend.

Lafayette kept his pistol trained on Jacob. Lafayette finally looked behind us and saw the four newcomers.

“What is this about?” Lafayette asked.

“It’s about me wanting revenge,” Jacob spat out. “But it’s about me wanting the sixty-five thousand British gold pieces King George promised me for your head even more. Seventy-five thousand if I bring you to him alive.”

Like a T.V. villain, he laughed and explained how much smarter he was than me. I was shocked that people did that.

“When we fought, I noticed your scar,” Jacob bragged. “I knew who you had to be. I also knew I was lucky to have survived our encounter. The next day, I sent a message to King George. When the report came to me that Lord North had been killed by an assassin with your same scar, I sent another messenger to the king, promising I could bring you to him. My men told me you were on the Ariel. The king has promised me I can keep the ship if I kill everyone on it. That will be my next chore after taking you back to England.”

I forced myself not to flick my gaze to Lafayette. "And my friends?"

"They may leave, or they may die," Jacob answered with a half-shrug. "I care not which. They are worth no coin to me."

"Marie, take Mr. Franklin and go," I threw over my shoulder.

"Never," Lafayette said, his French accent exaggerated with pride and loyalty. I had to give him credit for that, but I also needed him out of here.

"Marie, take Mr. Franklin and go, please," I said again. "There's nothing you can do except get yourself killed. It will be okay. Trust me."

I wish I had the confidence that I put into my words, but I didn't. I was as good as dead, and everyone, including me, knew it. Lafayette's jaw clenched as he slowly lowered his pistol, then turned to hug me, kissing both sides of my face. I slowly took off my sword belt, handing it to Lafayette. I drew both my knives, handing them to Lafayette as well. I left my boot knife where it was, hoping Jacob's men wouldn't find it. I then gave Lafayette a small push, and he trudged towards the carriage. As soon as he climbed in and shut the door, the carriage driver didn't hesitate but slapped the reins against his horses' backs. The carriage started away with a jerk.

"What now?" I turned and asked Jacob.

"Now we go for a ride," he said in his snide tone.

I smirked at him. "When you think back and wonder where you went wrong, right before I kill you. This is the moment you should think about. This is where you made your fatal mistake."

He ignored me. Waving his one good arm, he signaled for his own carriage. A bigger carriage pulled by four horses came to a stop behind me. I turned to face the carriage, and something struck my skull from behind.

I woke up sometime later inside the carriage with my hands tied together in front of me. Shifting my eyes to the side, I saw Jacob and four of his cronies were in the carriage, too. Jacob's men had searched me and found the boot knife.

The back of my head ached, and I let out a groan. Jacob's eyes flashed at me, and he moved forward and punched me in the nose. My head flew back and struck the seat back. I squeezed my eyes shut as they watered with tears. The sharp taste of copper filled my mouth, so my nose had to be bleeding. A second punch landed hard on my jaw, and blackness overtook me again.

I woke again not knowing how much time had gone by, but we were still in the carriage. Jacob sat across from me, but this time he didn't attack me. Instead, he smiled. Dried blood coated my upper lip, and a migraine headache throbbed behind my eyes.

Jacob's four men took turns holding a pistol on me for the whole ride. I glanced out the window and could see we were heading towards the coast. We rode without rest, all that night and the next morning. I pretended to sleep, constantly waiting for a chance to do something. My chance never came, and I was still trapped with my hands tied. We arrived somewhere along the coast near midday.

I had hoped we were going to the harbor where Captain Jones might have attempted a rescue, but we were nowhere near the harbor. We'd stopped somewhere along an empty beach. Jacob must have sent word ahead of our arrival, because a long boat rested on the beach with two sailors waiting for us. Climbing down from the carriage and looking around, I kept my head low as I took notice of two more of Jacob's cronies on horseback who had followed us.

We walked down a steep trail to the sandy beach. One of the thugs behind me pushed me towards the longboat waiting for us.

"Get in," Jacob ordered.

I managed to half-climb, half-fall into the boat, hands still tied together in front of me. My shoulder ached from the position of my hands, and unable to really support myself, I sat down hard on one of the benches.

Jacob climbed in next and sat behind me. His man, Robert, stood in the surf and handed Jacob his pistol. Jacob pushed the pistol roughly into the small of my back. Robert and the rest of the men grabbed a hold of the longboat and pushed us out into the surf. The men jumped into the boat one at a time as we got deeper in the water, with Robert being the first in and the two sailors jumping in after. Without a word spoken, the two sailors rowed the boat out into the ocean where one of Jacob's smaller ships waited for us.

"You never asked how I knew to sack your friend, Franklin," Jacob commented as the boat bounced up and down over the waves.

He was worse than any T.V. villain. I could tell he wanted to tell me to ask, so I did. "Ok, I'll bite. How did you know?"

"Robert here doesn't work for me," Jacob said, pointing to Robert. "He works for my father."

Why did that matter? "Well, good for Robert."

"No," Jacob said. "It's good for me."

"How's that?"

"When my men rushed me to a doctor's residence," Jacob explained, "Robert had the good sense to stay behind and observe you. He saw you talking to that man pretending to be a servant, who left with the two Americans."

"And?"

"The great and mighty Pale Rider who is from America, talking to a servant, who was also talking to two other Americans? Robert figured it out. The French sent you to save the minister in exchange for help killing Lord North."

"Isn't Robert the smart one?" I commented dryly.

"Yes, he is," Jacob said.

For his part, Robert didn't say a word through the exchange. He merely observed. When we reached the ship, a ladder was unrolled and lowered to us.

"Up," Jacob commanded, waving his pistol at me.

I thought about jumping overboard, but with no way to untie my hands and the weight of my vest, I would have drowned. I held my hands up to Jacob as if to ask him *how*? He nodded his head, and one of his men produced a knife to cut my bonds. With his pistol, Jacob motioned me upward. Having no other apparent options, I climbed the ladder to the main deck of the ship, favoring my right arm the entire way up. The captain of the ship and three of his men waited up top for me, with pistols in hand. They tied my hands together in the front again, while we waited for Jacob.

"Take him below and secure him," Jacob commanded to the captain.

"You heard him!" the captain yelled over his shoulder at his men.

Two of the crew shoved me forward to the steps leading below and took me into the cook's galley. One of the men opened the door to a small storage room. There was a slide bolt on the door. The second soldier rammed me forward, and I fell to the floor of the room, catching myself on my left arm. The door shut behind me, and I heard the clunk of the slide bolt moving.

Rolling onto my back, I sat up on my butt. I turned my head from side to side, trying to see where I was. The room was dark except for the dim light one single port hole gave me. The room was filled with burlap sacks containing coffee, tea, sugar, flour, and other cooking ingredients.

The pantry for the cook, I told myself.

The *clang, clang, clang* of a chain being dragged against wood, sounded from outside the ship. They were raising anchor and getting ready to sail. I would be in England tonight and probably hung several hours later at the King's pleasure, not to mention his delight, if I didn't figure something out.

I sat with my back against a bag of what felt like potatoes and hung my head against my knees. I gave it half an hour of waiting to see if Jacob was coming down to gloat some more or not. When no one came, I decided it was time to escape. The only problem was, I had no idea how I was going to manage that.

Getting myself to my feet, I gazed out the window and watched the churning ocean going by. Which brought me to my second problem. If I did escape the room, where would I go? I wasn't able to free my hands and couldn't see anything sharp in the small room that I might cut the ropes with.

I did have one thing going for me. They hadn't removed my black vest. My guess was, since I was known for having the vest, they wanted to make sure it stayed on so when the king first saw me, he'd have no doubt that I was indeed the Pale Rider.

What they could not have known was one of the large brass buttons on my vest was actually a small, C4 explosive. I originally had two of them, but I had used the first one when I rescued Annie's two daughters back in America.

I pulled the button shaped C4 explosive from my vest and examined it to make sure it was still functional. It was waterproof so I didn't have to worry about water ruining the explosive. It didn't look damaged. I'd worn it for months now, but it still looked good. Getting down onto my hands and knees, I peeked under the door as best I could. The bottoms of a pair of boots stood right outside the door, no doubt one of the sailors guarding me.

Removing the strip of plastic covering the tape on the back, I pressed the explosive up against the door right above the lock. The charge could be activated by motion or by a thirty second timer. I flicked the tiny switch on the back to the timer this time. I then put as much distance between the door and myself as I could. I piled a three-foot-high wall of burlap sacks filled with potatoes and beans. I activated the C4, and dove behind the burlap bags, and plugged my ears with my fingers.

Even behind the burlap, the explosion rocked my world. I was violently shoved back against the wall as if I'd been hit by a car. Suddenly, a cloud of flour burst in the air, choking me. When I was able to catch my breath, I climbed to my feet. There was a ringing in my ears.

The window was blown outward, and the door was propelled off its hinges into the galley. Stepping over twenty-pound bags of potatoes, I made my way out of the dark room. The dead body of one of the sailors laid on the floor, face down. Turning the sailor's body over onto his back, I grabbed his long, curved knife. Men shouted above deck as I grabbed the knife, cutting my hands free.

The first sailor came running down the stairs and using my left hand, I flipped the knife over and plunged it into his chest. He slumped to his knees, and pulling down hard, I yanked the knife free. More sailors rushed down the steps and I ran away from them toward the back of the galley.

There was an open flame under a boiling pot of water. Grabbing the pot by the handle, I threw it at the stairs as the first man reached the bottom. That man fell to the floor screaming when the pot hit him in the face and scalding water burned his bare chest. With my right hand, I threw the knife at the next man in line.

Throwing the knife didn't hurt me as much as it hurt the man on the floor who now had a knife sticking out of his chest. It did however hurt my shoulder enough, and I inhaled sharply at the pain that shot through me as I moved it. I wasn't going to do that again.

I ran down to the lower deck which I hoped had the magazine locker. Two sailors already on that level ran my way. I kicked the first one in his knee, and he tumbled to the floor. The second one was pulling a flintlock pistol out of his belt, and I slid to the side and grabbed his wrist. The loud snap was sharp and sudden as I twisted his wrist and pushed it towards him. As his wrist broke, his hand opened, and I nabbed the flintlock. Yanking it out of his hand, I then pistol whipped him in the temple, knocking him out.

The magazine locker came into my view as men flooded down the stairs, shouting. I shot the first one in the chest and then dropped the pistol. I kicked open the door that I had hoped was the magazine locker.

I was rewarded to find a room filled with pistols, swords, and barrels of gun powder. I grabbed a barrel of gunpowder and rolled it at the men coming at me. Grabbing a flintlock pistol, I cocked the hammer back and aimed it at the barrel. The men skidded to a stop, hands up, begging for me not to do it. They turned to run back the way they had come in a cluster, screaming.

Dumb asses. If they weren't so scared, they'd have remembered pistols were always kept unloaded in the magazine locker.

Now that I was alone, I strapped on a sword and loaded my pistols. I'd never loaded a flintlock pistol before, but I had watched Lafayette do it plenty of times. The sounds of men screaming for their lives, followed by splashes in the water, told me I only had to fight about half the crew now. I wasn't as fast or as smooth at loading the flintlocks as Lafayette, but I got the job done.

I made my way back up the stairs, with two pistols in my hands and vengeance in my heart. The floor above me was empty but feet running on the main deck told me that the ship wasn't deserted yet. I was done trying to outsmart people. I was going to kill everyone still on board. I climbed the next set of stairs and looked at the chaos around me.

Now standing in the pale sunlight, I got a good look at myself. I was white as a ghost, covered from head to toe in flour. I was an awful sight to behold. A wicked smile filled my face as I thought about how I had to look to these men. Pale Rider indeed.

Sailors were jumping over the side rails while the captain tried to stop them. I spotted Jacob, surrounded by the original six men who had been at the park with him. They were looking in different directions, trying to figure out what was going on. Jacob was shrieking at the captain to get his sailors under control.

I fired both pistols and the closest two bodyguards collapsed onto the deck, clutching their stomachs. I was shooting low and needed to adjust my aim higher. The four men still standing spotted me and fired their own pistols as I rushed to hide behind the main mast. Woodchips flew into the air and rained down on me as the mast took the lead balls meant for me.

The captain decided he'd had enough of this murder fest and followed the last of his men, jumping over the side and into the water.

I raised an eyebrow as I watched him. *So much for the captain going down with his ship.*

All four of Jacob's men dropped their expelled flintlocks, as did I. They drew their swords and approached me. I didn't draw my sword and instead pulled the two pistols in the front of my pants. Stepping from behind the mast, I raised both pistols. The matching surprised look on their faces right before I shot the next two was almost funny.

Dropping those two pistols, I drew another two pistols from behind my back. Shoot and drop was my plan. The man named Robert was one of the last two men standing. He and the other crony turned and ran for the side of the ship, hoping to jump overboard behind the captain before I got my shot off.

I could have let them jump, let them get away, let them live. They were, after all, no longer a threat to me. On the other hand, they had taken part in my kidnapping, in Franklin's kidnapping, and they were now taking me to King George, not for king and country, but for money.

Raising both pistols, I aimed my shots at both of their backs right before they made it over the side. My right arm chose that moment to give out on me, and I missed Robert. I did hit the other man who went skidding to a stop against the railing, as Robert flung himself through the air and into the water below. I muttered a curse at that poor timing.

Jacob now stood alone, sword in his left hand, and fear in his eyes. I didn't have any more pistols, so I drew my sword. My shoulder screamed in protest, and I switched my sword into my left hand.

I marched towards him resolutely as he searched around for help. Neither of us wanted to swim in the rough and violent water below with just one arm, so going over the side like the crew wasn't an option.

"This is the time," I growled, my voice hard.

"What time?" Jacob asked, confused.

"Remember when I told you back at the bridge that you'd look back and wonder where you went wrong?" I lifted my sword tip to him. "This is the time for you to think back. It was on the bridge."

The fear in his eyes turned to hatred and anger. He leaped forward and swung his sword down at my head. Raising my sword, I was able to block his. I could tell neither of us had practiced the sword left-handed. I didn't have time, and he hadn't thought he'd have the need.

I went on the attack, swinging my sword to the left and back to the right. He blocked the first and stepped back from the second. Using our left hands meant a loss of strength, speed, and dexterity. None of our attacks were skilled or powerful.

He went on the attack next, chopping down at me over and over. I blocked every swing but was forced backwards.

"You killed my brother!" Jacob screamed madly as he chopped down. "You took my right hand from me!"

I let him chop his sword at me. I let him scream. He was tiring himself out, while I spent half the energy blocking his attacks. I kept backing up while he kept attacking. Finally, my backside hit the railing, and I had nowhere to go.

At his next downward chop, I didn't just block it, I pushed forward. Blade rang against blade, and with a sickly scraping sound, like nails on a chalkboard, my sword slid down his until our sword handles met. Letting my sword fall from my hand and over the side of the ship, I grabbed his left hand. I wrapped my fingers around his fingers, squeezing as hard as I could.

With his left hand trapped in my grip, and his right hand uselessly hanging at his side, his eyes widened as he tried to figure out what to do next. His knee came up towards my balls. I kicked out with my left knee, blocking his. I pushed back on him, forcing him to take one step back. He pushed harder on me, forcing me towards the railing.

With a hard yank upward, thrusting his arm towards the sun, I twisted his wrist, pulling him off balance and onto his toes. Wrenching my upper body hard around, and pulling with everything I had left, I screamed in fury and bunched my back muscles tight. Jacob went flying over me, then over the railing, and finally over the side of the ship.

He screamed the whole way down, hitting the water headfirst with a splash. I silently watched as his head broke the surface of the water, and he pawed at the water, screaming for help. His tired legs, and one exhausted arm weren't going to save him.

His one good arm splashed frantically as he panicked. He went under the water again, then managed to shoot back up, spitting and screaming. His head went under a third time, and again his head broke the surface. He went under a fourth time but this time he didn't come back up. I stared at the water, waiting to make sure it was over. After another thirty seconds, I was satisfied he was gone.

Letting go of the railing, I crumpled to my knees. I rolled over onto my butt, with my back against the wooden railing. Tired? No, there was no word for exactly how tired I was.

Now what? I asked myself.

I took the ship; it was now mine. The only problem was I didn't know how to sail or know quite where I was. I was heading to England, that I did know, so I had to turn the ship around and go back the way we'd come. Then I needed to head down the coast until I came upon something familiar. Hopefully the harbor itself.

Other than me, the deck of the ship was empty. The crew was either dead or had jumped into the ocean. The wheel spun crazily around one way, then the other. Instead of the wheel controlling the rutter, turning the ship through the water, the water pushed and pulled on the rudder, and the wheel spun at the command of the current.

Rolling onto my hands and knees, I waited for a wave of nausea to pass before grabbing the railing with my left hand and pulling myself to my shaky feet.

Stumbling over to the wheel, I spun it to the left and the ship lurched as it turned with the rudder. I was still close enough to see the coast of France, and I straightened the ship when land was directly in front of me. I let the ship drift back a little to the right, heading south.

When the harbor was in sight, I veered away from it and towards an open beach. I was on a runaway train with no way to stop. Even if I knew how to stop the ship, which I didn't, one man had no chance of dropping the sails or anchor and whatever else needed to be done.

I stood at the bow of the ship and waited. If I couldn't stop the ship, I'd let it run itself up onto the sand. I didn't know it the ship would stop or if it would be wrecked, but fortunately for me, I couldn't have cared less. Right before the ship ran itself ashore, I jumped into the ocean. The waves were smaller this close to land, and I was able to swim one-handed the hundred feet or so to shore. The ship itself came to a sudden and violent stop in the shallows as mother earth took her into its packed dirt and sandy embrace.

Tired, I dragged myself to the docks. Walking up the gang plank, and with the flour washed off me, some of the sailors recognized me and ran to me with open arms, catching me after I collapsed to my knees but before I fell on my face. Sailors hollered for Captain Jones, and his shadow was suddenly standing over me, the last thing I saw before I passed out. Again.

***

In my sleep, I found myself with Annie. We were walking in a golden field, holding hands. She wore a white dress, with her hair hanging free over her shoulders. This time it was me, the real me, not an alternative, Pale Rider form of me. I couldn't hear what she was saying, but she was smiling at me, and her eyes sparkled. She was genuinely happy. Although I couldn't hear her words, I somehow knew what she was saying. We were talking about our future and discussing where we would like to live now that the war was over. The British had lost the war after General Washington's victory at Yorktown.

The vision of Annie faded as a bright light invaded my eyes, and the clattering of horseshoes against cobblestones reached my ears. I turned my head, looking for the horses but couldn't find them.

Pain flared, throbbing in my right shoulder, and the world came back to me as I started to wake. The sound of a carriage came to my ears. A real carriage, not one in my dream. Then piercing sunlight penetrated my eyelids. My hand moved of its own accord, covering my eyes. A moaning reached my ears. It took me a few seconds to realize it was me moaning in pain.

"How are you feeling?" the familiar voice of Jones asked.

"Where am I?" I croaked, cracking open my eyelids. That impossibly hurt more.

"We're in a carriage," Jones answered. "I figured you'd wake up and demand to go to Paris right away, so I got a carriage. You've been asleep for the last half day. We are in Paris already."

The carriage bounced to Franklin's house, against my protesting head and body, and we were told by the lady of the house that Franklin was at the Adams's residence. Another painfully jouncing ride to the Adams residence, we were met by a very surprised Franklin and Lafayette.

They thankfully settled me into a plush chair, and I regaled them with the story of what happened on the ship, leaving out the part about the C4 explosive, of course. I told them of killing Jacob Testa and crashing the ship.

We were talking and laughing when Charles Gravier knocked at the door. I relived the entire story of what had happened again for him. First, he was shocked, his hand clenched against his chest for the entire tale, then stunned, and then delighted.

"I almost forgot why I came here in the first place," Gravier said as he grinned at me. "The king has requested your presence."

I exchanged a look with Lafayette. He nodded. "When?"

"As soon as I'm able to find you, I am to bring you," he answered. "Now if you're able."

"You must go, Thomas," Franklin urged.

"The king wishes the presence of all five of you," Gravier clarified.

I glanced down at myself. Not for the first time, I found myself in need of a change of clothes. I realized I was a mess, and I hadn't seen my face. I could only imagine how badly I looked. Reading my mind, Adams coughed into his hand, gaining my attention.

"I may have some clean clothes that will fit you," Adams said.

***

Two hours later we stood in the King's Palace, waiting for the king. I half-leaned on Layfette for support.

King Louis XVI walked in with a broad smile on his regal face. The king appeared to be twenty-five years old. He was in good health, lean, and with no extra fat I could see. His hair was either naturally curly, or he had a much better wig than the one I had worn. He wore white pants, a white shirt, and a white coat. Several large, star-shaped medals shone on his chest.

"We welcome you," the king intoned. "We know it was short notice, but we wanted you five to be the first to know the news. Tomorrow, February 6, 1778, France will officially join our allies and cousins across the ocean in their war against the British. We'll be signing the Treaty of Alliance and the Treaty of Amity and Commerce."

"Thank you, your majesty," Franklin and Adams said at the same time, bowing slightly.

"And we thank you," the king said, focusing his gaze on me. "You reminded us of what is possible. After what you have done over the last few days, imagine what our two countries might do together."

Then the king's tone changed. He was polite about it but asked everyone to leave the room except me. The room went quiet. Gravier bowed and turned to leave as everyone else looked at me with concern painted on their faces. I motioned with my head for them to leave. Franklin, Adams, and Lafayette bowed deeply to the king, before turning to join Gravier and walk out of the room, leaving me alone with the King of France.

"That was impressive," King Louis said.

"Your majesty?" I asked, not understanding his implication.

"The king dismissed them, yet three of them looked to you for leave to go," he said. "That has never happened to us before."

"I'm sorry, your majesty," I said. "I don't think they meant any insult by it."

"We are sure they did not," the king agreed. "Still, it says a lot about you."

The king walked over to a delicately carved side table and filled two crystal glasses with red wine, which he poured from a large crystal decanter. Leaving the decanter on the table, he walked back over to me and held out one of the glasses. After I took the glass, he motioned with his now free hand for me to take a seat on the three steps that led up to his and his wife's extra-large royal chairs. He then dropped down next to me, as if we were two ordinary, everyday guys. I was even further surprised when he leaned back on his elbows and crossed his slender ankles.

"Thomas, do you know why we asked the others to leave?" the king inquired.

The fact he recalled my name meant he knew who I was the whole time. It also meant he knew a lot more than we thought he knew. Did he also know I was the Pale Rider? He saw the look on my face and burst into laughter.

"You didn't really think Madame Fournier could run such an enterprising operation without it coming to our attention, did you?" King Louis asked.

"You know about Madame Fournier and her pigeons?" I asked.

"Know about her?" he asked. "She is our eyes and ears. We know everything she knows. As soon as she reported you had contacted her, we instructed her to assist you in any way possible."

After thinking back on my time with her, her actions suddenly made more sense.

"Then I assume you asked my friends to leave because curiosity has gotten the better of you," I commented. "You want to know the whole story, the details of everything that had happened. But you don't… you can't let anyone else know you know the truth. Ignorance and deniability."

"Yes," he said, his face brightening. "France can't be involved. History must never know."

I rubbed at my upper lip. "Anything in particular you want to know?"

"How did you kill Lord North?" he asked excitedly, like a child. "In the king's castle no less? And what in God's name happened on Testa's ship? How did one man capture a whole ship by himself?" He dropped his formal speech and spoke to me like the eager young man he was.

We talked, drank wine, and laughed like two old friends. I told my story, and he asked question after question, mouth open with anticipation for each answer. I believe I truly liked him. Then it made sense to me. He saw me as something more than just a man.

To him, I was the larger than life, the Pale Rider. Sometimes, especially on a night like tonight, the night before you signed a treaty, dragging your country and your people into a war, a night when you carried the weight of the world on your shoulders, even a king needed to be inspired. For some crazy reason, he'd chosen me. For Louis, it was an opportunity to relax and be himself. It was bizarre he'd picked an outsider like me, someone who was an executioner, a destroyer, an assassin, to be that man. Perhaps it was because of the lives I had taken, or how I had changed the course of the war with one sudden act of violence.

Whatever the reason, the King of France decided to let his guard down in front of me.

The king stood up, and I thought he was going to refill his wine glass. He walked over to the table with the decanter on it but didn't stop. Instead, King Louis sat his wine glass on the table as he sauntered past it to the far wall where two swords hung, crossing each other in the form of an X. The king reached up and pulled one of the two swords down from the wall. He held the sword level between his hands, gingerly with adoration, like he was holding a priceless piece of art and remembering how he obtained it. Turning back around, he spoke as he slowly walked back to me.

"Two years ago, we were forced to disband our Musketeers," the king said softly as he walked. "The captain of the Musketeers presented us with these two swords as a gift. These were … these *are* the last two rapiers ever made for the Musketeers."

The sword was beautiful, a true piece of art. It was three feet of highly polished fine steel. Not a scratch or blemish marred it. Perfectly straight, about an inch wide, and deadly sharp on both sides. The handle was silver with a fancy, thick, intricate wire handguard. The handle itself was made to be held easily with one hand and had a black leather wrapping with silver stitching.

He held the weapon out to me. "For you. In gratitude for your service."

I jumped to my feet with my mouth hanging open, but no words came out as he presented the weapon to me. I didn't have my scabbard on me. I had left it and my pistols at the Adams's house.

"Thank you, your Highness," I whispered in awe.

He slapped me on my back like an old friend, and we sat back down on the steps. Lafayette was going to be so jealous when he saw the sword. Then it hit me. *I had a real fricking Musketeer's sword.* Did that make me a Musketeer?

The king then asked about my family. Since I no longer had one, I told him about my new family – Annie, her daughters, old Ben, and even Little Joe. He told me about his family and about growing up in a palace.

For the next few hours, the king allowed himself to be just a man, easy, casual, with no responsibilities. And I enjoyed every astonishing moment of it.

But as we chatted, I knew the moment was fleeting. As for me, I still had a country to return to, a woman to love, a war to win, and a timeline to change.

THE END

If you liked this book, please leave a review!

Look for book 3 Final Chance –coming soon!

Excerpt of *Final Chance*, Book 3

Prologue

February 8th, 1778

Windsor Castle

King George the Third of England sat in his throne room, up high on the dais in his oversized royal chair and leered down at the incompetent men before and below him. He wore his favorite, deep red and soft silk pants, a large golden coat, topped with a thick, crimson flowing robe. The sleeves of his magnificent coat folded back in huge, exaggerated cuffs. A pure white fur sat on and around his shoulders over the coat and robe. He had a gold decorative sword secured around his waist, its value in gold equal to its worthlessness as a weapon. He didn't care much for wearing it except to show his subjects and let them know when he was upset or displeased. The fingers of his right hand drummed absently on the armrest of the thick wooden chair. The room was quiet with everyone waiting for him to speak first.

Ten rough-looking and experienced soldiers lined the walls, muskets in hand. Five soldiers stood on each side of the room, their muskets loaded and bayonets fixed. The king had not gone anywhere since the assassination of his trusted Prime Minister without these soldiers. Two soldiers stood next to his bed as he slept at night, when he was able to sleep at all. His wife had taken to sleeping in another room. She refused to lay in bed with two armed soldiers standing near them. He believed it was her excuse to sleep without him.

"The French have joined the war in America," the king said, breaking the silence, his eyes boring down on them.

The four men who cowered before him did not respond. It was not a question, nor was he informing them of something everyone in the country didn't already know. He was letting them know what was on his mind. He was upset, displeased, annoyed, and yes angry. What many of his own men would call *mad.* The king snorted at that thought.

Several of his highest ranking naval and army officers now sat in a cold, desolate prison, stripped of their rank and property, soon to be hung. Their families had been forced into a destitute life of exile. No one in the palace was safe from his unpredictable and swift wrath.

The king had been forgetting names and dates as of late, but since this Pale Rider criminal (*ridiculous name*, the king thought) had sacked not one but two of his ships, he had been acting . . . crazy. Even he could admit that. Waking up in the middle of the night screaming. Running around in the palace in his underwear. Late nights talking with his most trusted advisor Lord North had been the only way to calm him down.

Since the assassination of Lord North, the king had become totally unhinged. There were rumors that the king had seen and actually talked to, or rather yelled at, the assassin the day before the criminal had killed Lord North. Since the murder, the king had sealed himself off in the palace, afraid for his life. Hence the soldiers by his side at all times.

There were plenty of chairs in the room, but the king had not given his subjects leave to sit. In the mood he was in this morning, sitting right now might cost the person his life. So, they all stood, unmoving and silent until the king let it be known that he wanted them to.

The king himself had declared war on France two days ago, the same day King Louis, that bastard King of France, signed the Treaty of Alliance and the Treaty of Amity and Commerce. Backing the colonists. *His colonists!*

"Our own Prime Minister, Lord North, was murdered," the king intoned, raising his voice. "Right here in this palace. In *our* palace. Not a hundred yards from where you now stand."

The four men stiffened and readied themselves for an outburst of anger and profanity from the king. It seemed like any mention of the murder of Lord North or of the assassin known only as the Pale Rider was enough to throw the king into a fit.

Two of the four men standing were in the service of the king. George Germain, Secretary of State for the American Department, and George Collier, Vice Admiral in the Royal Navy. The other two men were finely dressed merchants. The fact they were in the palace meant they were either men with power, or men who had something to offer the king.

The king focused his anger at Germain and Collier, as if this situation was all their fault.

"How did you allow all this to happen?" the king asked in a hard whisper.

Neither man opened his mouth. There was no right answer, only answers which would get a man hung. They had not even been in the palace when Lord North was killed. Assassinated. None of this was on them, but to voice this opinion might sound as if they were saying it was the king's fault – a costly and fatal disaster.

"Why haven't you captured the assassin yet?" the king screamed, his voice rising with the tension in the hall.

"My king," Secretary of State George Germain answered, "I've already ordered a dispatch to deliver a messenger to Joseph Brant. The message will leave with the next ship to Canada."

"Joseph Brant?" the king asked.

"Yes, your Majesty," Germain said, bowing. "Captain Brant. With the Mohawk Warriors in Canada. Your Majesty has met him once before. He leads a mixture of Mohawk warriors and colonial loyalists. They are known as Brant's volunteers."

"Is he the native they call Monster Brant?" the king asked.

"He is called that, your Majesty," Germain said. "Among other names. He's of the Mohawk tribe, fierce warriors and loyal to your Majesty."

"And what orders are you sending him?" the king asked in a calmer voice. The hall seemed to release a collective breath.

"To travel south," Germain answered. "Track down and kill the Pale Rider and anyone who has ever given aid to him."

"Washington's Assassin," the king bit out, speaking each word slowly, "is not in America? Is he? No. He's in France."

"Yes, your Majesty," Germain said quickly. "He is now, at this moment, but our spies tell us he will be sailing for America soon."

"Your plan is to let him sail away free, out of our reach, and hope to catch him at a later date in America?" the king queried, his eyebrows furling with anger.

"No, your Majesty," Vice Admiral George Collier said. "We have five of our ships ready to sail and sink any ship he sails on."

"How will you know what ship he will be on?"

"I will supply this information, sire," the older of the two merchants said, speaking up for the first time as he bowed before the king.

"And you are?" the king asked.

"Freiherr Bartolomeo de Testa, your Majesty," the finely dressed, middle-aged merchant answered. "I'm also the father of two innocent, young boys that this man has killed. Murdered. Like you, I, too, seek revenge."

Excerpt from Book 1 *Chain and Mace*

Descended

Most people seem to believe that angels do not have free will. The truth is that they do. Angels in heaven chose to follow God, just as those in hell chose to follow Satan. When an angel chooses to follow the Lord but breaks one of his commands, he is cast out from heaven, but not all are cast to hell. These angels are known as Fallen Angels. But where do fallen angels go?

August 18

David fled down the grassy hill as fast as his legs could carry him, looking over his shoulder every few seconds. He was breathing hard; his heart pounded in his ears, and he was so tired. *Where were they? What were they?* They were behind him a minute ago, and now they were gone.

He remembered how they silently came out of the darkness, these strange men, *no not men, they were too big.* Animals, or a kind of creatures, *but they walked on two legs, or some of them did.* Monsters? He tried to think of an argument against using that word but could not. They grabbed Jake, his cameraman, by the throat. Jake hung in the air by that giant hairy hand or paw that shook Jake like a rag doll. There were three of them, that much he was sure of. The first one stood about six and a half, maybe seven feet tall, the biggest bear David had ever seen, but it wasn't a bear. Bears didn't grab people by the throats. He thought perhaps they were wolves. They did look like wolves, but wolves don't walk on two feet.

They must be men in costumes, David thought. After all, that was the reason he was out here in the first place.

His editor had sent him and Jake out to investigate reports of a type of new religious cult. Well, they sure as hell found the cult, or the cult found them. Poor Jake was overweight at least by forty pounds. How could any person just pick up a two-hundred-and-thirty-pound man by one hand? Maybe they were on drugs, PCP, or something. David had done a report earlier in the year about how strong people can get when they are whacked out on drugs. They had heard rumors about a motorcycle gang in the area, maybe they had something to do with this. David's thoughts were interrupted by the rock he tripped on. He fell to the ground and fought to stay conscious as he rolled forward on the grass, the metallic taste of blood filling his mouth.

Kathy! His mind suddenly went to her. *What would Kathy do if he died here?* Crouched in the dirt, he decided he would live. He had to find a phone and call the police, and it was his most unfortunate luck that he dropped his cell phone when he ran. *Maybe a pay phone at a gas station?*

David forced himself to his feet and looked behind him, up the hill that he had fallen down, but it was too dark to see if anyone was still there. He must have run a mile by now. David had played high school football years ago, and he always kept himself in good shape. He thought he could move with decent speed, but these guys were faster. By God, they were fast. It was almost as if they were playing with him. David thought about his cat and how she would pounce on the bugs she would find in the house, only to let them go, then pounce again.

"Stop thinking and just run," David said to himself out loud. He turned to run but was stopped by the very large hand that grabbed him by the back of the neck

Chain and Mace – Book 1

About the Author

Michael Roberts is a Police Officer in Southern California. He also served in the United States Marine Corps for seven years. He wrote this story for himself twenty years prior to publishing it. It was not until he met the love of his life, and his motivation, Michelle Deerwester-Dalrymple, a published author herself, that he updated this story and published it.

Also the Author:

Alpha Team Paranormal Military Series:

Chain and Mace – Book 1

Chain and Cross -- Book 2.

American History Military Time Travel Series:

Second Chance – Book 1

Another Chance Book 2

Final Chance Book 3